KINGPIN

Also by Mike Lawson

MIKE LAWSON

A JOE DeMARCO THRILLER

KINGPIN

Atlantic Monthly Press

New York

FIRST EDITION

Published simultaneously in Canada
Printed in the United States of America

This book was set in 12-pt. Garamond Premier Pro
by Alpha Design & Composition of Pittsfield, NH.

First Grove Atlantic hardcover edition: February 2024

Library of Congress Cataloging-in-Publication data is available for this title.

ISBN 978-0-8021-6088-1
eISBN 978-0-8021-6089-8

Atlantic Monthly Press
an imprint of Grove Atlantic
154 West 14th Street
New York, NY 10011

Distributed by Publishers Group West

groveatlantic.com

24 25 26 27 28   10 9 8 7 6 5 4 3 2 1

KINGPIN

1

When the fine folks of Boston think about organized crime in their fair city, if they think about the subject at all, they think of Whitey Bulger. Or maybe Johnny Depp playing Whitey Bulger. They think of the Patriarca crime family, also called the Boston Mafia, most of whose members are dead or in jail. They think of thugs they've seen in movies, guys whose last names end in vowels, wearing tracksuits and stocking caps as they unload boxes from a hijacked truck.

What they don't think about is Carson Newman and Newman Enterprises.

Carson Newman doesn't wear tracksuits. He wears suits made by Dior that retail for five grand. His headquarters occupies the entire thirty-fifth floor of the Prudential Tower; he doesn't work out of the back room of a bar. He doesn't have a consigliere. He retains a white-shoe law firm with four hundred lawyers whose partners are all WASPs. He'll never go to jail for tax evasion like Al Capone, because his accountants help him evade paying taxes without breaking the law. There have been several years when Carson didn't pay any federal income tax at all, and he didn't commit a crime by not doing so.

Carson's father had owned commercial property all over the Northeast—office buildings, shopping malls, apartments occupied mostly by low-income families—and when he passed away, Carson inherited these. So Carson didn't exactly pull himself up by his boot-straps, but to his credit, he significantly expanded his father's real estate empire. In addition to acquiring more properties, he became a builder. He quickly learned that being a builder was a risky, complicated business where the chance of failure was extremely high. Something as simple as a four-story apartment building or a shopping mall could take years to construct; skyscrapers, football stadiums, and golf courses could take a decade or more. It took months to line up the financing. It took ages to acquire the land and obtain the necessary permits and do the environ-mental impact studies needed to demolish existing structures and erect new ones. And there was always some group that was determined to stop whatever you were trying to build, and it would stage protests and bombard you with lawsuits. And by the time you paid off the bankers and the union laborers and the lawyers and the architects and the engineers, a builder was just as likely to end up in the red as in the black. Twice, Carson had to declare bankruptcy—not that it affected his lifestyle—and had to regroup.

Carson soon learned that bribing the right people for permits was faster and cheaper than following the prescribed process. Blackmailing a city councilman who had a predilection for girls still in their teens was helpful when a zoning ordinance needed to be changed. And if he had stubborn, unreasonable tenants that he needed to vacate a space so it could be renovated and rented for a higher rate, there were people who could be hired to persuade them to move. Lawyers, not gunmen, became his foot soldiers. He sued his opponents and countersued whoever sued him, and he usually won because his adversaries rarely had the resources to endure legal battles that could stretch out for years.

What Carson also learned was that he had to take a different approach when it came to politicians. Politicians could either pave the way for success or become major roadblocks, and simply donating to their cam-paigns and socializing with them often didn't produce the right results.

So in addition to the lawyers and the accountants that he employed, Carson put a lobbyist on his payroll who helped him put politicians on his payroll.

But no one called Carson Newman a gangster; nobody called him Godfather or the don.

At the age of fifty-six, Carson was worth several billion dollars. He had a lovely, cultured wife who was five years younger than he was. She had raised his two attractive children and now sat on the boards of various charities. He had a twenty-seven-year-old mistress who resided in an apartment he owned in Boston. He owned a restaurant he'd named after his daughter that charged forty bucks for a salad. He owned a mansion in Brookline, a town house in the Back Bay within strolling distance of Fenway, where he had box seats, and vacation places on Cape Cod and in Naples, Florida. He was a member of The Country Club, where a membership reportedly went for as much as half a million dollars.

Yes, Carson was on top of the world—and he was not about to let some nobody employed by John Mahoney topple him from his perch.

2

"But what *exactly* does he know?"

"I told you, Carson, I don't know. All my source could tell me is that this kid is convinced he's uncovered a criminal conspiracy and wants to do something about it."

"Well, this is the last goddamn thing I need right now, with all the other shit that's going on."

"Carson, I really don't think you should be overly concerned. Brian Lewis is a summer intern. He probably gets lost walking around the Capitol, and I can't imagine him uncovering anything that could cause you a real problem."

"But you don't know that for sure."

"No, but—"

"And why in the hell does Mahoney even care? The bill failed more than half a year ago."

Patrick Grady wanted to say, *He cares because he's just like you. He's a vindictive son of a bitch who never forgives or forgets.* But instead, he said, "I don't know, Carson."

Grady could picture Newman sitting at his desk in Boston, scowling, his fists clenched, a human volcano about to erupt. The man was well over six feet tall with a big, slightly hooked nose; a thrusting, square jaw; and a wide mouth with thin lips. He wore his silver hair in what Grady thought of as a Julius Caesar haircut—short and combed straight forward—and Grady wouldn't have been surprised if Newman had selected the hairstyle because he thought of himself as a modern-day emperor. When Newman was younger, he had a barrel chest; his gut now formed the barrel. But with his size, he could be physically intimidating, looking as if he was barely restraining himself from attacking whoever angered him.

"Well, I want to know what that fucking kid knows. Put your guy on him."

"All right, Carson. I'll do that. It's probably not necessary but I suppose it's a prudent thing to do."

———————————◆◆◆———————————

Kellogg, Long & Meyer was the largest, most profitable, most influential lobbying firm in Washington, D.C. It was the king of K Street. It billed two billion dollars a year, and its clients included Fortune 500 companies, Wall Street investment banks, Russian and Chinese oligarchs, Saudi Arabian princes, and American tycoons, like Carson Newman, who had their own political agendas.

Patrick Grady had been made a partner two years ago. He was paid $375,000 per year, not including bonuses, but the job was actually worth much more than his nominal salary. Almost every meal he had in a restaurant was expensed to his firm's clients. Almost every airline ticket he bought—and these days he only flew first class—was expensed. He had a membership in a country club in Virginia that the firm had paid for because it was a venue for schmoozing clients and members of Congress. He was even given a clothing allowance because the firm didn't want him entertaining clients in a seven-hundred-dollar suit from Men's Warehouse. Last winter he and his wife—he hadn't been able to figure out a way to take his girlfriend—vacationed for a week in Barbados and he hadn't paid for anything, because it had been a working vacation where he'd spent the whole time buying drinks and dinners for five legislators and their spouses.

For Grady, becoming a partner at the age of forty-two was no mean feat, considering the cutthroat nature of the competition. He hadn't come from a wealthy background, like many of his coworkers. He hadn't attended an Ivy League university and didn't have the connections that came with a privileged background. But one thing that could be said about Grady was that he had *willpower*—enough willpower to overcome every obstacle that he'd ever faced. He took a job at KL&M as a lowly, underpaid associate right out of college and then clawed his way up the ladder. He worked eighty-hour weeks. He schemed to outdo his rivals. He groveled when he had to grovel.

He even overcame his physical limitations. He was man of below-average height who had a genetic tendency toward pudginess, so he stuck to a rigorous diet and sometimes even fasted. He went to a gym three times a week where a sadistic personal trainer pushed him to his physical limits. He had a full head of brown hair, thanks to transplants, and his teeth were capped. In a different life, Patrick Grady would have been a short, bald, fat man with crooked teeth—and never would have been made a partner.

But partnerships could be taken away if the firm's clients became displeased or their desires weren't met, and unfortunately, when he became a partner, he was given the Newman account—and Carson Newman was not an easy man to please. And what Newman would do if he didn't get what he wanted was fire Grady and his lobbying firm. He fired people he employed at the drop of a hat. And now what he wanted was to know exactly what Brian Lewis had discovered, and because Grady's source in Congress couldn't tell him, he did what Newman ordered. He called Dave Morgenthal and told him to get on top of Lewis, an intern who worked for former Speaker of the House John Mahoney.

Dave Morgenthal was a licensed private detective. He and his partner, who was now dead, had both been in military intelligence. They spent twenty years in the army in places like Afghanistan and Iraq, where they tracked down terrorists by listening in on cell phone calls and using drones. And what they did after they got out of the military was use the skills provided by Uncle Sam to follow people their clients, like KL&M, wanted followed. They recorded phone calls. They planted bugs in houses and cars. They took photographs using cameras with long-range lenses. They spied on folks from overhead using drones they'd bought on Amazon.

And that's what Morgenthal would now do when it came to Brian Lewis.

One thing Grady noticed when he spoke to Morgenthal was that the man's voice was hoarse and he sounded tired—but he didn't bother to ask how Morgenthal was feeling, because he didn't care.

He should have.

3

Sydney Roma didn't know how much Brian Lewis was paid, but whatever it was, it wasn't enough. The guy was a workaholic. All he did was work.

He was about her age, tall and slender, with short dark hair and a prominent Adam's apple accentuated by his long, thin neck. He was always serious, rarely smiled, and was glued to his iPhone when traveling on the Metro, seemingly oblivious to the people around him. He wore the same clothes to work every day: a blue sport coat, a short-sleeved white shirt, a plain blue tie that matched the coat, and stay-pressed khaki pants. Sydney imagined he had more than one shirt and one pair of pants, but she was positive the sport coat was the only one he owned.

In the four days she'd been following him, he'd leave his apartment at six, get a latte to go from a coffee shop near his place, and catch the Metro to the Capitol. What he did inside the building all day, she had no idea, but he didn't leave until seven or eight at night. He put in twelve-hour days. And on two of the days she followed him, instead of going home, he stopped at the same coffee shop where he got his morning coffee, took out a laptop, and worked on it until the place closed at ten.

The first day, the only person he called was his girlfriend, and the girlfriend, who sounded as if she might be nurse, told him a patient had died that day and she started crying because the patient had been a kid. Lewis, who seemed like a decent guy, naturally tried to comfort her. The next night, even though he didn't get off until eight, he met the girlfriend at a pub, and Sydney saw her for the first time. Her name was Elaine. She was a petite blonde, pretty, but not what you'd call a knockout. After they ate, they went back to her place, and Lewis spent the night. The next morning, he was up at six and off to the Capitol, like a hamster on a wheel.

On the third day, he called his mother, and sounding like a mother, she asked him if he was getting enough to eat and said she hoped he wasn't working too hard. The mother did say one thing that could have something to do with the reason Dave had been hired to follow Lewis. She said, "Are you still digging into that thing you told me about?" Lewis said yes, and his mom said, "Have you talked to anyone else about it?" Lewis said, "Not yet." Sydney recorded the call. That night he didn't see his girlfriend—when he'd called her earlier, he'd said that he just had too much to do—and again spent a couple of hours in the coffee shop tapping away on his laptop.

Sydney told Dave that what they needed to do was get a bug into the girlfriend's apartment to see what the two of them talked about when they were there. But Dave said he didn't want to take the risk. What he meant was that he didn't want *her* to take the risk. She knew that if Dave had been the one following Lewis instead of her, he would have done it.

On the fourth day, something finally happened. For the first time since she'd been following him, Lewis left the Capitol at lunchtime. Until then, he'd spent all day inside the building. Sydney had been waiting near the same entrance he'd used to enter the building, the one closest to the Capitol South Metro station, going out of her mind with boredom, sweltering in the ninety-degree heat. She took a photo of him with her cell phone as he walked over to a stone bench, where he sat for at least ten minutes with a worried look on his face, obviously stewing over something. Then he took out his phone.

All Sydney needed to listen in on and record Brian Lewis's phone calls was his cell phone number and the app Dave had installed on her cell phone. Now whenever Lewis made a call, it was a conference call, and she was part of the conference.

She heard him say, "Professor Lang, it's Brian Lewis."

"Hi, Brian. How are you doing?"

"Not, uh, not good. Professor, I'd like to come and see you this weekend. I—"

And the call failed. Lewis called Lang back.

Lang said, "Sorry, Brian. The reception here is pretty spotty. You said you wanted to see me?"

"Yes, sir. I've learned something here at work and I need to talk to you about it. It's important. It has to do with a bunch of politicians taking bribes."

"Bribes? Are you sure?"

"Yes, sir. Anyway, I really need to talk to you about it and figure out what to do. So I was wondering if I could drive down to Charlottesville and see you this weekend."

"Brian, I'm not in Charlottesville right now. I'm hiking with a buddy on the Appalachian Trail. I'm not going to be home for at least a week. And like I said, I'm not in a good spot for a long phone conversation. Can this wait until I get back?"

"Yes, sir. It can wait. And it's not really something I can talk about on the phone. I need to show you the . . . the evidence."

"Okay, call me in a couple of weeks."

"Thank you, Professor. I'll do that. Have a good time on your hike."

Whoa, Sydney thought.

She spent a few minutes researching Lang. If he was a professor and he lived in Charlottesville, he probably taught at the University of Virginia. It took her five minutes to learn that he was on the law school faculty at UVA.

She called Dave and said, "Brian Lewis just called a law school professor at UVA named Adam Lang. I think you better listen to the recording right away."

"Okay," Dave said.

"How are you feeling?"

"Aw, you know. Those chemo sessions just wipe me out. But send me the recording."

Dave Morgenthal listened to the recording and decided he'd better pass it on to Grady immediately. If Grady knew he was using Sydney to track Brian Lewis, he would have had a fit, but Morgenthal figured there was no way that Grady would ever know.

He had no doubt Sydney could do the job. She was brilliant. And helping him made her feel good about herself, and she stayed focused when she was working. The problem was that Sydney was prone to self-sabotage, and he could never be sure when that little switch inside her head would flip from normal to crazy.

Morgenthal didn't know how much of Sydney's problems were genetic and inherited from her parents, particularly her father, and how much could be attributed to the bitch who was her mother and had abandoned her when she was ten. Sydney's father had been Morgenthal's partner and his best friend. They'd met in the army, and Brad Roma had saved Morgenthal's life when he pulled him from a burning personnel carrier in Afghanistan. And like his daughter, Brad had been brilliant. And like his daughter, you could never tell who he'd be from one day to the next.

When they mustered out of the military, they set up their detective agency and began to spy for people like Patrick Grady who wanted subjects followed and bugged. The problem was that Brad suffered from depression, depression so bad that sometimes he'd crawl into a mental black hole and wouldn't emerge from it for days. He committed suicide when Sydney was fifteen, and to this day Morgenthal had no idea what pushed him over the edge. One day he simply went into his garage and hanged himself and Sydney was the one who found him.

Because he had no choice, because he owed it to his friend, Morgenthal became Sydney's guardian—and then had to endure the roller-coaster ride that was Sydney's life. She was suspended from school repeatedly. It was a miracle that she graduated. She was arrested for shoplifting. She experimented with drugs, alcohol, and sex. Three times she disappeared, and Morgenthal had to track her down. One time he rescued her from a creep who was abusing her and forcing her to have sex with his drug dealer. Thanks to Morgenthal, the creep was now in jail and walked with a permanent limp.

Like her father, Sydney suffered from depression and, when she was seventeen, made an attempt to kill herself. Morgenthal found her in the bathtub one day, blood pouring from both wrists, and it was only luck that he'd gotten there before she bled out. And like with her father, he didn't know what made her do it and she wouldn't tell him. She was now twenty-three and had been clean of drugs and alcohol for over a year. Morgenthal had paid for the month she spent in rehab, and she attended NA meetings semiregularly. But the main thing that kept her on track was that when he was diagnosed with cancer, he began to teach her what he knew and started using her in his business. And that, more than anything else, seemed to keep her demons contained. She enjoyed the work—it was more like a game than a job to her—and she enjoyed the risks she sometimes had to take.

Morgenthal had no idea what to do about her future. He had lung cancer—he'd never smoked a day in his life—but with the drugs they had these days, there was a chance he'd beat it. At least for a while. But one of these days he wasn't going to be there to watch over her, and he had to figure out what to do about her before that day came.

She didn't have a college degree and, because of her problems with addiction, had rarely held down a job for more than a couple of months. So he didn't know what she'd do for employment in the future. Nor did she have any money. Her father had spent everything that he'd made in his lifetime, hadn't had a life insurance policy, and all Sydney inherited from him was his car. Morgenthal would leave his house to her when he passed and all the money he had, though he didn't have that much. But a lack of funds wasn't Sydney's biggest problem. Her biggest problem was that she needed a purpose for living or she'd end up killing herself the way her father had. He wished he could turn his business over to her—she was smart enough to do the job—but his clients were going to balk at working with a twenty-three-year-old woman with a green-ink vine tattoo winding around her throat.

He called Grady and told him he was sending him a recording.

4

"Goddamnit. What evidence? What does that fucking kid know?"

"Carson, I don't think he really knows anything. I mean, I know what you did—what *we* did—and I don't believe you have any serious legal exposure."

"But you don't know that for sure. And like I told you last time, this is the last fucking thing I need right now, with everything else I've got going on. And if he spills his guts to some law professor, God knows what'll happen after that. Son of a bitch!"

"Carson, I think you should calm down."

"Fuck you, calm down. I'm in this mess because of you."

That was a lie. But it was also typical of Carson Newman to never accept responsibility for anything that went wrong. But there was nothing to be gained by arguing about who was responsible. Or in getting him more riled up.

Grady said, "Carson, what do you want to do? Personally, I don't think we should do anything other than continue to keep tabs on him. I'm convinced he doesn't really know anything. And I'll press my source on getting more information. And I suppose there's one other option. Morgenthal told me that Lewis spends a lot of time after work on his laptop. I don't know if Morgenthal will do it, but I could ask him to try and steal the laptop so we can see what's in it."

Newman didn't respond. He was silent for so long that Grady said, "Carson, are you still there?"

"Yes."

"So, do you agree? Should we just continue to watch him, or should I tell Morgenthal we need him to find out what's in the laptop? Maybe he knows a hacker who can get into it remotely."

Again, Newman didn't respond immediately, but this time Grady just waited.

Finally, Newman said, "Tell Morgenthal to stop following him. I don't want him to do anything else."

"Are you sure?"

"Yes," Newman said.

The situation with Brian Lewis was due to the egos of two egomaniacs—Carson Newman and John Mahoney—and Patrick Grady was caught in the middle of it.

About a year ago when Grady learned that a gaggle of progressives were writing a tenants' rights bill, he informed his clients, including Newman. He said if the bill passed, it would cause people like Newman, people who owned rental property, some aggravation and might cost them some money. They would have to pay larger fines if they didn't fix problems in their buildings, they wouldn't be able to easily evict some tenants, and it would be harder for them to raise rents. But he also informed his clients that they shouldn't be too worried, explaining how they could file lawsuits to delay any laws from being implemented and that when the Republicans took control of the House after the midterm elections, as it appeared they would, they could be persuaded to repeal the bill. Grady would, of course, do what he always did to change hearts and minds before a vote was ever cast. None of his clients were happy about the bill but none of them went berserk—except for Newman.

Newman's reaction was mild at first. He objected to the bill, but he wasn't overly concerned, because he thought he could persuade then Speaker of the House John Mahoney to bury it. The bill just wasn't that big a deal—it was hardly groundbreaking legislation—and Newman had what he thought was a close, personal relationship with Mahoney. He contributed generously to the man's campaigns and forced his employees to contribute. He and his wife socialized with Mahoney and his wife. Two years ago, he'd hosted a five-thousand-dollar-per-plate dinner for Mahoney in Boston to help him raise money. And Mahoney had accommodated him in the past when he'd asked for favors, and Newman was sure he would do so again.

So Newman had called Mahoney and, after asking about his health and lamenting a Patriots team without Tom Brady, told him he'd appreciate it if the bill never saw the light of day. He subtly reminded Mahoney of all the campaign contributions he'd made, adding that he could be counted on if Mahoney ever needed his help in the future.

And John Mahoney basically told Carson Newman to go fuck himself.

What Newman didn't seem to realize was that although it was possible to buy Mahoney's vote, it was never certain. Mahoney was unpredictable. He was irascible. And at the time, with the midterm elections looming and the possibility that the Democrats would lose the House, Newman's desires were the last thing on Mahoney's mind. Mahoney wanted the bill passed because he thought it would make the Democrats look as if they could actually do something to help people not as rich as Newman.

It was after that phone call that Newman went berserk. He was outraged that Mahoney would turn his back on him as if he were some ordinary constituent and not one of the richest men in Boston. He was offended by the brusque way Mahoney had dismissed his concerns before cutting the call short, saying that he had more important things to do. And that's when Newman told Grady that he wanted his lobbying firm to go to war over the bill. He wanted an all-out campaign to make sure it failed. Frankly, the bill at this point became irrelevant; the only thing that mattered to Carson Newman was jamming it up John Mahoney's fat ass.

Grady, because Newman was paying for it, did what he was asked. He put three of his bright, young underlings into a room and told them to develop a winning strategy. They needed ten Democrats to vote no on the bill but figured that a dozen would be better in case there were a couple of defectors. Grady's trio looked at every Democrat in the House—they had dossiers on all of them—and zeroed in on twelve men who could most likely be persuaded to vote no. Obviously, campaign contributions would be used as one mechanism to convince them, but in some cases, it would take more than campaign money. So they identified things that would appeal to the congressmen's egos, things that would benefit their wives and kids, things that would get them some positive exposure in the media. They developed a rationale tailored to each legislator that he could use to justify his vote. The process took a month, but in the end, Grady's bright employees came up with myriad clever ways to persuade and influence the twelve, and Grady flew up to Boston and presented his team's plan to Newman.

And the plan worked.

When the bill was voted on, the twelve all voted no, and the bill failed.

And that should have been the end of it.

But then it wasn't, because of Brian fucking Lewis.

Nonetheless, and as he'd told Newman, Grady was convinced that Lewis really didn't know enough to pose a serious threat. How could he? And it appeared as if Newman had finally come around to his way of thinking.

He called Morgenthal and told him to stop following the kid.

5

Elaine knocked on the door of Brian's small apartment, but he didn't come to the door.

She was worried. She hadn't talked to him in two days. She'd called Friday evening to tell him she'd be working late and wouldn't be able to meet him for dinner, but he didn't return her call. She called him twice on Saturday, and again he didn't call her back. Since they'd gotten together, she couldn't remember a time they'd gone two days without talking. And he always returned her calls. She knew he wasn't giving her the silent treatment because they'd had an argument—they hardly argued about anything—but if they had argued, Brian wouldn't have ignored her out of spite. He wasn't like that.

She knocked again. Maybe he was sleeping—it was Sunday after all—and maybe he hadn't heard her. Then she thought, *No, there was no way he'd still be sleeping at ten in the morning*. Brian was an early bird, always up before seven when he wasn't working.

She pulled a set of keys from her purse. One key opened the apartment building door, the other opened Brian's door. He'd given her the keys when he first rented the crummy apartment so she could come and go as she pleased. The truth was that she didn't really need the keys, as she hardly ever went to his place when he wasn't home. She'd come over a couple of times and fixed dinner for him before he'd gotten home from work, but those had been special occasions, one his birthday and the other to celebrate the two-year anniversary of the day they met. She stored a few of her clothes there for when she spent the night, but they usually spent the night at her place when her roommate, who traveled constantly, was out of town.

They'd talked about her moving in with him, but not seriously. His apartment consisted of only three rooms: a living room, a bathroom, and a small kitchen. There was no bedroom; Brian slept on a hide-a-bed couch in the living room. And it was a dump. Moldy carpeting, a toilet that was always running, a stove with only two of the four burners working.

She put the key in the lock, turned it, and slowly pushed the door open but didn't immediately step inside. For some inexplicable reason, she was hesitant to enter. Intuition, not logic, was telling her that something wasn't right. Her nerves were tingling.

From the doorway, she could see the entire apartment except for the bathroom, because the bathroom door was closed. The kitchen was visible—the noisy refrigerator, the small sink, and part of the stove. An ancient corduroy couch—the hide-a-bed that Brian had to pull out each night when he wanted to sleep—took up most of the living room. On the back of the couch was a blue sport jacket, a short-sleeved white dress shirt, and a tie. That was odd. Brian, who was a bit of a neat freak, always hung up his clothes or put them in the hamper.

She called out, "Brian, are you here?" She knew if he was there, the only place he could be was in the bathroom.

She walked over to the bathroom door and knocked on it, knowing, as thin as the door was, he should have heard her call out to him.

She hesitated again. She was afraid to open the door. She finally turned the knob and slowly pushed the door open—and then had to clamp her hands over her mouth to keep from screaming.

Brian was sitting on the toilet wearing a white T-shirt and the Docker khakis he usually wore to work. His body had fallen sideways and was leaning against the sink next to the toilet. His face had a waxy look, the skin a bluish tinge, and his eyes were half open. Wrapped around his arm, above his left elbow, was a piece of rubber tubing. On the sink was a hypodermic needle, an empty small plastic bag, a book of matches, and a charred spoon.

If anyone else had found him, that person most likely would have backed away immediately and called 911. But Elaine was a nurse in training, and even though she knew it was pointless, she reached out a trembling hand and touched his throat to feel for a pulse.

There was no pulse.

6

Brian Lewis's body had been found on a Sunday morning. The next day, a little before noon, an Uber driver delivered a white cardboard box sealed with packing tape to the building on K Street that housed Grady's firm. The Uber driver gave the package to a receptionist, who gave it to Grady's administrative assistant, who didn't open it, because written on the box in black marker were the words *Confidential. Patrick Grady, Eyes Only.*

Grady didn't open the box immediately. He couldn't help but recall stories of packages being delivered to politicians containing anthrax and pipe bombs. But then he told himself he was being paranoid. He wasn't a politician; the crazies didn't know his name. He was the wizard behind the curtain.

Using a letter opener, he sliced through the packing tape and opened the box. Inside was newspaper that had been used for padding and a faux leather laptop case with a shoulder strap and a carrying handle. On the handle was a tag with Lewis's name, address, and telephone number.

"Son of a bitch!" Grady said out loud.

Grady knew that Lewis was dead. He'd placed a Google alert on his phone to notify him if Lewis's name popped up online, like if he was about to be interviewed on *60 Minutes*. When he learned that Lewis had died of a drug overdose, he'd been . . . Well, *happy* probably wasn't the right word, but he'd certainly been relieved. All his concerns of Lewis talking to someone in the media or a law professor at UVA about whatever it was he'd learned evaporated.

But now Lewis's laptop case was sitting on his desk.

The first thought that occurred to him was that Newman had hired someone to kill the kid, but Grady found it hard to believe that Newman would do something so drastic. Newman may have been the type of person who would do anything to protect himself, but in Newman's world that meant throwing money at problems and throwing other people under the bus and using lawyers to skirt the law. Murder was in a whole different league, and Grady doubted even Newman would be willing to take the risks that went with having someone killed. Plus, he'd told Newman that the likelihood of Lewis, an intern, being able to prove that anything illegal had happened was remote. It was beyond remote. Grady had figured that the worst thing Lewis would have been able to do was make some outrageous accusations that Newman's lawyers would have swatted away like pesky flies.

But maybe Carson Newman had thought otherwise.

Grady took the laptop out of the case. It was a silver MacBook Air with a thirteen-inch screen. He started to open it, then stopped. He didn't want to touch it.

He called Newman and said, "Someone sent me a laptop."

"Find out what's in it and let me know," Newman said.

"Why did you have it sent to me?"

Newman said, "Who says I sent it to you?"

One thing that Grady had noticed as soon as he started working with Newman was that he was usually very careful about what he said on phone calls, as if he was afraid that a third party might be listening in. Newman also rarely texted or emailed people, again maybe thinking ahead to the day when someone might get a warrant to look at his records.

Grady wanted to ask, *Did you have Lewis killed?* But he didn't. There was no way he was going to ask a question like that on a cell phone. Instead, he said, "Do you know that the owner of the laptop is dead?"

"Let me know what's in it," Newman said.

And with that, the bastard hung up.

Grady was now back to the question: Had Newman hired someone to kill the kid? He wouldn't have done it himself, of course. But Grady still found it hard to believe that Newman would go to that extreme. It was possible that he had hired someone to steal the laptop—Grady had even suggested doing that—and that the theft of the laptop wasn't connected to Lewis's death. Yeah, maybe. But if Newman had hired someone to kill Lewis, and since Grady had hired Morgenthal to follow Lewis before he was killed, could a prosecutor conclude that Grady was in some way an accomplice to Lewis's death? Yeah, maybe.

Grady sat for the longest time just staring at the laptop. What he should do was drop the damn thing into the Potomac, no matter what Newman had said. On the other hand, he wanted to know exactly what Lewis had learned and if he'd passed on what he'd learned to anyone else.

He raised the lid on the laptop—and up popped a prompt asking for a password.

Grady called the IT guy the firm used. His name was Don Janovich and he worked out of a loft in Dupont Circle with a couple of other geeks. The firm had hired him for years to deal with routine computer problems, and Janovich had installed the software to protect KL&M from cyberattacks. One time, after one of Grady's associates had died unexpectedly from a massive heart attack, the firm used Janovich to get into the dead man's password-protected devices.

He told Janovich to come to his office immediately. Janovich's hourly rate was three hundred bucks, but Grady said because he needed something done urgently, he'd pay him five hundred per hour, and if it took him less than an hour, he'd pay him a thousand. And whatever it cost, he'd bill Newman for it.

While waiting for Janovich, he searched the laptop case. The only other things in it were a power cord for the computer and an external hard drive that Lewis had probably used to back up his files. He would ditch the hard drive along with the laptop after he learned what was in it.

Janovich arrived half an hour later. He didn't look like a guy who lived in his mother's basement and spent twenty-four hours a day eating Cheetos while roaming the Dark Net. He looked like someone who could have been used on army recruiting posters, a Captain America with clear blue eyes, a strong chin, a muscular build, and short blond hair. But that didn't make him any less a geek.

Grady pointed at the laptop sitting on his desk as if it were a dead skunk that someone had dumped there. "All I need you to do is get around the password and fix it so I don't have to enter it again." Janovich took the computer to an empty conference room and was back twenty minutes later. Grady thanked him, wrote a check for a thousand dollars, and sent him on his way.

The first thing Grady did was look at the file names in the Documents folder, and he found what he was looking for in less than five minutes. It was a Word document with a grandiose name: "Tenants' Rights Conspiracy."

He printed out the document; it was ten and a half pages long. He was shocked by how much the kid had pieced together—and in some cases, he couldn't easily figure out how he did it—but it was as he'd expected.

If Lewis's findings had been made public, it would have caused Newman some embarrassment, but not much more than that.

He shredded the document, then looked at Lewis's emails to see if he'd attached it to an email and sent it to anyone. He hadn't. He could have snail-mailed it to someone, but in this day and age, that seemed unlikely. Grady spent an hour looking at other files in the laptop and saw several that were related to Lewis's conspiracy theory—background information on congressmen, rough drafts, research notes, online articles he'd cut and pasted related to campaign finance laws. He couldn't help but admire the kid's thoroughness and persistence.

He called Newman and told him what Lewis had learned. Newman, like Grady himself, was shocked by some of the things the kid had uncovered.

"How in the fuck did he find that out?" Newman said more than once.

Grady told him that in addition to Lewis's main report, thesis, theory, analysis, whatever the hell you wanted to call it, there was also some related background information that supported Lewis's conclusions.

"The good news," Grady said, "is that he didn't email it to anyone." Then, because he couldn't help himself, Grady added, "And even if he did send it to someone and it became public, it was like I told you in the first place: he didn't find anything that could have caused you a major problem."

What he was really saying was: *If you had that kid killed, you really fucked up.*

When Newman didn't respond to the I-told-you-so, Grady asked, "Do you want me to email it to you?"

"No," Newman said.

Of course he didn't want it sent to him. He didn't want it on *his* computer.

"In that case, I'm going to get rid of the laptop."

"No, don't do that. Hang on to it for a while," Newman said.

"Why?"

"Why not?"

Grady wanted to scream *Because it's fucking evidence!* And he didn't know if it was evidence of theft or murder.

Newman said, "If the report pops up someplace, we might need whatever else is in the laptop to show that Lewis conducted some sort of rogue, illegal investigation and anything coming from it is illegal. You know, what lawyers call 'fruit of the poisonous tree.' I kind of doubt that will happen, but you never know, so just hang on to it for a bit."

Grady didn't like the idea of keeping the laptop, but he wasn't overly concerned. How would anyone even know that he had it? The only ones who knew it was in his possession were Newman and the person who sent it to him, who probably worked for Newman, and they wouldn't tell. And he now knew that if Lewis's report ever did see the light of day, it wasn't a problem for him and the firm.

But what he didn't know was if Lewis had accidently OD'd, as had been reported.

Well, whether he had or not, Grady wasn't going to dwell on the subject.

That was Newman's problem, not his.

He hoped.

7

—◆◆◆—

John Mahoney was sitting behind his desk in a high-backed, black leather chair. He was wearing a white shirt with gold cuff links and red suspenders. In his meaty right paw was a tumbler filled with ice and bourbon. He wasn't doing anything—other than drinking and brooding.

Mahoney was a handsome, heavyset man with a shock of pure white hair. He had a florid complexion and broken veins in his cheeks and nose, thanks to the amount of alcohol he consumed on a daily basis. His eyes were bright blue—eyes that could twinkle with amusement and charm, or that would turn into daggers to stab whoever needed stabbing. For him to be having a drink at eleven a.m. on a Monday while at work wasn't at all unusual. He was an alcoholic. But normally he drank his bourbon out of a coffee cup in the morning.

Perry Wallace approached Mahoney's desk cautiously, like a man afraid to disturb a hibernating bear. "I need to talk to you," he said.

Mahoney didn't respond. He just sat there glowering.

Mahoney had been the Speaker of the House for eight years, but when the Republicans gained the majority in the November midterm elections, he lost the top spot and another man, a bitter rival, was now called Mr. Speaker. Mahoney's new title was House Minority Leader, a title he absolutely hated. And because he no longer had the power and the prestige that went with the speakership, he was almost impossible to be around these days.

Mahoney blamed everyone—but himself—for the Democrats' failure to keep the House. He blamed the president, a Democrat. He blamed the Democratic Senate Majority Leader, who'd miraculously managed to keep his job. He blamed the idiots on the Democratic National Committee. He blamed the talking heads on MSNBC and CNN for getting the spin wrong on every important story. He blamed every lawmaker who lost his or her seat in the House for not following his advice and for running incompetent campaigns. He didn't really blame the Republicans for lying, cheating, and gerrymandering—he blamed his fellow Democrats for failing to lie and cheat and gerrymander more effectively.

So Mahoney no longer sat in the Speaker's plush office with its balcony, where he could stand in the afternoons with a drink in hand and gaze out at the National Mall. He no longer held the gavel when Congress was in session. He no longer decided what hearings would be held that could be used to embarrass the other party. He could no longer fulfill campaign promises by passing legislation that his constituents wanted. And it seemed as if every day, in his role as second banana, he was forced endure another humiliation from the man who had replaced him. And every day he took his wrath out on those closest to him—one of those people being Perry Wallace, his chief of staff.

Perry said, "I've got some bad news."

"So what else is new?" Mahoney said, without looking at Perry.

"That kid you had me hire, Brian Lewis? He's dead."

Now Mahoney looked at Perry. "Christ," he said. "How the hell did that happen?"

"Drug overdose," Perry said.

"Aw, geez," Mahoney said.

The only reason Mahoney had told Perry to hire Brian was because Brian's mother had been married to one of the last U.S. servicemen killed in Afghanistan. The man had been at the airport in Kabul when Afghan citizens, fearful of the Taliban, stormed the airport trying to get on the last U.S. planes leaving the country, and a bomb exploded. The bomb killed one hundred and sixty-nine Afghans and thirteen American soldiers. Brian's father was one of the thirteen.

Mahoney had his faults—he had many faults—but he was a veteran and always willing to do what he could to help those who'd served and their families. He'd met Brian's mother at her husband's funeral at Arlington National Cemetery—he often attended the funerals of veterans—where he'd hugged her and said that if there was anything he could do, she shouldn't hesitate to ask. The woman had been almost catatonic with grief, and he wasn't sure she'd even heard him, so he was surprised when she wrote him almost two years later and asked for a job for her son.

Perry said, "This is the last kid I ever thought would have been using drugs. He worked his ass off, always getting here early and leaving late. He never once looked hungover or like he was high on something."

"Fucking drugs," Mahoney said, unable to think of anything more profound to say. "Find out when the funeral is and arrange my schedule so I can drop by to tell his mom how sorry I am."

⁌———◈———⁍

Five days after his body was discovered, and after an autopsy had been performed, a funeral service was held for Brian Lewis at an Episcopal church in Silver Spring, Maryland. A reception was held after the service in the basement of the church, and about thirty people attended. There were plates of cheese and crackers on a long folding table, and on the floor were coolers filled with soft drinks and bottles of water. On a card table by a wall was a vase filled with drooping lilies and photos of Brian at various stages of his life, from toddler to college student.

Mahoney timed his visit to arrive after the reception had started. There was no way he would have taken the time to attend the service, nor was he a man who felt comfortable inside a church. He was Catholic but the only time he went to Mass was when he was campaigning.

He caused the expected stir because most of the people at the reception recognized him, as he was on the news about every other night complaining about something the Republicans had done. He came with two security people—big guys dressed in suits with guns barely visible in shoulder holsters—and they parted the crowd for him as he walked over to Brian's mom.

She was a small woman in her forties with dark hair and a thin face. For whatever reason, maybe because of the way her hair was styled, she made Mahoney think of the famous photo of Jackie Kennedy in her blood-stained pink suit, standing next to Lyndon Johnson as Johnson was sworn in as president after JFK's assassination. Caroline Lewis had the same haunted look in her eyes, the same I-can't-believe-I'm-standing-here expression on her face. She was wearing a simple black dress; it was the same dress she'd worn at her husband's funeral, the only formal black dress she owned.

People were standing in a line waiting to speak to her and express their sympathy. Mahoney ignored the line and walked up to her. He took one of her hands into both of his, looked into her eyes, and said, "Caroline, I'm so sorry. Brian was such a wonderful young man." Mahoney said this having met Brian only once, on the day he reported to work. "I know the pain you must be feeling and—"

Caroline interrupted him. "I need to talk to you. Alone."

She turned and walked toward a door that was behind where she'd been standing, and Mahoney, having no choice, made a gesture to his security people to stay where they were and followed her.

She opened the door, and she and Mahoney stepped into a small office. There was desk with a computer on it, a single chair behind the desk, and three four-drawer file cabinets against a wall. It looked like an office used by the church's bookkeeper.

Caroline closed the door and looked up at Mahoney, who was six inches taller than she was.

She said, "Brian was murdered."

Knowing he was talking to a grief-stricken mother, Mahoney said, "Aw, Caroline. I know you're—"

"Listen to me. Brian didn't do drugs. Ever. He barely drank."

Mahoney was thinking, *I kinda doubt he'd tell you he was mainlining heroin*, but had the good sense not say that. He said, "I know you're distraught but—"

"You're damn right I'm distraught. My husband's gone and now I've lost my only child. But you better take me seriously, Congressman. We had dinner a couple of weeks before he died, and I could tell something was bothering him. He was distracted and fidgety and— Anyway, I asked him what was going on and he said that he'd discovered something at work."

"At work?"

"Yes. He said he had proof that a bunch of politicians had committed crimes and he was trying to figure out what to do about it."

Now she had Mahoney's complete attention.

"What kind of crimes?"

"I don't know exactly. He told me it had to do with people taking bribes but said the laws were complicated and it was hard to prove that what they did was illegal, but he had no doubt he was right."

Mahoney figured the kid had probably seen something related to campaign contributions. He also figured that Brian wouldn't have had a clue as to what was legal and what wasn't. Hell, there were lawyers who specialized in campaign finance laws who couldn't agree on how the laws should be interpreted. But before he could say that, Caroline said, "Now, I know what you're thinking. You're thinking that since you were the politician he worked for, that one of the people he may have been talking about was you."

That was true. That had also occurred to Mahoney. That was actually the first thing that had occurred to him.

Caroline said, "So I asked him. I asked him if you were one of the congressmen he was talking about, and he told me no."

Mahoney almost blurted *Thank God*, but didn't. Instead, he said, "Caroline, I have no idea what Brian was doing in my office. He may have worked for me, but he got all his assignments from my chief of staff or someone who works for him. But I do know that he never reported uncovering any sort of crimes, or his boss would have told me."

Caroline said, "Well, I don't know who he told. All I know is that he was convinced that he'd found something significant. And since I know he didn't use drugs, I think whatever he found was the reason he was killed. There couldn't have been any other reason. He didn't have any enemies. He was only twenty-two years old, for Christ's sake. And that's what I told the police."

Aw, Jesus. She'd already talked to the cops about this.

Caroline said, "I told them that they needed to look into what he was doing at work, but they blew me off. The detective I spoke to said there was no evidence that he'd been murdered. He also said that lots of kids kill themselves with drugs and about half the time their parents have no idea they're using. Well, I *know* he wasn't using drugs, goddamnit, and I'm convinced his death is connected to whatever he'd learned at work. And what I want is for you to lean on the cops to make them do a real investigation."

"I'll do that," Mahoney said. *The hell he would.* The last thing he was going to do was allow the cops to look into anything his staff was doing.

Caroline pinned him with her red-rimmed eyes. "Like I said, you better take me seriously, Congressman. I'm angry. I'm *really* angry. And if you don't do something and if I'm not satisfied that the police are looking harder, I'm going to talk to the press."

"Caroline," Mahoney said, "I am taking you seriously." And he was. "But you need to give me some time. I'm going to assign the best guy I've got to look into his death and see what the cops are doing, and I promise either he or I will get back to you."

Back in the car with his security detail, he pulled a silver flask from the inside pocket of his suit, took a swig, put the flask back, then called his secretary.

He said, "Mavis, track down DeMarco and tell him and Perry that I want them sitting in my office when I get back."

8

Joe DeMarco was not in his office in the Capitol when Mahoney's secretary called.

DeMarco owned a narrow town house on P Street in Georgetown made of white-painted brick. The grass, as usual, needed cutting. He was standing in his backyard, next to his air conditioner, yelling at a short, swarthy, balding guy who was wearing gray work pants and a grease-streaked blue shirt with the name Rick in red letters over the breast pocket.

DeMarco was saying, "I bought this fuckin' unit less than two years ago. The last air conditioner I had lasted fifteen years."

DeMarco was almost six feet tall and had a broad-shouldered, muscular build. He had a full head of dark hair he combed straight back, blue eyes, a prominent nose, and a cleft chin. He was a handsome man but a hard-looking one, and he could be intimidating if he chose to be. Rick wasn't the least bit intimidated.

"Well, they don't make 'em like they used to," Rick said.

"No shit," DeMarco said.

"And the warranty on the compressor is only good for a year. You should have paid for the extended warranty. That would have covered the compressor for five years."

"Why the hell should I have to pay for an extended warranty? Why would the goddamn thing fail in less than two years?"

"Hey, I don't know what to tell you."

"What do you mean, you don't know what to tell me? You're the goddamn expert and I'm paying you seventy-five bucks for this service call, and all you can say is 'they don't make 'em like they used to'?"

"Look, I'm sorry," Rick said. "But you're going to have to replace the compressor."

"Why does it have to be replaced? Why can't you fix it?"

"I don't know how to fix it. Nobody does. They make the compressor for this unit in China—or maybe it's Korea—and all the information about it is proprietary. And the circuit boards for these things, you gotta have a degree in electrical engineering to understand how they work. When something fails, like the compressor, the only thing we can do is replace it."

"And how much will that cost?"

"Thirty-five hundred."

"Thirty-five hundred! Are you shitting me? That's half of what the whole unit cost."

"Well, the compressor is the main part in the unit."

Knowing he was screwed, and knowing that yelling at Rick was futile, DeMarco took a breath and said, "Fine. Replace the compressor. How long will that take?"

"It only takes two or three hours to put in a new one, but we don't have any new ones for this model in stock. It'll probably be a couple of months before we can get one."

"A couple of months!" DeMarco screamed. "I can't go all summer without an air conditioner."

"Sorry, but we got these supply chain problems. You may have heard about 'em."

DeMarco's phone rang. He pointed at Rick and said, "Don't move."

He answered the phone, saying, "This is Joe," and Mahoney's secretary told him he was to come to Mahoney's office immediately. He said, "I'll be there as soon as I can, but Mahoney has me working on something and I had to go to Fairfax and the traffic's really bad."

He hung up and glared at Rick.

"So what do you wanna do?" Rick said.

"What can I do? Replace the damn compressor. But I'm going to be calling you about every other day to find out where the new one is."

Rick wrote up the paperwork and asked if DeMarco wanted to pay the additional two hundred and fifty bucks for the extended warranty. "You thievin' bastards," DeMarco muttered—but he got the extended warranty.

As Rick was leaving, he said, "Oh, by the way, you'll be getting an email asking you to complete a survey, to tell my boss how I did today. I'd appreciate it if—"

"Get away from me," DeMarco said.

———————————◆◆◆———————————

DeMarco arrived at the waiting room outside Mahoney's office forty-five minutes later. The white golf shirt he was wearing was soaked with sweat; he looked as if he'd run a marathon instead of walking fifteen minutes from his parking place. In D.C., in July, the humidity percentage was usually about the same number as the temperature, and if you stepped outside any air-conditioned structure for more than a minute, you immediately began to sweat like a stevedore unloading the hold of a cargo ship.

Perry Wallace was already in Mahoney's waiting room, going through a stack of papers in his lap. Perry had thinning dark hair and dark circles under his eyes because he worked about sixteen hours a day to keep Mahoney happy. He no longer had a wife. He had no kids. He had no hobbies. He didn't have a life. He was about DeMarco's age and height but outweighed DeMarco by fifty pounds. The only exercise he got was running from his office to Mahoney's, and he lived on Diet Coke and fast food and whatever he could find in vending machines. DeMarco had always thought that Perry should be the subject of a medical study to find out if he had some previously undiscovered gene that explained why he hadn't yet had a heart attack.

Perry had worked for Mahoney longer than any person on his staff except for Mahoney's secretary, Mavis. And Mahoney would never have been able to do his job if he hadn't had Perry. Perry managed Mahoney's large staff. He wrote Mahoney's speeches. Mahoney was a big-picture guy, not a details guy. Perry handled the details. Most important, Perry understood the operating rules of Congress. The procedures for passing laws and appropriating money are complex—they're so complex that Congress has a person called a parliamentarian to interpret and referee all the rules—and Perry understood the rules and how to get around them.

When Perry saw DeMarco, he asked Mavis, "Can we go in?"

She glared at DeMarco. "What took you so damn long? He's hard enough to be around these days without you aggravating him."

Mavis had worked on Mahoney's first campaign and then had stayed with him in the decades that followed. In her twenties, she'd been a gorgeous, long-legged redhead, which was probably the main reason Mahoney had hired her. Now she was gray-haired and whip thin and cantankerous. The reason Mahoney had kept her by his side long after her looks had faded was because she was bright and efficient and protective; she would step in front of a bullet for him. Why she was so loyal DeMarco didn't know, but at this point in her career, she knew all of Mahoney's secrets, and if she ever turned on him, she'd become the star witness for the prosecution. And no one who worked for Mahoney, including Perry, had more power or more influence over Mahoney than she did. She definitely outranked DeMarco.

"Hey, I told you. I was in Fairfax and—"

"Shut up and get in there," she said.

Mahoney was behind his desk, sipping bourbon but this time from a coffee mug. Today his shirt was blue and his suspenders were black. His eyes were bloodshot, and DeMarco could smell the booze on his breath from four feet away.

He looked at DeMarco and said, "Where the hell were you?"

"I was—"

"Never mind. I don't have time for whatever lie you're about to tell me." Looking at Perry he said, "It's Brian Lewis. The kid who died."

"Who's Brian Lewis?" DeMarco asked.

"An intern who worked for me," Perry said. "He OD'd." To Mahoney, he said, "What's the problem?"

"His mother. I dropped in on his funeral and his mother takes me aside and tells me she thinks he was killed."

"Oh, for Christ's sake," Perry said.

"That's not the worst of it," Mahoney said. "She said that he'd uncovered some kind of criminal conspiracy involving a bunch of politicians."

DeMarco was thinking that only Mahoney would consider that the murder of a young man was less important than a potential political scandal. He also understood why Mahoney felt that way and so he asked, "Is she saying you're one of the politicians?"

"No," Mahoney said. "In fact, she asked her son if I was one of them and he told her I wasn't, and she believed him."

"So which politicians?" Perry said. "And what kind of crimes?"

"His mother said it had to do with guys taking bribes but—"

"Like that would ever happen," DeMarco said, rolling his eyes.

"Shut the fuck up," Mahoney said. "I'm not in the mood for your smart mouth. But he probably saw something related to campaign contributions or campaign financing and didn't have any idea what he was looking at." Pointing at Perry, he said, "What I want you to do is look at whatever you had him doing and see what he might have found. Or thought he found." To DeMarco, he said, "And what I want you to do is meet with his mother right away and convince her that we're working our asses off to get to the bottom of this thing and keep her from talking to the TV people. And when you go see her, don't wear a fuckin' golf shirt."

"I better go see the cops first," DeMarco said.

"No," Mahoney said. "Go see her first. Finding out what happened to her son isn't the priority. The priority is keeping this thing contained until I know what the hell's going on."

Perry and DeMarco, having been given their marching orders, rose to leave, but Mahoney said, "By the way, what did I have you working on before this came up?"

"Budnick," DeMarco said.

"Oh, yeah, that little prick. Why haven't you taken care of him?"

"Do you want me to work on Lewis or Budnick?"

"Lewis. But get the damn Budnick thing done."

As they were walking down the hall to Perry's office, Perry said, "Are you actually doing anything when it comes to Budnick?"

"No," DeMarco said.

A few paces later, DeMarco asked, "Is the drinking getting out of control?"

"Yeah," Perry said. "It's bad. There've been a couple of times I've had to stop him from going to meetings and have his detail take him home.

I'm going to have to get together with Mavis and Mary Pat and do an intervention."

Mary Pat was Mahoney's long-suffering wife. The woman had given him three daughters and put up with his unfaithfulness and his self-centered nature for more than forty years. As far as DeMarco was concerned, she was a living saint.

"An intervention?" DeMarco said. "You mean talk him into going into rehab?"

"He'd never go into rehab. But we gotta convince him to get the boozing back to less than a bottle a day before he destroys himself."

There was barely room to move in Perry's office. Paper was stacked *everywhere*: on Perry's desk, on the floor, on top of file cabinets, on windowsills, on one of the two visitors' chairs. Bills passing through Congress can be hundreds and sometimes thousands of pages long. Mahoney never actually read the bills, but Perry did, and then briefed Mahoney on what they said. And then there was all the paperwork supporting all the crap that was in the bills. Studies from think tanks; estimates—usually pulled out of thin air—regarding how much it would cost the taxpayer if the bills were actually made into law. There were memos from other legislators, glossy brochures prepared by lobbyists packed with lies, scholarly papers prepared by eggheads who worked in ivory towers. Perry read these, too. DeMarco figured that Perry must have a system for organizing all the stuff in his office so he could find whatever he needed to find, but if there was a system, it wasn't obvious.

Perry walked through a narrow aisle of paper, like he was moving through a minefield, and took a seat behind his desk. He pointed to the one visitor's chair that had a stack of red three-ring binders on it that was two feet high and said to DeMarco, "Clear that shit off the chair." Before DeMarco could ask why, since the other visitor's chair was usable as a chair, Perry picked up the phone on his desk, punched a button, and said, "Come to my office. Now."

DeMarco picked up the stack of binders, looked around for a place to put them, and finally dumped them on top of a two-foot pile of paper, creating a four-foot Leaning Tower of Pisa that would collapse if anyone brushed against it.

A woman rushed into Perry's office; she was panting as if she'd run from wherever she'd been. She was in her forties and a bit overweight. Her dark hair looked as if she'd combed it with a fan, and she was wearing a white blouse and the pants from one of those pantsuit outfits that Hillary Clinton always wore. The color of the pants was turquoise.

Perry said to DeMarco, "This is Jane Rosen. She was Brian's immediate supervisor."

To Jane, he said, "This is DeMarco."

"Yeah, I know," Jane said. "I've seen him around here before, but I don't know what he does."

"That's because you're not supposed to know what he does," Perry said. Before Jane could respond, he said, "This is about Brian."

"Oh, that poor kid," Jane said. "I just can't believe he's gone. He was so young."

"Yeah, yeah," Perry said. "What did you have him working on?"

Jane said, "Can you tell me why you're asking?"

Perry hesitated, then said, "You need to keep what I'm about to tell you to yourself."

"Then why tell her?" DeMarco said.

"Because if she knows, she'll be better able to help us figure out what's going on. And because I trust her. She's worked for me for seven years."

"Eight," Jane said.

Perry said, "Brian told his mother before he died that he learned something that pointed to a bunch of politicians committing crimes and—"

"What?" Jane said.

"—and his mother thinks someone killed him because of whatever it was he learned."

"That's absurd," Jane said. "I mean, the part about him uncovering something illegal. I would have known."

"So what did you have him doing?"

She shrugged. "Intern shit. He probably spent half the day running things from our office to some other office. He made copies. We sent him out for sandwiches. We had him make the coffee. Once I had him go to Mahoney's condo and get him a clean shirt when Mahoney spilled barbecue sauce on the one he was wearing."

"Yeah, but what else?" Perry said. "I know you had him doing other stuff."

"Let me think," Jane said. "I had him update all the personal stuff on the big-shot donors' list. He spent two weeks, off and on, doing that. There were over four hundred names."

The big-shot donors were those who contributed significant amounts to Mahoney's campaigns, and the list contained personal information on each donor—like the names of spouses and kids, where the kids went to school, what kind of hobbies the donor had, any notable achievements recently accomplished by the donor, and so on. To get this information, Brian would have scoured the Internet for articles, looked at Facebook and Twitter and Wikipedia, and updated the information on the list if necessary. The reason the information was compiled was so that when Mahoney called to ask them for money, he could pretend he actually cared about them. *I'm so sorry to hear your mother, Agnes, passed away last year. She was such a wonderful teacher and I know her students at St. Mary's all loved her.*

"What else?" Perry said.

"The water thing. You know the clean-water thing. H.R. 7300."

"What did you have him do?"

"Compare the budget estimates from the first time we tried to pass it to the current ones. You wanted to know what costs had increased and why. So I had him make up a spreadsheet and I sent it you."

"Oh, yeah, I remember," Perry said. "But I didn't know he was the one who put it together. He did a good job on that."

"But all he did was look at numbers, see which ones had changed, then call whoever he had to call to get an explanation."

"What else?" Perry said.

Jane rolled her eyes. "The dirty dozen. You told me to get going on that and I assigned an intern because I knew you didn't think it was important, but he only spent a little bit of time on it."

"The dirty dozen?" DeMarco said. "What's that mean?"

Perry said, "Aw, it was something Mahoney had a hair up his ass about. I was hoping he'd forgotten about it, but a couple of months ago, when he was three sheets to the wind, he bugged me and I told Jane to get it done."

"Get *what* done?" DeMarco said. "I don't know what you're talking about."

Perry sighed—the sigh of a reasonable man who worked for an unreasonable one. "This was right before we lost the House, right before the midterm elections. There was this bill that had to do with tenants' rights. It made it harder to evict people not paying the rent if they got laid off or got sick and couldn't work. Like during the pandemic. It made it harder to raise rents. It was also intended to tighten up the laws related to holding landlords—meaning slumlords—accountable for fixing shit. You know, these guys that own these crummy buildings in housing projects where you got rats running all over the place and the elevators and the furnaces never work. Under the current laws, the landlords get citations and get fined, but about half the time it's cheaper to pay the fines than actually fix anything.

"So that's what the bill was about, and Mahoney wanted it passed because it would have shown we actually cared about helping ordinary people and because it would make the Republicans look bad if they voted against it, which they all did. In other words, it was just business as usual. But the bill didn't pass. There were twelve Democrats who voted against it and Mahoney went apeshit. He wanted to know why they voted no. He wanted to know why they'd betrayed him. His gut told him there was something weird going on and he wanted to know what."

"Maybe some of them got bribed to vote no," DeMarco said.

"No one got *bribed*," Perry said. "There was no reason to bribe anyone. If the bill had passed, fifty lawsuits would have been filed the next day claiming that everything in it was unconstitutional. Plus, there was the fact that everyone—but Mahoney—could see we were going to lose the House and the Republicans would have just repealed the bill. So why bribe anyone?"

Perry shook his head. "Anyway, Mahoney wanted me to figure out why these guys voted the way they did. I told him that some voted no because they were in purple districts and didn't want to come off as socialists. Some thought the bill didn't go far enough. Some thought it went too far. And this vote happened while people were campaigning, trying to keep their seats, and they were doing a lot of squirrelly things. But Mahoney wasn't satisfied and he told me to dig deeper.

"But I didn't do anything right away, and after the midterms he was so depressed and pissed off and drinking like a fish that I thought he'd forgotten about it, and I didn't bring it up. Then the new Congress gets seated after the first of the year and there's a million things going on, but for whatever reason he brings it up again. But he was so drunk at the time, I figured he wouldn't remember even talking to me about it and again I didn't do anything. It just wasn't that important. But then a couple of months ago, something must have jogged his memory, and he got really pissed when I told him I hadn't gotten around to it. I reminded him that more than half a year had passed since the vote was taken, but he said he didn't give a shit. So I told Jane to put together something that might make him happy, and as you heard she assigned one of the new summer interns."

"That sounds like something pretty complicated to give to an intern," DeMarco said.

"Not really," Jane said. "I just told Brian to look at their voting records, to look for patterns and anomalies, to see how they justified their vote on the bill based on what they put in *Congressional Record.* That sort of thing."

To Jane, Perry said, "Did Brian give you anything?"

"No, he was still working on it when he died. With all the normal intern shit I had him doing, he hadn't made much progress on it."

"Well, get into his computer and print out whatever he came up with and give it to me," Perry said. "For that matter, print out everything in his computer—emails, notes he made on things, articles he cut and pasted—so I can take a look. Anything else he was working on?"

"No," Jane said.

DeMarco said, "Did he ever say anything to you about crooked politicians?" He paused before adding, "Talk about an oxymoron."

"No," Jane said.

"Nothing about kickbacks? Nothing about people violating campaign finance laws?"

"No," Jane said.

No one spoke for a moment.

DeMarco said, "Tell me what you know about him. What kind of kid was he?"

Jane said, "He was a first-year law student at UVA. He was only going to be here for the summer, to earn some money before school started again in the fall. He was bright. Also, very intense. He took the job seriously. And he was inquisitive, always asking questions about how things worked. There were lots of times when he'd still be here when I left for the day because he liked to read about how the committees functioned and the procedures for getting laws passed."

"Huh," Perry said. "I wonder what else he could have been doing when you weren't watching over him."

"I don't know," Jane said, "but I will tell you one thing about him and maybe it explains in a way what he told his mother."

"What's that?" Perry said.

"Brian didn't like seeing how the sausage was made. He didn't like all the trade-offs. He didn't like the influence of the special interest groups. And he really didn't like how lawmakers would compromise on things he didn't think they should compromise on. What I'm saying is, he was an idealist, and he was naive, and he found the whole process distasteful. One time he told me he couldn't believe how unethical most politicians were."

"And what did you tell him?" Perry asked.

"I told him, 'Welcome to the NFL, Buttercup. This is the real world and it's how things get done.'"

DeMarco asked Jane, "Did he use the word *unethical* or did he say *criminal*?"

"He said *unethical*. But the point I'm trying to make is that maybe he saw something that offended him but was just business as usual and that's what he was telling his mother."

Perry nodded. "That makes more sense than him uncovering some conspiracy." Turning to DeMarco, he said, "Go see his mother. Convince her that we're digging like coal miners to find something that could have gotten him killed, but so far we haven't found anything and she needs to hold off on talking to anyone until we're done digging. And since I don't think we're ever going to find anything, you need to start thinking about some way to settle her down."

9

The inside of DeMarco's house was like a pizza oven—and he silently cursed Rick, the air-conditioning guy, and all his swarthy offspring. After he shaved and took a quick shower, he put on a lightweight gray suit, a white shirt, and a tie, following Mahoney's directive not to wear a golf shirt when he went to see Brian's mother.

Mahoney had told DeMarco to see her before he talked to the cops, but DeMarco decided not to. He wanted to know the circumstances surrounding the kid's death and find out what the cops were doing. Ignoring an order from Mahoney didn't bother him. He ignored Mahoney's orders all the time, particularly when he knew that Mahoney would either never find out or forget that he'd given one. Sometimes working for an alcoholic had its benefits.

But before going to see the police, he called Caroline Lewis. She didn't answer the call, maybe thinking it was a robocall, or maybe she was still too grief-stricken to feel like talking to anyone. So he left a message saying, "Mrs. Lewis, my name is Joe DeMarco. I'm a lawyer who works for Congress, and John Mahoney asked me to look into your son's death. I'd like to meet with you today if you're available."

Caroline called back five minutes later. "I got your message. You say you're a lawyer?"

"Yes, ma'am, but I don't practice law. I serve members of Congress on an ad hoc basis and I'm a guy Congressman Mahoney sometimes uses when he doesn't want to use his staff."

This was all true and at the same time very misleading.

DeMarco continued, "Congressman Mahoney, considering what you told him, thought it would be best if someone independent like me conducted the investigation. Mahoney is taking this very seriously, Mrs. Lewis, and I'll be reporting directly to him."

"I see," Caroline said.

"So can I meet with you today?"

"Yes, of course. Come to my home," she said. "I live in Silver Spring."

"I'll be there as soon as I can," DeMarco said, "but I want to talk to the police before I talk to you, and I don't know how long that will take."

"It doesn't matter. I'll be here," Caroline said.

"Good. Give me your address, please."

Caroline did and DeMarco punched it into the map app in his phone.

"The other thing I need is the name of the police officer or detective who investigated your son's death. Congressman Mahoney told me you'd talked to the police."

"His name is Olivetti. I don't remember his first name. He works out of the Fifth District or Fifth Precinct, whatever you call it."

"Thank you," DeMarco said. "I'll see you in a little while."

What DeMarco had told Caroline about his job was mostly accurate with one major exception. He didn't work for Congress; he worked for John Mahoney and wasn't the least bit independent. Years ago, Mahoney had decided he needed someone not directly connected to his office that he could use to do things that he could later deny if necessary. In other words, Mahoney wanted a bagman and a fixer, and if that individual broke the law, Mahoney could claim that he was in no way responsible. So he set up a civil servant position for DeMarco's predecessor, a man who had passed away years ago. The stated duties of that position were to serve members of Congress on an "ad hoc basis," meaning if, for whatever reason, a legislator needed a free in-house lawyer, one would be available. But the truth was that DeMarco was only available to Mahoney.

———◆———

The District of Columbia is divided into seven police districts. The Metropolitan Police Department's Fifth District is located in Northeast D.C. on Bladensburg Road in a long, white two-story building. Across the street is a lot where broken-down city buses are parked. In front of the building are two flagpoles, one displaying the American flag, and the other the flag of the District of Columbia, both flags hanging limply on a stifling, windless day. D.C.'s flag consists of three red stars above two red bars on a white background, and DeMarco had been told that it was based on the design of the coat of arms granted to one of George Washington's British ancestors. DeMarco didn't know if this was true or not, but he'd always thought that D.C.'s flag should be emblazoned with the words *No Taxation Without Representation*, a common bumper sticker, and a poke in the eye at Congress for its refusal to make Washington, D.C., a state.

The building's entryway was packed with a dozen people, some standing, others sitting on benches. One old man was holding a bloody handkerchief to his forehead; a couple of women, both wearing short skirts and halter tops—and who DeMarco suspected might be hookers based on the brevity of the skirts—were yelling at each other at the top of their lungs; and a girl who couldn't have been more than sixteen was clutching a baby that was screaming its head off. The place was bedlam. DeMarco got in a line behind three people and when he finally reached the head of the line, he flashed his congressional ID at a uniformed officer and said, "I need to speak to a detective named Olivetti."

The officer passed him a clipboard, on which there were already half a dozen names listed, and said, "Write your name down and take a seat, and I'll get to you when I can. As you can see, I'm kinda busy here."

DeMarco said, "Maybe I should clarify something. The guy who sent me is John Mahoney, the guy who used to be the Speaker of the House."

The cop smirked. "But, like you said, Mahoney's no longer the Speaker. The Democrats got their asses handed to them."

"Do you really want to test me here?" DeMarco said. "I'll bet you five minutes after I make one phone call, whoever you work for is going to be in your face telling you what a dumb fuck you are for pissing off the highest-ranking Democrat in Congress. You know, Congress, the group that controls the District of Columbia's budget."

"Yeah, okay, don't have a hissy fit. What was that name again? Olivetti?"

Santos Olivetti was a lanky guy in his thirties dressed in jeans, a faded red polo shirt, and high-top black tennis shoes. A gray sport jacket hung from a hook in his cluttered cubicle. On his desk was a photo of a pretty woman and two cute little girls with curly dark hair. Olivetti also had curly dark hair and sported a neat goatee. He reminded DeMarco of a point guard who'd played for the Wizards.

DeMarco confirmed that Olivetti had investigated Lewis's death, then explained that Brian had worked for Mahoney and that his mother was a friend of Mahoney's, and that's why Mahoney had sent him.

The detective shook his head. "I'll bet this has to do with his mother thinking her son was killed."

"That's right," DeMarco said, figuring there was no point in being evasive. "What did she tell you?"

"She said that her son would have never used drugs, but he had information about a bunch of crooked politicians and that's why he was killed. I tried to explain to her that there wasn't any indication whatsoever that the boy had been murdered. His girlfriend found the body after she let herself into his apartment with a key because the door was locked. All the windows were locked, too, and on top of that, he lived on the third floor and there was no fire escape ladder outside his windows. Spider-Man couldn't have climbed up to his windows. There was no sign of a break-in. The door hadn't been jimmied. There was also no sign that anyone did anything to force him to take drugs. He didn't have any bruises on him. There were no defensive wounds like there would have been if he'd tried to fight someone off. His apartment hadn't been tossed like someone had been searching for something." Olivetti took a breath. "Brian Lewis wasn't killed, Mr. DeMarco. He died, instead of having a nice mellow high, because he injected himself with heroin laced with fentanyl, which happens fairly often these days."

"I see," DeMarco said.

"And there's one other thing. I didn't tell his mother this, because I felt sorry for her and I didn't want to add to her misery, but there were other drugs in his apartment. I found a bag of heroin that looked as if came from the same batch as the stuff that killed him. I also found a couple of joints and three tabs of ecstasy."

Olivetti stopped speaking long enough pull a bottle of Rolaids from his desk and pop two tablets into his mouth. He said, "I don't want to do this, but if his mother runs to the press like she threatened to do, I'll have to tell them that her son was in fact a drug user. And, like I said, there was no evidence whatsoever that anyone killed him, other than himself."

"Where did you find the other drugs?"

"In a drawer in an end table near his couch. I wasn't searching for drugs. The drawer of this end table was open, and I could see them sitting there, like he'd forgotten to close the drawer before he went into the bathroom to give himself a fix."

"Did he have track marks, old needle marks, to show he was a frequent user?"

"No. I suspect he snorted the stuff most of the time and he'd just recently started injecting it. That's what usually happens. People go from snorting to mainlining."

"Could you trace the heroin?"

Olivetti shook his head. "It came in a little bag, like the little ziplock bags you'll see screws or nuts in if you're assembling something, but the bag wasn't marked. Sometimes the bags will be marked with a trade name or a symbol. You know, a dealer marketing his brand, but not this time. I asked his girlfriend where he could have gotten the drugs from, because we'd really like to trace the shit before someone else gets killed, but his girlfriend was like his mother. She insisted he never used drugs.

"So, DeMarco, I don't know what else to tell you. But you can tell Congressman Mahoney that the department has no reason to believe the kid was murdered and that's what we'll tell the press if we're asked. But can I ask you something?"

"What's that?"

"Do you know if he found anything at work that would have given some politician a reason for wanting him dead?"

Now it was DeMarco's turn to shake his head. He wasn't going to tell Olivetti about anything that Brian was working on, or at least not until after he and Perry had investigated further. He said, "No. Brian was an intern and he wasn't assigned to work on anything sensitive. He was basically a gofer. His supervisor is going back over the jobs he was given, but so far hasn't seen anything out of the ordinary."

DeMarco got Olivetti's cell phone number and left a couple of minutes later.

10

Olivetti watched DeMarco walk down the hall. DeMarco had said he was a lawyer, but he didn't look or act like a lawyer. He didn't have the glibness, or the patina of oily slickness exhibited by most attorneys Olivetti had encountered. And he hadn't made any legal threats, like suing if the department had gotten it wrong when it came Lewis. He'd acted as if he just wanted to hear the department's side of things and didn't have any ulterior motive or axe to grind. On the other hand, he was a lawyer, so nothing he said could be taken at face value. After DeMarco turned the corner, Olivetti walked over to his boss's office.

Harry Coleman was on the phone and Olivetti heard him say: "You gotta be shittin' me. Last week a pressure-treated eight-footer was twelve bucks. How did the price go up a buck and a half in a week?" He listened to whomever he was talking to, then said, "Well, I'm gonna look around. You ain't the only lumberyard down there. And the quantity I'm buying, I should be gettin' the kind of discount you give to contractors."

Olivetti knew his lieutenant, who was six months away from pulling the plug, was building a cabin in the Blue Ridge Mountains—and he spent more time thinking about it than anything else at work. He saw Olivetti standing in his doorway and said, "What's up?"

"You told me to let you know if anyone took an interest in the Lewis case. Well, a guy name DeMarco, who's working for John Mahoney, just talked to me."

"What did you tell him?" Coleman asked.

Olivetti told him what he'd told DeMarco.

Olivetti wasn't surprised that the brass wanted to know if anyone was asking about Lewis. Since the kid had worked for Congress, and for a heavyweight like Mahoney in particular, the bosses would naturally want to know if anyone took an interest in the investigation.

After Olivetti left his office, Coleman picked up the phone and called the chief of detectives. He said, "You told me to let you know if—"

Former congressman Jimmy Cooper was sitting in his office fighting to stay awake after a three-martini lunch when the chief of detectives called him. The chief said, "You asked me to let you know if anyone took an interest in—"

Jimmy Cooper loved his job. He'd been a cop for twenty years before he decided to run for Congress, then spent eighteen years in representing the Eleventh Congressional District of the great state of Florida. His last ten years in Congress he'd had a seat on the Crime, Terrorism, and Homeland Security Subcommittee. When he decided to retire at the age of fifty-eight, the lobbying firm of Kellogg, Long & Meyer made him an offer.

While a congressman, Jimmy had earned $174,000 a year. Now his annual compensation, not including all the perks that went with the job, was $250,000. His area of expertise was law enforcement and terrorism, thanks to his prior subcommittee experience, and there's a *ton* of money in law enforcement and terrorism: KL&M's clients provided equipment for cops—which included helicopters, drones, and armored personnel carriers. Other clients provided communication systems and physical and cybersecurity systems. And it wasn't just hardware. Some clients were involved in managing police department pension plans. Some were law firms that made their money defending or suing cops.

So this was Jimmy's bailiwick, and one of his jobs was maintaining and grooming contacts in various police departments, which, of course, included the hometown cops, D.C.'s Metropolitan Police Department. These contacts were almost always compensated for their services; some were basically on retainer and given monthly stipends. But most often, currency wasn't used to pay a contact. Hard-to-get tickets to sporting events, a low-interest loan, a nudge given to the admissions department of a prestigious school, or landing a job offer for a son or daughter in a well-paying company were all used to compensate useful contacts. In the case of MPD's chief of detectives, a man who considered himself a wine connoisseur, Jimmy would send him a bottle of a California pinot noir that retailed for three hundred bucks for the phone call the chief had just made.

Jimmy pulled a bottle of mouthwash from his desk, gargled with it, spit the blue liquid into a trash can, then took the elevator to the top floor. He had no idea why Grady wanted to be kept apprised of anything related to the death of Brian Lewis. And he had no intention of asking why.

Grady's secretary—who Jimmy suspected had been hired solely for her looks—told him that Grady wasn't available. He was at the White House, meeting with the president's chief of staff. Name-dropper.

Jimmy said, "Tell him to call me."

"Can I ask what this is related to?" she said. She had a British accent, but Jimmy had learned that she'd been raised in Omaha and had spent only two years in London when her husband worked for the U.S. embassy there. She came back with the accent but without the husband.

Jimmy said, "Just tell him it's about Brian Lewis. He knows who that is."

Two hours later, Grady called.

Jimmy said, "A guy named DeMarco—"

11

Caroline Lewis lived on a quiet, tree-lined street in a small, white clapboard house. The house had a carport instead of a garage and a neatly mowed front lawn that wasn't much larger than a pickleball court. DeMarco noticed that every house on the block was identical to Caroline's, and he wondered if the neighborhood was or had been military housing.

DeMarco rang the bell, and the door was answered by a woman in her sixties with short gray hair, sharp gray eyes, and no makeup. DeMarco thought she looked the way nuns looked these days when they no longer wore a habit.

He said, "Mrs. Lewis? I'm Joe DeMarco."

"I'm not Caroline," the woman said. "I'm Irene, her big sister. I'm staying with her for a while. She told me you were coming. I'll go get her." Irene shook her head. "She's going through Brian's things, trying to decide what to keep. She saved every award he was ever given, every trophy, every ribbon. She saved papers he wrote in grade school. She saved pictures he drew in kindergarten. She saved toys he played with when he was young and books she used to read to him, thinking that one day he'd have children and she'd give the toys and books to her grandkids. All she's doing is making herself even more depressed than she already is. I told her to wait awhile before going through his things, but there's no talking to her."

DeMarco, not able to think of anything else to say, said, "I'm sorry."

Irene left DeMarco standing in the living room. He noticed a picture on an end table of a dark-haired woman posing with a young man. DeMarco recognized the setting: it was an area called the Lawn at the University of Virginia and he could see a domed building with white columns in the background. The building was called the Rotunda and had been designed by Thomas Jefferson. DeMarco assumed the photo was one of Brian and his mother. He was a good-looking kid. He had short dark hair and a slim build and was a foot taller than his mom. In the photo, he was smiling and so was Caroline.

The woman in the photo stepped into the living room. Her face was haggard—she looked exhausted—and her eyes were swollen and red from weeping. She was in her mid-forties, maybe fifteen years younger than her sister. She was wearing jeans and a gray T-shirt that had *ARMY* emblazoned on the front in yellow letters. Perry had told DeMarco that her husband had been one of the last servicemen killed at the end of the Afghan war. He couldn't imagine Caroline's pain, losing first her husband and then her son.

She said, "Let's go into the kitchen."

DeMarco followed her into a kitchen that was painted a cheerful yellow. She pointed him to a small table by a window that looked out onto a cherry tree in the backyard. On the windowsill were small cactus plants in red clay pots.

Caroline asked, "Would you like a glass of water or a soft drink?"

"No, I'm fine," DeMarco said.

Getting right to the point, Caroline said, "So. What did you come to tell me?"

"Like I told you on the phone, Mahoney assigned me to look into Brian's death. I've interviewed Brian's immediate supervisor at work, and

I asked her what Brian had been working on. Because he was an intern, he was mostly used as a messenger, picking up documents or delivering them. He'd only had a couple of real assignments. One of them had to do with updating a call list of donors, you know, a list that Mahoney would use to call people and ask for campaign contributions. He developed a spreadsheet for Mahoney's chief of staff, doing a cost analysis for a bill. I mean, he didn't do the analysis—he didn't have the background for that—but he put the data together. Perry Wallace, Mahoney's chief of staff, told me he did a good job on that, by the way. He was also doing a study for Mahoney looking at how individual lawmakers had voted on a particular bill and the reasons they gave for voting yes or no. Mahoney was interested in this because the bill didn't pass, and he wanted to understand why so he could twist some arms the next time it came up for a vote."

There was no way DeMarco was going to use the term *dirty dozen* or tell Caroline that Mahoney suspected these lawmakers had conspired when it came to voting on the bill.

"So far," DeMarco said, "I haven't seen anything that he was working on that would have pointed to politicians doing anything illegal. But I've told Brian's supervisor to print out everything on Brian's work computer—emails, Word documents, spreadsheets—so I can look it all over and see if there's something there."

DeMarco figured it wouldn't hurt to tell Caroline he was doing things that Perry and Jane were doing. His job, as Perry had said, was to convince Caroline that he was digging hard and deep.

"The other thing I've done," DeMarco said, "is talk to the detective who handled the investigation. He told me, as he told you, that there's no evidence that Brian had been murdered. The door and windows of his apartment were all locked when Brian was found, and there was no indication that an intruder had been in his apartment."

Caroline said, "But that doesn't necessarily mean—"

"I agree," DeMarco said. "So I'm going to look at Brian's place myself and talk to his girlfriend, since she's the one who discovered the body, and see if I can think of anything the cops might have missed."

DeMarco had decided not to tell her about Olivetti discovering other drugs in Brian's apartment. Like Olivetti, he didn't want to make Caroline more miserable than she already was. But he figured that at some point he was probably going to have to tell her.

Caroline said, "Good. I'm glad to see you're not taking the cops at their word."

"I'm not," DeMarco said. "But I need a couple of things. I need Brian's girlfriend's phone number and I'd like you to talk to her before I call her and ask her to speak with me. And I need the keys to get into his apartment if you have them. I'm assuming no one's moved in yet."

"No one has. The rent is paid up until the middle of next month and I told the landlord that it was probably going to take me until then to get Brian's things out of there."

DeMarco said, "The other thing I need is for you to tell me about Brian. I never met him, and I don't really know anything about him. Like why did he want a job working for Mahoney?"

Caroline said, "He was a law student at UVA. He hadn't decided what kind of law he wanted to practice but he was interested in public service. Not necessarily politics but something on the federal side, like maybe a job at DOJ. He figured that a summer job on Mahoney's staff would look good on his résumé, but he also wanted to learn more about the way Congress operated. I have to tell you, from the little bit he told me, he wasn't that impressed."

DeMarco gave her a small smile. "Yeah, I can understand that," he said. "No one has a lower approval rating than Congress."

"Who was he close to?" DeMarco asked. "I mean, other than his girlfriend. Was there anyone he might have confided in?"

"I can't think of anyone. He didn't have a roommate at school. I mean, he had one during the first semester, but his roommate dropped out of school, and he lived alone after that. And as far as I know, he hadn't become good friends with anyone at UVA and he didn't stay in touch with the kids he knew before law school. To tell you the truth, Brian wasn't very outgoing, and he could be kind of a grind. I got the impression that all he did was study because he had to study hard to keep his scholarship. He liked to jog but he wasn't into team sports. He didn't have any hobbies. He wasn't a party animal. He was into politics, but he didn't belong to any political clubs. He just studied."

DeMarco was thinking that there was no college kid on earth who spent all his time studying but didn't see any point in saying that.

"Oh," Caroline said. "There was one person he might have been close to at school. It was one of his law professors who was also his adviser. He spoke about the man as if he really admired him."

"What's his name?"

"Adam . . . Adam something. I can't remember his last name. Elaine might know."

"His girlfriend?"

"Yes."

"Okay," DeMarco said. "I'll go talk to Elaine tomorrow and take a look at his apartment. And I might talk to this professor at UVA and see if Brian talked to him about what he was doing at work."

Caroline said, "I appreciate what you're doing. And frankly I'm surprised that Mahoney assigned you. I always figured that he was the type who would be inclined to bury anything that might make his fellow politicians look bad."

DeMarco said, "Mahoney doesn't mind making other politicians look bad at all. He does it all the time. Himself, that's a different story. Which is the reason I know that when it comes to Brian, he doesn't have anything to hide. If he had, he wouldn't have assigned me."

At least DeMarco hoped that was the case.

12

Grady sat with his eyes closed, massaging his temples in a futile attempt to prevent the migraine he felt coming on. He was prone to stress-induced migraines, and they could be debilitating. When he got one, he'd have to close all the blinds in his office and turn off the lights and just lie on his couch with a cold pack on his head until the pain subsided. Goddamnit. He'd figured that the Lewis problem would go away after Lewis had gone away. But it hadn't.

And now that he'd actually seen the document that Lewis had titled "Tenants' Rights Conspiracy," the Lewis situation was even more galling. As he'd told Newman, there really wasn't anything in it that would have caused Newman a significant problem.

But what the kid had done was amazing. He had traced campaign contributions from Newman to the twelve legislators who voted no on the bill, and this was somewhat surprising in that Newman hadn't contributed personally or directly to the congressmen. The contributions came from people who worked for him or from companies that did business with Newman Enterprises but that were not directly controlled by Newman. Yet, somehow, the kid had managed to trace every contribution and to link every one of them in some way to Newman. He had to have spent *days* doing that, maybe weeks. But there was nothing illegal about the contributions.

In other cases, Grady couldn't figure out exactly how Lewis had uncovered the information. For example, a congressman's kid was admitted to an exclusive preschool, one that cost thirty grand a year and that had a full waiting list. Somehow, someway, fucking Lewis was able to determine that at the same time the kid was admitted to the school, one of Newman's construction companies donated the labor to install a new roof on the school. Lewis had concluded, based solely on the timing of the two events, that Newman had put the new roof on the school just to get it to admit the congressman's brat. Which he did.

Another example was the daughter of one of the congressmen, a guy who was practically broke, being awarded a partial scholarship to an Ivy League school. The scholarship came from a newly formed foundation based in the congressman's district that had no apparent connection to Newman. But if you pulled the string—*really* pulled the string—you would find that the new foundation received its initial funding from the Newman Foundation, the charitable organization managed by Newman's wife. Lewis concluded that the new foundation had been established only for the purpose of giving money to pay for the congressman's daughter's tuition. Which was true.

In a third instance, a congressman was admitted to a pricey country club as an "honorary" member in recognition of his "service to the public." This happened right after the country club's parking lot was given a new coat of asphalt, with labor and materials donated by a Newman Enterprises subcontractor.

In order to get some of the information Lewis had obtained, it would have taken more than a public records or Internet search, and Grady concluded Lewis must have contacted and questioned some of the people involved. He wondered if Lewis had passed himself off as someone with the authority to ask questions, like claiming he was working for the

House Ethics Committee. Or he might have even bluffed people with congressional subpoenas, which would have really taken some balls. Lewis had even obtained copies of emails between a congressman and one of Grady's employees, but Grady had no idea how he'd gotten them. The only thing Grady could conclude was that Lewis had convinced a member of the congressman's staff to give him the emails, maybe claiming that he was acting on behalf of Mahoney. Whatever the case, an investigative reporter from the *Washington Post* couldn't have done a better job than Lewis in tying Carson Newman to all the things done to influence the twelve congressmen.

On the other hand, Lewis couldn't prove—beyond a reasonable doubt—that the lawmakers had voted no on the tenants' rights bill because they'd been compensated in some way by Newman. Like in the case of the preschool. Just because the school got a new roof at the same time the congressman's kid was admitted wasn't proof that the two events were related. Lewis could *surmise* that this was the case—which he did—and he could make a powerful, well-reasoned argument that this was the case—which he did—but there was no direct proof of a quid pro quo, and a coincidence isn't a crime.

Newman's lawyers would have made mincemeat out of Lewis's conspiracy theory, and there was no way that Newman would have been indicted, much less convicted.

If the kid's report had been made public, it would have been *embarrassing* for Carson Newman—but that would most likely have been the worst of it. Papers like the *Boston Globe* and the *New York Times* would have dragged Newman through the mud. Sanctimonious editorials would have been written about rich men and their lobbyists undermining democracy for their own self-interest. Newscasters would have shaken their handsome heads in dismay as they rambled on about influence peddling in the swamp. But those were probably the worst things that would have happened.

But now Lewis was dead—and if Newman *had* had the kid killed, he'd done it for no good reason. And because the kid was dead, now Mahoney's guy, DeMarco, was poking into things. Son of a bitch!

Grady said, "There's a guy named DeMarco looking into Brian Lewis's death."

"Who's DeMarco? A cop?"

"No, Carson. He's a lawyer who works for Congress. But you remember Lyle Canton, the congressman who was shot by a Capitol cop a few years ago?"

"Vaguely," Newman said.

"Well, DeMarco was arrested for killing Canton. It turned out he was innocent, but because of the investigation into Canton's death, the media learned that DeMarco is really John Mahoney's personal fixer, although both he and Mahoney have always denied that."

"That fuckin' Mahoney," Newman said. "But why's he got DeMarco looking?"

"Because Lewis's mother thinks her son was killed and she asked Mahoney, who assigned DeMarco, to investigate."

Newman didn't say anything in response to that, and when he didn't, Grady asked, "What do you want to do about DeMarco?"

Newman again didn't respond but this time Grady waited. Finally, Newman said, "Get your guy on him. We need to know what he's up to."

Grady thought that over and said, "Yes, that's probably prudent. But, Carson, this can't end the way it did with Lewis."

"I don't know what you're talking about," Newman said.

13

———◆———

Carson Newman's office on the thirty-fifth floor of the Prudential Tower was more than three thousand square feet. There was a bathroom that included a shower stall, a closet where he kept changes of clothes, a wet bar stocked with expensive bottles of booze, a seating area with couches and armchairs that could accommodate a dozen people, and a gleaming conference table that could seat twenty. A top-of-the-line Peloton bike—that Carson had used maybe four times—sat in one corner. Persian rugs covered the floor, and on the walls hung an art collection that was worth two million bucks. A glass case contained a silver serving plate that had been hammered into shape by Paul Revere.

Carson sat alone in his vast office, his chair turned so he could look out a window at the Back Bay and Fenway Park. The Sox were playing that evening at Fenway, and from his perch, he could see part of the crowd. He rarely used his box at Fenway, because the truth was that baseball bored him to tears. The box was almost always occupied, however, because he let people he wanted favors from, or people he owed favors to, use the box, but he probably didn't use it himself more than two or three times a year. He couldn't remember who was using it today. He'd thought about selling the box after his kids had grown up, but having a box at Fenway was a status symbol, similar to owning a helicopter and having a membership at The Country Club. Symbols of his affluence were important. They made it clear for all to see that he was a man who'd reached a pinnacle that common folk could only dream about.

Today, Carson was doing something he rarely did. He was second-guessing a decision he'd made. He was beginning to think that it had been a mistake to have Lewis killed.

But Lewis had been the proverbial last straw, the one that broke the camel's back.

When he'd first heard that Lewis was digging into the votes on the tenants' rights bill, he'd had two other major issues going on and he'd felt like a king in a castle under siege, like Gulliver being attacked by the Lilliputians from all sides.

A crane owned by one of his construction companies had partially collapsed and dropped a load of steel beams, killing two people on the ground. Naturally, a lawsuit was filed. Carson's lawyers blamed the calamity on the company that had built the crane, saying the design was faulty and the materials were bad, but from out of the woodwork crawled a whistleblower. The whistleblower was a foreman who worked for the construction company—and also the uncle of one of the people killed—and he said that he'd filed a report stating that he'd seen stress fractures in the crane's structure and recommended that the crane be taken out of service. Carson, although he denied it, had been informed of the foreman's recommendation. But the project had been behind schedule, and if the crane was repaired or replaced, it would get further behind, and each day the project was delayed, he would lose over two hundred grand. So Carson, although he again denied it, told the man managing the construction company to keep using the crane. He didn't tell him directly but made sure he got the word. The damn crane had been in use for seven months and only had to last two more months, and Carson had figured it would be fine for that long.

The lawsuit turned into a criminal investigation of negligent homicide. Carson was subpoenaed to testify that he'd personally been informed of the crane's condition, which he, of course, denied. The foreman's report had disappeared, and no one could prove that anyone had talked to Carson about it. Nonetheless, the lawsuit and the attendant criminal investigation were moving forward, work on the project had come to a standstill, and the insurance company was refusing to pay for damages.

That was part of the load the camel was carrying.

A second thing that was going on at the time the Lewis problem raised its ugly head had to do with an ambitious and tenacious Massachusetts attorney general. The woman, who had her beady eyes set on becoming governor, had accused Newman of inflating the value of a property to get a loan and then undervaluing the property to evade taxes. Newman's lawyers claimed he had nothing to do with how the property was valued—his accountants handled those sorts of mundane matters—but again a whistleblower, an attorney he'd fired for incompetence, came forward and claimed Newman was lying. The case was so complicated that it would take years to resolve, and Newman was certain he'd never be indicted—although he might have to pay a fine or some back taxes—but that was the second load being borne by the camel.

On top of these two specific issues were just the normal headaches that went with an operation the size of Newman Enterprises. Projects behind schedule. Loans coming due that needed to be refinanced. Routine lawsuits making their way through state and federal courts. Employee shortages that could be solved with immigrants waiting at the U.S./Mexico border. Supply issues with the fucking Chinese who made most of the steel he needed. Environmental nuts in California determined to stop work on a project there.

So at the time he was informed that this pip-squeak congressional intern was looking into how he'd manipulated a bunch of avaricious, unscrupulous lawmakers, he was already overwhelmed with problems while making headlines for his alleged role in the deaths of two workers and how he was avoiding paying Uncle Sam his fair share. The last fucking thing he'd needed was to have muckraking journalists start writing stories filled with half-truths and unnamed sources about how he'd cor-rupted a few lawmakers.

Brian Lewis was simply the last straw.

And when he'd heard about Lewis, he admittedly went a bit crazy, and that's when he decided to make the problem go away by making Brian Lewis go away. Had he overacted? Yeah, probably. But now what was at stake wasn't him manipulating politicians. What was at stake was the possibility of being indicted for first-degree murder.

Hopefully, it wouldn't come to that. There was no evidence Lewis had been killed—the cops had said so—and the laptop containing Lewis's report was in safe hands. And without the report, there was no motive for anyone to have killed Lewis.

No, DeMarco wouldn't be a problem.

And if he started to become one—

Well, there were ways to deal with Mahoney's thug.

14

<hr/>

The morning after meeting with Caroline Lewis, DeMarco was on his way to see Brian's girlfriend and was only half listening to the car radio. He was thinking about what to do about Rick, the air-conditioning mechanic, who hadn't returned any of his calls to tell him when his new compressor would be arriving. Then he heard the newscaster say, "According to Karl Budnick, Congresswoman Diane Meadows habitually forces herself to vomit after lunch to maintain her weight."

DeMarco slammed the steering wheel. Fucking Budnick. He'd told Mahoney that he was working on Budnick, but the truth was that he was just letting time and nature takes its course. But if Mahoney heard the so-called news about Meadows, he'd be on DeMarco's back again to do something to silence the crazy asshole.

Karl Budnick had been on the staff of a California congresswoman, and she fired him for numerous valid reasons. He'd sexually harassed female coworkers; he'd shown up at campaign events drunk and high on cocaine, his drug of choice; he'd lied to the congresswoman about various things he'd done; and he'd leaked information to journalists to make them think he was more important than he really was. So she fired him—and he did not take being fired well. The Capitol Police had to forcibly remove him from the Rayburn House Office Building.

Being unable to find employment and not able to afford his rent, thanks to his alcohol and cocaine habits, Budnick moved into his mother's basement in Fairfax and now had a new profession. He was a podcaster. His podcast was called the *Budnick Hour* and it consisted of Karl Budnick screaming into a microphone and dishing dirt on politicians. He'd tell unflattering stories about legislators he'd encountered while working, and the stories inevitably made them look like fools, liars, and hypocrites. And after he ran out of personal stories to tell, he started hanging out in bars where congressional staffers drank and gossiped, and he would get a seat close to them and eavesdrop on their conversations. That was probably how he learned about Congresswoman Diane Meadows's weight-control technique. He also began to follow politicians and take unflattering photos of them, which he showed on his Facebook page. One photo was of a seventysomething congresswoman with her dress hiked up, exposing her thick thighs, as she struggled to get out of a car. Another was of a congressman who appeared to have his hand on the backside of a young woman; the congressman hadn't actually touched the woman, but the photo made it appear as if he did. But the photo that mattered—and the one that explained Mahoney's interest in Budnick—was a photo he'd taken of Mahoney. Mahoney had been vacationing at a wealthy constituent's home, using the pool in the secluded backyard, and Budnick scaled a fence and photographed Mahoney in a bathing suit—and it was not a flattering picture. Mahoney, with his big gut and his spindly legs and his whiter-than-chalk complexion, looked like a beluga whale.

But Budnick was rapidly going downhill both mentally and physically, his addictions most likely contributing to his decline. While a congressional staffer, he'd been clean-shaven and kept his hair short. He now sported an untamed beard and long, tangled, unwashed hair. His clothes were often soiled and appeared as if he'd slept in them. He was beginning to look like a homeless person and his podcast was becoming increasingly incomprehensible. He made no money off his show, couldn't get guests to appear on it, and his audience, as best DeMarco could tell, was about fifty people—most of them congressional staffers who tuned in only to see if Budnick would say anything about their bosses.

But after the photo of him came out, Mahoney, who was drunk at the time, told DeMarco, "I want you to do something to shut that asshole up." DeMarco thought Mahoney should have simply ignored Budnick; he had no credibility and no real audience. He also thought Mahoney's order was just another sign of Mahoney's own decline, his booze consumption and his perpetual frustration with having lost the Speaker's gavel affecting his ability to think rationally.

DeMarco, however, contrary to Mahoney's desires, had decided that he wasn't going to do anything personally when it came to Karl Budnick because Budnick was rapidly destroying himself. The congresswoman who'd fired him had gotten a restraining order against him because he'd started following her and harassing her. Another congresswoman was talking about suing him for defamation, and complaints about his profane podcast had been made to the FCC. DeMarco figured it wouldn't be long before Budnick did something so stupid and outrageous that he'd be arrested. Or he'd simply disappear into a black hole of his own making. And DeMarco's plan was to simply wait until that happened—but he had no intention of telling Mahoney that.

DeMarco immediately liked Elaine Patterson. She was studying to be a nurse and he liked nurses. How could you not like nurses? There might be a few Nurse Ratcheds out there, but in general, nurses were caring and compassionate, people who devoted their lives to helping the suffering. And during the pandemic, they'd been genuine heroes, soldiers on the front lines, working until they dropped, risking their lives on a daily basis.

DeMarco met Elaine in a diner across the street from the hospital where she had a summer job as a nurse's aide. She was a petite twenty-year-old with small features and brown eyes. Kind brown eyes. She wore her blond hair in a ponytail and was dressed in blue hospital scrubs. He noticed her fingernails were trimmed short and bare of polish. She struck him as a bright, sensible young woman mature beyond her years—and he concluded that she would have made Brian a fine partner if he'd lived long enough to marry her.

After explaining that he'd been assigned by Mahoney to look into Brian's death because of Brian's mother's concerns, he said, "I know you loved Brian. His mother told me the two of you planned to get married as soon as you both got your degrees. And I know you're hurting right now, but there's something I need to know." DeMarco paused. "The main reason Brian's mom is convinced he was killed is because she's certain he didn't use drugs. But if he did use drugs, I doubt he'd tell his mother. I figured if anyone would know, it would be you."

"He didn't use drugs," Elaine said. "Ever. I knew him for two years. He wouldn't even smoke a joint. He'd have a beer if we went to a party, but he'd never have more than one or two. One thing his mother probably didn't tell you was that Brian's father was an alcoholic. He'd been sober for ten years before he died, but before he started going to AA, he drank heavily and he was abusive when he did. So maybe it was because of his father, but Brian was very careful when it came to alcohol. And like I said, as far as drugs go, Brian wouldn't touch them."

DeMarco said, "Elaine, I'm sorry to have to tell you this, but the detective who investigated Brian's death found drugs in his apartment. He found a couple of joints, a bag of heroin like the one that killed him, and three tabs of ecstasy."

"That's bullshit," Elaine said—the word *bullshit* coming from her shocking DeMarco.

She said, "Either the detective's lying, or someone planted the drugs. I'm telling you that Brian never used drugs. Ever."

"Okay," DeMarco said.

"No, it's not *okay*. You're just saying *okay* to pacify me. You need to believe me. Brian would never have used drugs, which proves someone killed him."

It didn't, but DeMarco decided not to say that. He said, "Let's talk about him finding something at work that pointed to politicians committing crimes. What did he tell you about what he'd found?"

"He told me he'd been assigned to do a study of how some politicians voted on some bill, and he'd found proof that they'd been bribed. Or that they'd been given illegal campaign contributions, although I'm not sure what the difference is."

"Did he name any of these politicians? Or did he say exactly how they'd been bribed?"

"No. He said it was complicated, and in some cases he wasn't sure how the law applied to some of the things they'd done. All I know is that he was working on this thing nonstop the last two weeks before he died. He'd stay late at work to get the information he needed, and when he got home, he'd spend hours trying to get more information online and documenting everything he found. I hardly saw him the last two weeks."

Elaine shook her head. "The thing about Brian, and sometimes it would annoy me, is he could get fixated on something and wouldn't be able to think about anything else. And if he thought someone was doing something wrong, he could be relentless. About a year ago, his mother got into a fender bender and the insurance company totaled her car and wouldn't give her enough to buy a new one. Well, his mom gave up, but Brian just wouldn't let it go. He wrote to the CEO of the insurance company and everyone on the company's board, telling them that his mother was an army widow and they were cheating her. And in the letters, he made it sound as if he already had a law degree and was planning on suing them. He also found complaints against the company that were like his mother's, and he went to the office of the Maryland state insurance commissioner in Baltimore and wouldn't leave until the guy saw him." Elaine smiled, but tears welled up in her eyes. "In the end, the insurance company gave his mom enough to get a new car."

DeMarco said, "It sounds like he would have been a good prosecutor."

Elaine brushed away the tears and said, "He would have been a *great* one."

"But you said he was documenting whatever he'd learned about these politicians. How was he doing that?"

"I don't know. In a report or a memo of some kind, I guess. Or maybe in a brief, like they taught him in law school."

"What did he plan to do with the information? Go to the press?"

"He didn't know. He hadn't figured that out. He was going to talk to his adviser at UVA."

"Do you know if he did?"

"No."

"Well, one of the things I'll be doing is looking at all the stuff he had in his computer at work."

"You need to look in his laptop. That's where you'll find something. I'll tell you something else. Before he died, Brian acted as if that laptop was made of gold. We were going out to dinner one night, and when we started to leave my place, I saw he was carrying his laptop case. I asked why he was taking it with him, and he said he didn't want it out of his sight. He'd never had a problem leaving it in my apartment before."

"Do you know where his laptop is?"

"I imagine it's in his apartment. I didn't look for it when I . . . I found him."

Elaine returned to the hospital and DeMarco left the diner and walked to his car. He unlocked the doors and tossed his suit jacket onto the back seat, then started the car and set the air conditioner to the lowest setting and turned the fan on high. While the car was cooling down, he stood next to it and made a call.

He didn't notice the striking young woman parked down the block in a black Ford Focus staring at him.

15

Sydney watched as DeMarco made a call and heard him say, "Perry, it's me. Did you look at the stuff in his work computer yet?"

Who the heck is Perry?

Perry: "Yeah, there's nothing there."

DeMarco: "Well, whatever he found is almost certainly related to the dirty dozen."

The dirty dozen? What the hell does that mean?

DeMarco: "I got that from his girlfriend. So you didn't see anything incriminating connected to those guys?"

Perry: "No. All that was in his computer was what I knew already. Statements people made to the press on why they voted the way they did. Copies of speeches they gave on the floor before they voted."

DeMarco: "And he didn't have any kind of memo summarizing anything he learned?"

Perry: "No."

DeMarco: "Something's off. According to his girlfriend, he was working nonstop on whatever he found before he died, and he was writing up some kind of report."

Perry: "Well, there's no report here. In fact, I'm surprised at how little progress he made on the assignment. He was supposed to look deeper than the stuff that was already on record. Anyway, there was nothing in his computer here at work pointing to anyone doing anything illegal."

DeMarco: "His girlfriend said he had a laptop and that's most likely where he would have put something. Ask Jane if she ever saw him using a personal computer at work."

Perry: "All right. But she should have been on his ass if he did. He wasn't allowed to use his own computer here."

DeMarco: "Yeah, but remember Jane said lots of times he stayed after she left. I'm going to call his mom and see if she has his laptop or if the cops have it. And I'm going to take a look at his apartment to see if it's there."

Sydney watched as DeMarco got into his car and took off. She followed him. While he was driving, he made another call. The call went to voice mail. She heard him say, "Mrs. Lewis, it's Joe DeMarco. I'm trying to find Brian's laptop. Do you have it? Please call me."

A few minutes later, he got a call from some woman named Leah saying that she wouldn't be able to see him this week because she had to drive to Cleveland to see her mother. Who was Leah? A girlfriend? DeMarco was a good-looking guy and she figured he must have some sort of love life—or sex life—but she'd also noticed that he didn't sound too disappointed that Leah wouldn't be able to see him. Whatever. It didn't sound as if Leah was involved in the Brian Lewis thing.

Half an hour later, DeMarco pulled into a parking spot on a street of run-down brownstones in Northeast D.C., and Sydney watched as he walked to one of the buildings and let himself in with a key. It was the apartment building where Lewis had lived.

She called Dave. "He spent half an hour talking to Lewis's girlfriend—I don't know what she said to him. Now he's at Lewis's place. But before he went there, he called someone named Perry. I'll text you the recording and you can hear what he said, but the bottom line is, he's looking for Lewis's laptop."

"Okay," Dave said.

"How you feeling?" Sydney asked.

"Aw, you know. How are you doing?"

"Great," Sydney said.

When Lewis was found dead in his apartment, Morgenthal had been shocked. He knew that Lewis had uncovered something to do with dirty politicians, but that's all he knew. And when Grady told him to stop tracking Lewis, he didn't think twice about it, thinking that Grady had obtained whatever he was after.

He supposed Lewis could have OD'd the way the papers said, but when he asked Sydney if Lewis struck her as a junkie, she said no. She said that Lewis was totally straight—that he reminded her of those Mormons with their white shirts and skinny black ties who knock on the door and try to hand you pamphlets—and she never saw him approach anyone who looked like a drug dealer. Which left the possibility that Lewis in fact had been murdered, and taking it one step further, that he and Sydney were accomplices because they'd provided Grady information on the kid's routines that could have been used to plan a murder.

But Morgenthal had a hard time believing that Grady would have had Lewis killed. Morgenthal had done a lot of jobs for Grady's firm over the years, following and spying on people. And he knew Grady's firm used the information he provided to manipulate and maybe even blackmail people, but Grady had never struck him as someone who'd be willing to kill. Grady was just your average D.C. lobbyist, a slick talker who would take any position on any issue his clients wanted him to take. He would lie, he would twist statistics, he'd take politicians on vacations they couldn't afford, and do whatever else he needed to do to get politicians to vote the way his clients wanted—but murder? Morgenthal didn't think so. But then again, Morgenthal didn't know exactly what Lewis had learned, so maybe it had been something so damaging that Grady had been forced to kill him.

When he'd first accepted the job to track DeMarco, he hadn't known that DeMarco was looking into Lewis's death. When he found out what DeMarco was doing, he could have told Grady he didn't want anything to do with the job but then decided to have Sydney stay on DeMarco to make sure that DeMarco didn't uncover anything that pointed to him and Sydney. Plus, they needed the money. He hoped he'd made the right decision.

16

DeMarco didn't immediately see a laptop or a laptop case inside Brian's apartment. Remembering Elaine's comment about how he'd acted as if his computer was made of gold, he wondered if Brian would have hidden it. So he searched for it, and as small as the place was, that took him only ten minutes. He looked in the only closet, looked in all the drawers, looked in the cabinets over and under the kitchen and bathroom sinks, looked inside the oven. He even pulled out the bed from the hide-a-bed couch to see if the laptop was stashed inside. It wasn't. Brian's laptop wasn't in the apartment.

Now what?

As he stood there, not knowing what to do next, he thought about Brian. The kid had been driven and ambitious and had worked his ass off. He'd lived in a cramped, shabby apartment because he couldn't afford better, and when DeMarco looked in the cabinets over the sink, he noticed packages of Top Ramen and cans of tuna fish and not much else. His mom had said that Brian had to study hard to keep his scholarship at UVA, and DeMarco imagined that without the scholarship, he wouldn't have been able to attend a first-rate law school. Yeah, he'd been a hardworking kid, willing to make whatever sacrifices he had to make to succeed, and DeMarco couldn't help but admire him. But according to

Elaine, Brian could also be obsessive and relentless. The story she'd told about him writing letters to the insurance company pretending to be a lawyer intent on suing also showed that he wasn't a complete Boy Scout when it came to getting what he wanted. He wondered if Brian could have done something similar, something somewhat underhanded, when researching the dirty dozen and if that could have made someone think he posed a threat. But to figure that out, he had to find the damn laptop.

As he was thinking about this, Caroline returned his call and told him that she didn't have Brian's laptop. She said the only possessions of Brian's that the police had given her were his phone, his watch, and his wallet. She said she assumed his laptop would be at his place or at Elaine's.

DeMarco's next call was to Detective Olivetti. He asked Olivetti if he had Brian's laptop. Olivetti said he didn't.

———◆◆◆———

Sydney recorded the call from Caroline Lewis and the one to Detective Olivetti.

She texted the recordings to Morgenthal, who relayed the information to Grady.

Detective Olivetti called his boss after he spoke to DeMarco and told his lieutenant that DeMarco was looking for Lewis's laptop.

Olivetti's boss passed this on to the chief of detectives, who passed the information on to former congressman turned lobbyist Jimmy Cooper—who also passed it on to Patrick Grady.

17

Unable to think of anything better to do, DeMarco decided to go see Perry and talk things over with him. But Perry wasn't in his office, nobody on his staff knew where he was, and he wasn't answering his phone. DeMarco eventually found him in the House Chamber.

The vast room where the State of the Union is held was almost empty. There was one congresswoman at the podium giving a speech that no one appeared to be listening to. The half a dozen other lawmakers present, probably waiting their turn to get their opinion on the record, were all looking at their phones except for one guy who was sleeping soundly. Democracy in action was not an inspiring sight.

Perry was sitting alone in the gallery above the chamber floor watching the congresswoman—making DeMarco wonder what sort of plan he and Mahoney could be hatching that involved her. When he saw DeMarco waving at him, Perry got up and joined him in the hallway, where they stood beneath a portrait of a long-haired guy named Robert Pothier. Why the portrait of an eighteenth-century French jurist would be hanging there, DeMarco had no idea. Nor did he have the curiosity to find out.

DeMarco told Perry what he'd learned, the punch line being that he'd had no luck in finding Brian's laptop.

Perry said, "I think we should just end this whole thing. There's nothing to show the kid found anything that would make anyone want to kill him. And you need to go tell his mom that. You tell her that he was a kid with an overactive imagination who thought he was seeing criminal conspiracies when all he was really seeing was politics as usual. You tell her what Jane said, that he didn't like seeing how the sausage was made. You also tell her how he didn't know enough about the law to know what was criminal and what wasn't, and that a campaign contribution isn't a bribe even if it sometimes looks like one. And if she doesn't accept that—"

"Which she won't," DeMarco said.

"—then you drop the bomb on her about the cops finding other drugs in his apartment, and tell her if she goes to the press, no one is going to believe her, and unfortunately, as much as we'd hate to do it, we'll have to side with the cops."

"The problem, Perry," DeMarco said, "is that *I* believe her. And I believe his girlfriend. I don't think that kid was using drugs. And I'm bothered that his laptop has disappeared."

"So what are you going to do?"

"I don't know."

"Well, whatever you do, you need to keep Caroline Lewis contained. That's what Mahoney wants."

"Yeah, I know. How's he doing? Did you have the intervention?"

"Yeah, last night. We sat him down and tried to talk to him. Mavis was actually screaming at him at one point. But he told us all to mind our own fucking business and leave him alone. And then he went and sat on the balcony at his condo and drank until he passed out. This morning, he looks like the walking dead. I don't know what I'm going to do about him."

"Well, I've got an idea," DeMarco said.

"What's that?" Perry said.

"Send him to the most dangerous war zone you can think of."

Perry looked at DeMarco for a long moment, then said, "Now I don't know why I didn't think of that."

There was nothing Mahoney liked better and that energized him more than being around American armed forces, particularly Marines, since he'd been a marine. Mahoney loved talking to the young servicemen and -women. He loved putting on a helmet and body armor. He loved being photographed landing in a helicopter at some forward-deployed military base and emerging from the chopper in the dust created by the prop wash. He loved eating in a mess hall with the troops, listening to their stories, and telling his stories of Vietnam. And the closer the soldiers were stationed to an actual combat zone, the better Mahoney liked it. He'd made more than two dozen visits to see the troops in Afghanistan and Iraq while those wars had been active—and every time he went, he scared the hell out of the military brass and his own security people because they were terrified that he was going to be killed on their watch. On one trip to Afghanistan, a mortar round hit a tent a hundred feet from the mess hall where Mahoney had been eating with a group of Special Forces guys, and instead of taking cover, and before anyone could stop him, he ran to the tent to see if he could assist the wounded. He nearly gave the general who'd been assigned to accompany him a heart attack.

And when Mahoney was with the troops, he controlled the drinking. He didn't care what people in Washington thought about his booze consumption, but there was no way he was going to be seen glassy-eyed drunk and slurring his words in front of the young soldiers he'd come to see. Yeah, sending Mahoney on an overseas tour of military bases was almost as good as putting him into a rehab facility.

Perry said, "I'm going to have his ass on a plane by tomorrow, and the mood he's in, I don't think it will take much to convince him. I just need to pick a spot and invent a reason for him to go there. I just hope to hell that he doesn't make me go with him."

18

Grady canceled a lunch meeting with a client—which pissed off the client, as he'd driven down from Philadelphia to see him—and called Carson Newman.

"DeMarco is looking for the kid's laptop."

"Why?" Newman asked.

Grady said, "Because Lewis's girlfriend convinced him that if Lewis had written some kind of report, that's where it would be."

"What's with this son of a bitch?" Newman said. "Why does he give a shit?"

"I don't know. From everything I've heard about the guy, he spends more time on golf courses than he does on Capitol Hill."

"Goddamnit," Newman muttered.

"So what do you want to do?"

Newman didn't answer.

"Carson," Grady said, "what do you want to do?"

Another long pause.

"Carson?"

"Give it to him."

"What?"

"Give him the laptop. I mean, after you delete everything in it we don't want him to see. Once he sees there's nothing there, he'll stop poking around."

"Are you sure?"

"Yeah, I'm sure. Find a way to get the laptop to him. Now aren't you glad I told you to keep it?"

———◆———

No, he wasn't glad.

What he had to do now was sanitize the computer. He had to delete the kid's report and everything in the machine related to it. As for the external hard drive that Lewis used to back up his files, he'd toss it into a dumpster.

He told his secretary to cancel all his appointments, then removed the laptop from the closet in his office, where it had been sitting since the day he'd received it. He could almost feel the heat coming from the machine as if it were radioactive. He turned it on and went to Finder, the program that showed all the files. Jesus Christ, there were over five hundred files. Most of them were related to Lewis's law school studies: papers he'd written, class notes, copies of case files related to subjects he was studying. There were, however, all the files related to campaign finance laws and background information on the twelve congressmen.

The first thing Grady did was send Lewis's summary, the stupid "Tenants' Rights Conspiracy" file, to the Trash folder. He sent all the documents related to campaign finance laws to Trash. Every file on the congressmen went to Trash. Every file that had a name that showed it might be related in any way to Lewis's screwball conspiracy theory, he sent to Trash. He then did a word search of all the files, searching for the words *Newman*, *Grady*, *tenants*, *contributions*, and *bribes*. Two dozen files containing those words were all dumped into the Trash folder. It took him three hours to complete the search, and by the time he was finished his head was throbbing. The last thing he did was empty the Trash folder.

But he didn't know enough about computers to know if what he'd done was good enough. He didn't know if the things he'd deleted— the things he'd sent to Trash—were really gone. For all he knew, little bytes of information were still floating around inside the machine like the parts of a dismembered corpse. So he called Don Janovich, the Captain America computer geek, and told him he needed him again. Right away.

When Janovich arrived, he pointed to the laptop and said, "I need you to do a couple things for me. I deleted a bunch of files from that computer. I sent them to Trash, then emptied the Trash folder, but I want you to make sure that everything I deleted is gone from that computer. Forever. Can you do that?"

"Sure," Janovich said.

"Then I want you to wipe out the search history on that machine."

"Okay," Janovich said.

"When those things are done, I want you to restore it to the way it was before. You know, put the original password back in place."

"Okay," Janovich said again, and half an hour later Grady wrote him another thousand-dollar check.

Grady then told his secretary, who was about to leave for the day, that he needed her to find him a pair of latex gloves and a spray bottle of whatever people used to clean computers.

"Latex gloves?" she said in her phony British accent.

"Just do it," Grady said.

When the gloves and the cleaning solution arrived, Grady put on the gloves and sprayed the laptop keyboard with the blue liquid his secretary had found and wiped off every key. He then wiped all the other surfaces of the laptop. He put the laptop back in its case and then sprayed the case and wiped it down. The whole time he was doing this he couldn't help but feel like some low-life car thief wiping his prints off the steering wheel. Fucking Newman.

Lastly, he called Morgenthal and said, "I need you to do something for me."

19

Grady had told Morgenthal to meet him at a coffee shop a block from KL&M's office.

Morgenthal got there fifteen minutes early because he didn't want Grady to see him walk into the place and see how feeble he was. He was only sixty-two, but these days he was moving like he was ninety-two. His complexion was the gray of cigarette ashes, and he looked exhausted because he'd been getting only about three hours of sleep a night since he started chemo.

He'd taken an Uber to the coffee shop because he didn't trust himself to drive a car. Sydney had offered to take him, but he'd insisted on going alone. When he arrived at the shop, he ordered a cup of coffee but didn't drink it. He was afraid if he tried to drink it, his hands would tremble so much he'd spill half the coffee from the cup. And then there was the fact that coffee, which he loved, now made him nauseous.

Cancer was a bitch.

Grady arrived right on time. Morgenthal noticed that Grady appeared flustered and his tie was undone and his hair looked as if he'd been running his hands through it. He saw Morgenthal and walked over to him, and Morgenthal saw he was carrying what looked like a laptop case. The odd thing was that Grady had a handkerchief in the hand holding the case handle.

Grady set the laptop case down by the chair where Morgenthal was seated and sat down in the chair across from him. Without any preamble, he pointed at the laptop case and said, "That's Brian Lewis's laptop, and as you know, DeMarco is looking for it. I want you to find a way to get it back to either the cops or Lewis's mother, some way that explains why it wasn't in his apartment with him when he OD'd."

"How did you get it?" Morgenthal asked.

"You don't need to know that."

Morgenthal didn't say anything for a moment. "Mr. Grady, I provide information to people. And sometimes I do things that aren't completely legal."

He meant things like breaking into someone's home to plant listening devices or cameras.

"But I draw the line at murder."

"As far as I know, Lewis wasn't murdered," Grady said. "And if he was murdered, I didn't have anything to do with it. I'm a lobbyist, not a criminal. I asked you to follow him because he was doing something that affected one of my clients and I passed on the information you gave me to this client, but that's all I did."

"But you've got his laptop."

"Can you do what I want or not?" Grady said.

"Yeah, I can do it. But I want more than my normal rate. A lot more." He not only wanted to be paid more considering the risk he would be taking, but he also wanted more money to leave to Sydney in case he didn't beat the cancer.

"Not a problem," Grady said.

After Grady left, Morgenthal remained sitting at the table.

He still believed that Grady hadn't killed the Lewis kid. Grady, little slimeball that he was, didn't have the balls for murder. The kid had been killed by Grady's client, whoever that was, and it was the client who had stolen the laptop after he was murdered. Well, not the client personally. The client—who could be an individual or a corporation—was probably a rich son of a bitch who'd paid to have the job done. Whatever the case, it was probably smart to get the laptop to the cops. It would be better for everyone—including him and Sydney—if this guy, DeMarco, stopped poking around.

Morgenthal sat for a few minutes longer thinking about the best way to handle the problem, then called Sydney and asked her to come pick him up.

20

———◆◆◆———

Sydney watched the barista named Bob come out of the coffee shop, walk a few paces from the door, lean against a wall, and light a cigarette. She wondered for a moment if *barista* was the correct term for a male coffee server, if maybe there was some masculine version of the word, like maybe *baristo*? Whatever the right word, Bob was taking his smoke break, which he did about once an hour.

Sydney looked at her reflection in the rearview mirror. She thought she looked good—certainly good enough for ol' Bob. She'd removed her nose ring and the ring from her left eyebrow—the nose ring tended to turn some guys off—applied a little more glossy magenta lipstick, and ran her fingers through her gelled hair to spike it up a bit more. The whites of her eyes—since she'd stopped drinking—were not the least bit bloodshot, and her green irises were like two cut emeralds. She was wearing skintight jeans with designer-cut holes in both knees, a T-shirt without a bra so her nipples were evident, and black combat boots. Yeah, she was definitely hot enough for ol' Bob.

She grabbed the handle of Lewis's laptop case with a Kleenex and got out of her car. When she placed the case on the ground near Bob, she'd palm the Kleenex so Bob wouldn't see it. She crossed the street and walked over to him. She could see him gawking at her as she moved toward him.

She said, "Hi."

"Hey," Bob said, clearly surprised she was talking to him. Bob was a tall, stringy dork with a bad complexion and red hair that reminded her of a clown's wig. He needed to use some kind of whitener to get the yellow out of his nicotine-stained teeth, and his arms were two strands of spaghetti. Sydney would have pinned him in two seconds in an arm wrestling match.

"Can I bum a smoke off you?" Sydney asked.

"Yeah, sure," Bob said, then dropped his pack of cigarettes on the ground trying to fish one out for her.

Sydney took a cigarette and caressed Bob's hand as she held it while he lit the cigarette for her.

She blew out a stream of smoke and said, "I was wondering if you'd be willing to do me a favor, Bob."

"How do you know my name?"

She pointed at his name tag and said, "Duh. And actually, you wouldn't be doing the favor for me as much as for a sweet girl who doesn't deserve to be hurt."

"What are you talking about?" Bob said.

"Did you know Brian Lewis?"

"No. Who's he?"

While Sydney had been following him, Lewis had stopped every morning at the coffee shop on his way to the Metro station and had spent hours in there after work—but Sydney wasn't surprised that a doofus like Bob didn't know who his customers were.

Sydney said, "Brian used to come to your coffee shop almost every morning to get a latte on his way to work."

"Oh," Bob said. "But—"

"Well, Brian's dead."

"Dead?"

"He OD'd. Heroin."

"Geez," Bob said.

"Well, the thing is, and I hope you won't hold this against me, but Brian spent a night at my place the weekend before he died. And he forgot his laptop case there. The thing is, Brian had a girl he was engaged to. This nice little nurse. Well, I want to get Brian's laptop back to his family, but I don't want to have to explain that he left it at my place. What I'm sayin' is, fucking Brian wasn't a big deal to me, but I know it'd really hurt his girlfriend if she found out."

"I imagine his girlfriend's nowhere near as hot as you."

Sydney shrugged.

"But I don't understand what you want from me," Bob said.

"Well, I was hoping you might be willing to call the cops and tell them you have Brian's laptop. I mean, you say he left it at the coffee shop and you found it. You meant to call him and tell him you had it, but then you forgot, and then came the weekend and you totally forgot about it. But then today some customer, you didn't know his name, tells you that he'd read that Brian was dead. So you call the cops and tell them you've got Brian's laptop, because you didn't know who else to call. The other thing is, I sort of have a history with cops and I'd just as soon not have to talk to them at all."

"Gee, I don't know."

Sydney stroked one of Bob's skinny arms. "Come on, Bob. It's not complicated, and I'd really appreciate it. And like I said, you'd be sparing his girlfriend, his fiancée, a lot of pain. It's simple. Brian left his laptop at the coffee shop, you found it, stuck it in the back room, and forgot to call him, and then you remembered you had it when one of your other customers told you he'd OD'd. I even got the phone number of the station you need to call."

"Yeah, okay," Bob said. "Uh, what's your name?"

"Miley," Sydney said. She'd been listening to Miley Cyrus's "Wrecking Ball" just before she left the car.

"Uh," Bob said, "do you think we might be able to get together for a drink when I get off work."

Sydney smiled, her sparkling green eyes boring into Bob's dull brown ones. She was surprised that ol' Bob had mustered the courage to ask her out. She was almost impressed. "I can't do it today, but tomorrow will work. Give me your phone and I'll put my digits in it."

She wasn't worried about leaving fingerprints on his phone; he'd smear her prints with his own when he used it.

21

After talking to Perry and not knowing what to do next when it came to Brian, DeMarco spent the next day mowing his lawn and washing clothes and paying the bills that were almost overdue and ignoring those that weren't. Chores completed, he walked to a bar in Georgetown that had air-conditioning and drank beer and ate chicken wings as he watched a rerun of a golf tournament that Xander Schauffele won in a playoff by sinking a fifty-foot putt that even Xander knew was mostly luck.

The next morning, he woke up feeling tired and grumpy, as he'd hardly slept because his bedroom was so damn hot. He'd thought about buying an AC unit he could stick in the window but didn't want to spend the money on one, so he bought a fan, but all it did was push the hot air around and he had a hard time sleeping with the air blowing directly on him. The first thing he did, after he made a pot of coffee, was call fucking Rick. When Rick didn't answer, he left a voice mail saying: "When will my new compressor be delivered? I want a date. And you better return this call."

After five minutes, when Rick didn't return his call, he called the company that Rick worked for intending to speak to his boss. His call was answered by a recording, one left over from the pandemic, saying the company was experiencing higher-than-normal call volumes and to please be patient. He listened—impatiently—to elevator music for fifteen minutes before cursing and finally giving up.

He trudged to his front door and picked up his copy of the *Washington Post* off the porch. He still had the paper delivered because he didn't like reading the news on his phone or on a tablet. On the front page of the *Post* was a photo of Mahoney. A highly motivated Perry Wallace must have gotten him on a plane the same day DeMarco talked to him.

Mahoney was standing in a sunflower field in front of a crumpled Russian tank that had been destroyed when Putin invaded Ukraine. Standing next to him was the American ambassador to Ukraine, who looked nervous, and a couple of smiling, bearded Ukrainian soldiers dressed in camo, holding rifles. Mahoney was wearing a combat helmet and, hopefully, a bulletproof vest. He had a hand on the shoulder of one of the soldiers and a broad grin on his ruddy face. He was obviously enjoying himself. The accompanying article said that Mahoney would be visiting several bases where American troops were stationed after he left Ukraine. Which bases and when he'd be there weren't being disclosed for security reasons.

DeMarco scanned the sports pages next. He saw that the Nationals were in last place in their division, the best pitcher they had needed surgery on his throwing shoulder, and an outfielder they were paying twenty million bucks a year was going into rehab. It was going to be that kind of summer.

He couldn't figure out what to do about Brian. He was almost positive that he hadn't been using heroin. Which meant that he had most likely been killed, as his mother and his girlfriend thought, and that somebody had planted drugs in his apartment. And that same person had stolen his laptop, which probably contained information on whatever conspiracy Brian had uncovered.

He figured that there were a dozen members of Congress—some of whom were now ex-members—who had a possible motive for killing Brian, but he considered it highly unlikely that any of those weasels would have committed a murder to cover up whatever crime Brian thought they'd committed. If they were accused of taking bribes, what they would do first is lie and deny, and then if they thought a crime could be proved, they'd hire a good shyster to avoid going to jail. They wouldn't kill anyone. At least DeMarco didn't think so.

Then there was the fact that if Brian had been murdered, it would have taken someone with a special skill set. The killer had to break into Brian's apartment without leaving any evidence that he'd broken in. He had to subdue a healthy young man in such a way that he didn't leave any bruises before injecting Brian with the heroin. He also had to be able to find a supply of fentanyl-laced heroin. DeMarco found it hard to imagine that any of the dirty dozen—the majority of them being overweight and middle-aged—would have had the ability to do those things. They—or one of them—could have hired someone who had those skills, but he also found it hard to imagine that they would go to that extreme.

On the other hand, depending on the circumstances, the stakes were high. DeMarco remembered reading an article in the *Washington Post* talking about members of Congress who had been indicted since 1980 for various crimes. There were more than three dozen lawmakers on the list, and they were pretty much equally divided between the two parties. Amazingly, John Mahoney's name wasn't included.

A few were indicted for sex-related offenses, but most were nabbed for taking bribes. One guy was sentenced to thirteen years in prison when ninety thousand dollars was found in his freezer. The $90K was only a part of the half million he was accused of receiving in return for political favors. Another guy got eight years. But these stiff sentences were outliers. The other sentences varied from three months to three years, and many of those indicted were never convicted, or their convictions were overturned, or they avoided jail time by pleading guilty and resigning. In one case, a sitting president commuted a guy's sentence. Nonetheless, the possibility of serving time in prison might be enough to cause one of the dirty dozen to commit a murder or pay someone to do it.

But how would he ever prove one of the congressmen had Brian killed? He certainly couldn't do it by himself. The FBI could do it. They could look at phone records and bank accounts and trace people's movements, but those things would take warrants—and DeMarco didn't know enough about what Brian had uncovered to provide justification for warrants. He needed to know what the dirty dozen had done—or what Brian thought they had done. What he needed was Brian's laptop. But since he couldn't find the laptop, the only other thing he could think to do was talk to the one person he hadn't talked to: Brian's professor at UVA.

Brian's mother had said the professor's name was Adam something. He went online and looked at the names of the university's law school faculty. There was only one Adam. Professor Adam Lang. It took him a half dozen phone calls before he finally reached a woman who told him that Lang wasn't teaching summer classes. When he asked for Lang's home or cell phone number, the woman refused to give it to him. She wasn't the least bit impressed or intimidated by the fact that he worked for Congress. Why should she be? Congress didn't seem to be able to do anything to people who ignored subpoenas and committed perjury when they testified before its committees. What could Congress possibly do to her for refusing to give out a phone number?

He called Perry and said, "Who's the rep from the district that includes the University of Virginia?"

"Stan Wood."

"Democrat or Republican?"

"Republican."

"Well, shit."

"Why? What do you need?"

"I need a telephone number for a Professor Adam Lang who teaches at UVA. He was Brian's adviser at the law school and, according to his mother, someone Brian might have confided in. But the university won't give me his number. I was hoping the congressman might be able to call someone, like whoever is in charge down there, and get the number for me."

"Stan might do it. He's a good guy."

"What reason will you give him for wanting the number?"

"Hell, I don't know. I'll come up with some kind of lie."

"Good. When you get it, give me a call. By the way, I saw that Mahoney is in Ukraine. How's he doing?"

"Great. I sent an aide with him, and I've been talking to him. He said Mahoney only had a couple of drinks on the flight over, and since he's been there, the aide hasn't seen him take one in public. I'm sure he's got a bottle with him, but today when he woke up, the aide said it didn't look as if he'd spent the night sipping from it."

"I'm surprised he's not having DT's."

"Maybe he is, but so far he's holding himself together. The biggest problem right now is he wants the military to let him shoot one of those Javelin anti-tank missiles. Not at a real tank, of course, but at one they use for target practice. Well, the damn missiles cost about eighty grand each, and they don't want to waste one to entertain Mahoney. Anyway, that's the Pentagon's problem."

DeMarco laughed. "Call me when you've got a number."

After he finished talking to Perry and since he couldn't think of anything more productive to do, he decided to go to a driving range and whack a bucket of balls. Golf ball whacking was therapeutic.

He'd hit about half the fifty balls in the bucket when his phone rang.

It was Caroline Lewis.

She said, "I have Brian's laptop."

22

When DeMarco arrived at Caroline's place, he found her and her sister in the living room packing household items into cardboard boxes. Most likely to give DeMarco and Caroline some privacy, her sister picked up an empty box and said, "I'm going to deal with some of the stuff in the second bedroom."

Caroline said to DeMarco, "We're getting this place ready to sell. There's nothing to keep me here and I'm going to get a place near Irene in Colorado. She and my nephews are the only family I have now."

On the floor near one of the boxes was a polished wooden case with a glass cover containing a folded American flag and a dozen military medals. It was her husband's shadow box, and the flag was probably the one they'd given Caroline when they buried him at Arlington. DeMarco couldn't help but think that Brian might be alive today if Mahoney hadn't attended that particular funeral.

Pointing at the shadow box, DeMarco said, "It looks like your husband had an impressive career."

Caroline glanced at the shadow box and said, "Yeah, he fought in one pointless war after another."

Not knowing how to respond to that, DeMarco said, "How'd you get Brian's laptop?"

"That detective, Olivetti. He said he got it from a barista at a coffee shop that Brian used to go to. The barista said Brian forgot it there on the Friday before Elaine found his body. He meant to call Brian—his phone number was on the laptop case—and tell him he'd left the computer at the shop, but then he put it in the back room and forgot all about it. Yesterday, someone told the barista that Brian was dead and that's when he remembered the laptop."

"Huh," DeMarco said. "Did Brian go to this coffee shop very often?"

"Elaine said he went there almost every day. He'd get his coffee there in the morning and sometimes he'd work there in the evening because the Internet connection in his apartment was so slow. But Elaine said she couldn't imagine him forgetting his laptop there."

"Huh," DeMarco said again.

Caroline said. "I tried to see if there was anything in it related to what Brian had learned at work, but it's password-protected."

"Well, give it to me. I know a guy who can probably get around the password."

"Have you learned anything since the last time we talked?" Caroline asked.

"No," DeMarco said. "I've been through all the stuff in his work computer, and there wasn't anything there that pointed to anything illegal. But maybe there'll be something in the laptop. The other thing I'm planning to do is talk to that professor at UVA you mentioned. The guy isn't at the school this summer and I'm trying to run him down. But don't worry, I'll find him."

He left Caroline's house shortly after that. Caroline, although not happy with his results, at least appeared satisfied that he was trying and keeping her informed.

The story about the barista suddenly remembering that he had Brian's laptop nine days after Brian died bothered him.

But what really bothered him was that as soon as he started looking for the laptop, it appeared.

DeMarco decided he wanted to talk to Olivetti, but when he called his cell phone, the call went to voice mail. He called the precinct and after a little back-and-forth was eventually transferred to Olivetti's boss, who told him that Olivetti was at the courthouse on Indiana Avenue waiting to testify in a trial that would be going on all day.

"Which trial?" DeMarco asked.

"Morehouse," Olivetti's boss said, and hung up.

DeMarco drove to the courthouse and then wasted fifteen minutes trying to find a place to park. Once inside the building, he asked a bored guard standing near the metal detectors where the Morehouse trial was being held and found Olivetti sitting on a bench outside the courtroom reading a Donna Leon paperback.

He looked up in surprise when DeMarco sat down next to him.

"What are you doing here?" Olivetti asked. Before DeMarco could answer, he said, "The prosecutor just told me they'll probably call me in the next fifteen minutes, so you better make it quick."

Curious, DeMarco asked, "What's the trial about?"

Olivetti shook his head. "This doctor, Shirley Morehouse, has spent the last five years writing scripts for opioid addicts. And that's all she does. I mean, she wrote like thirty thousand last year alone—that's more than a hundred scripts a day—and two dozen of her so-called patients have OD'd. This goddamn woman went to med school at Johns Hopkins and could probably get a job anywhere in the country that would pay her two or three hundred grand a year for treating actual sick people, but instead she sets up a so-called pain clinic where she dispenses pills to addicts like popcorn. She's a fuckin' drug dealer, not a doctor, but she's smart and her lawyer's even smarter than she is, and I wouldn't be surprised if she didn't serve a day in jail. Anyway, what do you want?"

"How'd you get Brian Lewis's laptop?"

"Like I told his mother, he left it at a coffee shop. A barista found it, meant to call Lewis, but then he forgot. This barista isn't the sharpest card in the deck. Anyway, he learned about Lewis's death yesterday, remembered the laptop, and since he didn't know who else to call, he called me."

"How'd he know you were working on the case?"

"I don't know. I'm guessing he called the precinct, talked to whoever answered the phone, and asked for the guy handling Lewis's case."

"I'm just curious," DeMarco said. "Did you tell anyone I was looking for the laptop?"

"Yeah, my lieutenant. And the only reason I told him was because you work for Mahoney, and he asked to be kept informed of anything going on with Lewis."

"But no one else?"

"No. Why are you asking?"

"Because I'm troubled by the coincidence of me asking about his laptop and it magically appearing."

"Well, I don't know what to tell you, DeMarco. What the barista told me makes sense, and coincidences do happen. You know, you and Lewis's mom have got to quit thinking there's some big conspiracy going on here. The kid was experimenting with heroin, got some bad shit, and killed himself. Last year, in this country, ninety-two thousand people OD'd. That's like two hundred and fifty people OD'ing every single *day*. Lewis's death wasn't an anomaly."

"What's this barista's name?" DeMarco asked.

Olivetti hesitated. "Bob. I don't remember his last name."

"Do you call male baristas *baristas*?" DeMarco asked.

"How the fuck would I know?" Olivetti said.

DeMarco drove to Georgetown and, carrying Brian's laptop case, entered a four-story office building near the banks of the Potomac River. He took the elevator to the fourth floor, went to an unmarked door, and pushed on the doorbell, one of those Ring doorbells that contain a camera. A voice said, "What do you want, DeMarco?"

"Let me in, Neil," DeMarco said.

A latch clicked and DeMarco pushed the door open.

He'd had no doubt that Neil would be in his office, as Neil hardly ever left his office. Neil didn't even usually go out for lunch, preferring to have his food delivered. DeMarco found him where he almost always was, sitting behind a long table that served as a desk and held four jumbo-size monitors. Beneath the table were computer towers and an assortment of black boxes with blinking lights. DeMarco had no idea what the black boxes did.

Neil was an overweight white man who tied his thinning blond hair in a short ponytail. He was wearing a Hawaiian shirt decorated with red hibiscus flowers, cargo shorts, and sandals. Neil was a criminal, although he didn't consider himself one, and the computers and the black boxes were the tools of his trade. He didn't use his tools to steal money or people's identities, however. What he did was steal information and sell it to folks interested in buying it. DeMarco had used him in the past when he needed records buried in databases protected by insubstantial firewalls.

Without looking at DeMarco, and while tapping on a keyboard, his fingers moving like a concert pianist's, Neil said, "I'm busy, DeMarco. I'm up against a deadline."

"You're probably just looking at porn."

Neil stopped typing. "I am not," he said, genuinely offended. Neil was a bit of a prude. "I'm helping shut down a hacker in Nigeria."

"A hacker? You mean someone like you?"

"Yeah. I've got a contract with Homeland Security to help stop cyber-attacks on defense contractors."

"Homeland Security? Are you shitting me? Does Homeland have any idea what you normally do?"

"I don't know if they do or not. I suspect they do. But they needed someone with my, uh, *skill set*, and they came to me. I didn't apply for the job."

"I don't believe it," DeMarco said.

"This Nigerian planted ransomware on the computers of a company that makes parts for cruise missiles, and Homeland wants to know exactly where he is. And I wouldn't be surprised that when I locate him, they send in some guys wearing ski masks to drop a hood over his head and snatch him."

"This is like a bad movie," DeMarco said. "Use a thief to catch a thief. Homeland must be desperate."

"What do you want, DeMarco?"

DeMarco took Brian's laptop out of its case and placed it on Neil's table. "I need you to get around the password that's on this machine so I can see what's inside it. This is important, Neil. The person who owned the laptop was a twenty-two-year-old intern who worked for Mahoney. He's dead now, and I think he might have been murdered for whatever is in this computer."

"Murdered?"

"Yeah."

"Okay," Neil said. "I'll get to it as soon as I can, but I gotta deal with the Nigerian first." Neil sat back and smiled. "You know, this job is paying so much, I just might make this a full-time thing."

DeMarco shook his head.

23

DeMarco's next stop was the coffee shop where Brian had supposedly forgotten his laptop. He'd gotten the name from Elaine. And like Elaine had said, the coffee shop was only a block from Brian's apartment.

DeMarco went inside the shop. There were only two customers in the place. One was one guy with a mop of uncombed hair and a tangled beard who was on a computer. DeMarco thought he looked like Ted Kaczynski, the Unabomber. Or like the way Karl Budnick, the fired congressional staffer turned podcaster, now looked. The other customer was a middle-aged woman reading a Kindle as she sipped an ice tea. Behind the counter was a pretty girl with short blue hair looking at her phone. DeMarco liked the blue hair; it looked good on her. And it made him smile.

DeMarco said, "There's a guy who works here named Bob. Is he around?"

The barista rolled her eyes. "Yeah, although *works here* may be a stretch," she said. "He's outside having a smoke."

DeMarco walked outside. When he'd entered the shop, he hadn't noticed the skinny redhead leaning against a wall smoking. DeMarco walked over to him.

———◆◆◆———

Sydney was parked in a no-parking zone half a block from where DeMarco had parked.

She'd followed him to Caroline Lewis's house in Silver Spring. When he came out of Caroline's house, he was holding Brian Lewis's laptop case. From Caroline's house, he'd gone to the courthouse on Indiana Avenue. She'd followed him inside, where she saw him sitting on a bench talking to a good-looking guy with a goatee, who she suspected was Detective Olivetti based on DeMarco's phone calls. From the courthouse, he'd driven to an office building in Georgetown near the Potomac. When he went into the building, he was holding the laptop case. She'd waited a minute, then walked into the lobby of the building and looked at a sign that identified the building's occupants: real estate agents, a website designer, a PR firm, a couple of lawyers, a CPA, and a graphic artist. She'd noticed that all the occupants were on floors one through three, but no one was listed as occupying the fourth floor. She'd wondered who DeMarco could be seeing and used her phone to take a photo of the sign before returning to her car. When DeMarco came out of the building, he wasn't holding the laptop case.

From the office building, he drove to the coffee shop.

And when she saw him walk up to Bob, she said, "Aw, shit."

———◆◆◆———

DeMarco said, "Bob, I need to talk to you."

"Who are you?" Bob said.

DeMarco flipped open his wallet, showed his congressional ID to Bob like he was flashing a badge, and said, "My name's DeMarco. I'm an investigator who works for Congress."

"Congress?" Bob said.

"Yeah. And I'm investigating Brian Lewis's death."

"But what do you want with me?"

"I want you to tell me about finding Brian's laptop."

"Oh," Bob said, and looked away—and DeMarco knew that Bob was about to lie to him.

Bob said, "There isn't much to tell. He left his laptop case in the shop one day, by the table where he'd been sitting, and I found it. I saw his number was on it, and I was planning to call him, but it got busy and I stuck the case in the back room and then forgot all about it. Then when someone told me he'd died, I remembered it and called the cops and told them I had it."

DeMarco stared at him for a moment without speaking. "Bob, I happen to know that there's no way Brian would have forgotten his laptop. He'd have been more likely to forget his head. And before you say anything else, let me tell you something. Like I said, I work for Congress, and what I'm going to do is get the FBI down here and have them ask you the same question I just asked. You know why I'm going to do that?"

"No," Bob said, gulping like he was trying to swallow a baseball.

"Because if you lie to me, Bob, it's not a big deal. But if you lie to the FBI, it's a crime and you go to jail."

"I don't want to talk to you anymore. And I don't think I have to. I mean, legally."

Bob started to walk past him, but DeMarco put his hand in the middle of Bob's skinny chest and pushed him up against the wall.

———◆———

"Aw, shit," Sydney said again.

"Bob, do you want to go to jail?"

"No. And let me go."

DeMarco took his hand off Bob's chest. "Tell me the truth, Bob, or your shitty life is going to get really shitty."

Bob looked away again, but this time DeMarco interpreted the gesture as *I give up.*

"There was this babe," Bob said. "This really hot babe, and she—"

Bob's story was that a young woman came up to him the day before while he was having a smoke and told him that Brian had spent the night with her and forgot his laptop at her apartment. The woman said she knew Brian was engaged and she wanted to spare his fiancée the pain of learning that he'd left his computer at another woman's place, so she asked Bob to call the cops and tell them that Brian had left it at the coffee shop.

"What's this woman's name?" DeMarco asked.

"She said it was Miley. And she gave me her phone number because she said she'd like to get together for a drink, but when I called the number, a guy in a Korean restaurant answered the phone."

"Did she give you a last name?"

"No. Just Miley."

DeMarco doubted the woman would have given Bob her real name.

"What did she look like?" DeMarco asked.

"I told you. She was smokin'. Really hot."

"Yeah, but can you be more specific? Like how old was she?"

"I don't know. Twentysomething. About my age."

"What else?"

"She had gelled hair, that was, you know, all spiky. And she was built. Oh, and her eyes were this incredible green, like jade green."

"What color was her hair?"

"Oh, black."

"And that's it? I need to identify this woman, Bob, and if I don't get something more from you, I'm going to let the D.C. cops know that you lied to them about finding the laptop. Trust me when I tell you that you don't want to spend even a single night in a D.C. jail."

"I don't know what else to tell you," Bob whined. "Oh, wait a minute. You know that Australian actress Ruby Rose?"

"No, never heard of her."

"Well, look her up. That's who she looked like, except she was younger, and she had tats like Ruby. Ruby's all tatted up."

"Well, shit, Bob. What kind of tattoos?"

"She had one of a green vine with little green leaves winding around her throat. It was cool. And she had a couple of tats on her arms, symbols of some kind, like Chinese letters."

"Are there cameras in the coffee shop?" DeMarco asked.

"There's one behind the counter. It looks down at the cash register. I think they installed it to see if any of the baristas are stealing. But she never went into the shop."

"Okay, Bob," DeMarco said. "You can go back to work now."

Bob said, "I should've known a babe like her wouldn't be interested in me."

"Maybe if you stopped calling women *babes* they'd be more interested," DeMarco said.

━━━◆━━━

Sydney saw Bob slink away from DeMarco and she had no doubt that Bob had given her up. DeMarco had acted like a cop. Or like a Mafia leg-breaker. Yeah, more like a leg-breaker than a cop. *Shit, shit, shit.*

She watched as DeMarco stood on the street for a couple of minutes in front of the coffee shop, just looking around, and then he crossed the street. He went into the sushi place that was directly across from the coffee shop, came out a minute later, and went into a nail salon next to the sushi place.

When he came out of the nail salon, he took out his cell phone and made a call, and Sydney heard DeMarco say—

"I've got Brian's laptop. Whoever had it, or stole it, arranged for it to be returned to the police."

"Arranged? What are you talking about?" Perry said.

"I'll give you the details later, but I got a lead on one of the people involved."

"Who is it?"

"A woman. I don't have a name, but I've got a description of her. What I need right now is someone with a badge to squeeze a couple of store owners who have cameras that might have caught her on video. I don't want to use D.C. Metro, because I don't think they'd do it. And because I don't trust them. So send me a Capitol cop."

"What do I tell the cop?" Perry asked.

"You tell him that someone on Mahoney's staff might have been killed. And you tell him to keep his mouth shut about it until we know more. But in the meantime, I want a scary-looking cop to meet me and then squeeze these store owners and get them to show their surveillance tapes without a warrant."

"Yeah, okay," Perry said. "Where will you be?"

DeMarco gave him the name and address of the sushi place across the street from the coffee shop.

24

"Aw, fuck," Sydney said.

She called Dave. "DeMarco knows I gave the barista the laptop."

"What? How did he figure that out?"

"I don't know. I'm guessing he didn't buy the story the barista gave to the cops and then he went and leaned hard on the barista. He acted more like a cop than a lawyer, and I could tell he scared the shit out of the barista. Anyway, he doesn't know my name, but he knows what I look like, and right now he's trying to look at surveillance cameras near the coffee shop to see if he can spot me."

"Where are you right now?"

"I'm still watching him. He doesn't have a clue that I've been following him."

"Sydney, get out of there. You're pretty distinctive-looking. And you have a record. If they start comparing video footage to police mug shots, they'll ID you."

"You think DeMarco has enough clout to make that happen? You know, to get the cops to use facial-recognition software or something to ID me?"

"I don't know how much clout he has but he works for John Mahoney, who definitely has clout. And the son of a bitch is persistent. You need to get out of there and go to ground until I can decide what to do next. But I'm inclined to drop this whole thing. We're making good money, but I think the Lewis kid might have been killed and we need to back away from this before the cops tie us into that. Anyway, hole up in a motel someplace. Call me later and let me know where you're staying."

———————————

Morgenthal was lying on the couch in his living room, willing himself not to throw up. He didn't have the energy to vomit one more time today.

Like he'd told Sydney, it was time to stop tracking DeMarco. Lord knows they could use the money, but the risk of being tied to Lewis's death wasn't worth it. If he was in any shape to follow DeMarco himself, he probably would have kept going—but he wasn't and he couldn't take the chance of Sydney ending up in a cell. She'd go insane in prison and he couldn't let that happen to her.

He called Grady, who of course wasn't available. He was probably in a meeting with one of his high-paying clients trying to figure out a way to bend some lawmaker to the client's will. An hour later, Grady called him back.

Morgenthal said, "I'm through with the DeMarco thing."

"Why? What happened?" Grady asked.

"I got the laptop back to the cops like you wanted, but DeMarco didn't buy the story I came up with and right now he's trying to track down a person I used."

"What are you talking about?"

Morgenthal told Grady how he'd used a woman to convince a barista at a coffee shop to say Lewis had left his laptop in the shop. "But DeMarco saw through the story, and he's managed to get a description of the woman I used. If he can ID her, he might be able to use her to get to me, although I doubt it. The gal I used is a hooker, one that was good-looking enough to convince the barista to do what she wanted. I figure the odds of DeMarco being able to ID the hooker are pretty small, and if he does, the hooker doesn't know my name and I look like a million other middle-aged white guys. But I'm still dropping this thing. You said you didn't murder the kid, and I believe you, but someone stole his laptop and I just don't want anything more to do with this."

"What if I increased your fee to—"

"Nope," Morgenthal said. "I'm done." And he hung up.

Grady was pissed that Morgenthal had quit on him.

He wanted to know what DeMarco was going to do next, and if Morgenthal wasn't following him, he wouldn't be able to find out. On the other hand, there was a good possibility that DeMarco wouldn't do anything. Once he learned that there was nothing in the laptop, what could he do? DeMarco still had no idea what Lewis had uncovered, and without the files that had been erased from the laptop, he'd never know. And DeMarco, as best as he could tell, had found no evidence that Lewis had been murdered, and the cops weren't treating Lewis's death as a homicide. And if DeMarco asked the cops to do anything, Grady would know. So maybe Morgenthal's quitting wasn't a problem.

Morgenthal, however, was a liability. If the cops or DeMarco ID'd him and started squeezing him, Morgenthal might confess that Grady had hired him to return the laptop. Or even worse, that Grady had hired him to follow Lewis before Lewis was killed. But what was the likelihood of Morgenthal being identified? Morgenthal said he thought it was small and he was probably right.

He'd call Newman and tell him that he'd returned Lewis's laptop to the cops as he'd asked, and that DeMarco now had it. And since the laptop had been wiped, he'd tell Newman that there was nothing to worry about. But he wouldn't tell Newman that DeMarco didn't buy the story of how the laptop turned up and that he was now looking for the hooker that Morgenthal had used to deliver the laptop. He was afraid if he told Newman . . . Well, he just couldn't predict what Newman might do. He wanted the whole Lewis problem to end, and the last thing he needed was Newman doing something that could escalate the situation.

———◆———

"Okay, I got the laptop back to the cops and DeMarco now has it," Grady said. "And since there's nothing in the computer we care about, DeMarco's not going to be able to learn anything that will cause us a problem."

"Good," Newman said. Based on the background noise, it sounded as if Newman was in a restaurant, and he was probably with other people.

Grady said, "And if he goes to the cops, I'll know it. But I don't think he will. I think this thing is over with and we can relax."

"I am relaxed," Newman said.

25

DeMarco hadn't had lunch, and the only place to eat near the coffee shop was the sushi place across the street—and he didn't like sushi. As far as he was concerned, raw fish had another name, that name being *bait*. He looked at the menu above the counter and saw they had egg rolls that were fried and contained vegetables. Fried was good. He ordered four egg rolls.

He'd just finished eating when a woman walked up to him. She was wearing a gray pantsuit with a white blouse and had light-brown skin and pale blue eyes. Her dark hair was very short, no more than an inch long. She was tall and had the kind of broad shoulders that Olympic swimmers tend to have, and DeMarco would have bet that she spent a lot of time in a gym. She looked fit.

She said, "Are you DeMarco?"

"Yes," DeMarco said. "Who are you?"

"Celeste Honoré. Capitol Police."

She had a slight Southern accent, and with a French-sounding name like Honoré, he wondered if she could be a Creole from Louisiana.

DeMarco had told Perry he needed a scary-looking Capitol cop. He'd figured that Perry would send a man, a big guy with a bent nose who looked like he would enjoy whacking people with his nightstick. But he was thinking Honoré would do. The woman was intense—he could sense it—and he had the immediate impression she could be intimidating if she chose to be.

DeMarco gestured to the seat across from him and she sat down. "What do you need?" she asked.

DeMarco said, "I need you to get the owners of this place, the nail place next door, and the coffee shop across the street to show you their video footage. They all have cameras. And you need to make them do it without a warrant. Tell them you're a Capitol cop. Show 'em your badge. Show 'em your gun. Tell them you're involved in a big-deal case trying to track down a bad guy. Imply it's related to a threat against a senator or anything else you can think of. Tell them it's time-sensitive and you don't have time to get a warrant, but if they make you get one, you're gonna come down on them like a ton of bricks. You're gonna get ICE to see if any of their employees are illegal. You're gonna get health inspectors to go through their kitchens looking for rat droppings. You're gonna—"

"Yeah, yeah, I get the idea," Honoré said. "What am I looking for?"

"Yesterday, a woman in her twenties with short, spiky hair and tattoos gave a laptop case to a barista named Bob who works in the coffee shop. Bob's a skinny redheaded dork. He's in the coffee shop now and you can get the exact time from him. According to Bob, the woman looked like a younger version of some Australian actress named Ruby Rose. You know who that is?"

"Yeah."

"That's good, because I don't. Anyway, I want you to see if you can spot her on video and then ID her."

"All right."

"And did Perry tell you that you need to keep this thing to yourself for now?"

"Yeah."

DeMarco wrote his phone number on a napkin and handed it to her. "Call me as soon as you have something."

DeMarco left feeling confident that Honoré was going to scare the shit out of the store owners, because she kinda scared him.

———— ✦ ————

As DeMarco was leaving the sushi place, Neil called.

Neil said, "I got into that computer like you wanted. Cracking the password was a piece of cake. But you need to know something. Somebody, somebody like me, somebody who knew what he was doing, got into it before I did and wiped out a lot of the information that used to be there."

"How do you know that?"

"If I told you how I know, DeMarco, do you think you'd be able to understand the explanation?"

"No."

"Then just take my word for it. Somebody permanently wiped out a bunch of files and the user's Internet search history."

"Okay, I'll swing by and get it."

As he was heading toward Neil's place, Perry called.

DeMarco said, "Thanks for sending the cop. Why did you pick her?"

"During the insurrection, she escorted me and Mahoney to a safe place, and I watched her take down three of the rioters with her baton. And I could tell she enjoyed doing it. I got to know her a bit after that, and figured she'd be just what you needed. Anyway, I have a phone number for that UVA professor."

"Can you text it to me? I'm driving."

"Yeah."

DeMarco said, "I had a guy get into Brian's laptop for me. I'm going to go pick it up now. After I talk to this professor, I'll come to your office."

"Okay," Perry said. "Mahoney called today. He asked if we were making any progress on Brian. I told him not really, but so far you were doing a good job when it came to keeping his mom in line. I didn't want to tell him you thought the kid might have been murdered. I didn't want to give him any bad news and spoil the fun he's having."

"Is he still behaving himself?"

"Yeah. But he's having such a good time that now I'm starting to wonder if he'll ever come back."

———————◆◆◆———————

DeMarco picked up the laptop from Neil, then called the number for Professor Lang. When Lang answered, he said, "Professor, my name is Joe DeMarco. I work for Congress and I'm looking into Brian Lewis's death."

"Brian's dead?" Lang said.

"Yes, sir. You didn't know?"

"No. My God, what happened?"

DeMarco wasn't surprised Lang didn't know about Brian. The death of a young man OD'ing in Northeast D.C. was hardly unique and barely newsworthy. DeMarco started to tell Lang about Brian's death—but then he didn't. He said, "Professor, where are you right now? I'd like to discuss this with you in person rather than over the phone."

"I'm at my home in Charlottesville," Lang said.

Charlottesville was a two-hour ride from D.C.

"Can I come and see you today? This is rather urgent."

"Urgent?"

"Yes, sir. I'll explain when I see you. I can be there in two hours."

"Well, okay," Lang said, sounding unsure. Or maybe he was still thinking about the fact that Brian was dead.

"Could you please text me your address?"

DeMarco had decided on the spot that he wanted to talk to Lang in person. If Brian had discussed something sensitive with him, DeMarco figured Lang was more likely to be forthcoming if he spoke to the man face-to-face. You can't hang up on someone sitting in front of you. The other thing was, he was still bothered by the fact that Brian's laptop had shown up as soon as he started looking for it. He thought it pretty unlikely that someone could be monitoring his phone calls but, well, these days, with cell phones, you never knew.

To speed things up, DeMarco decided to drop the laptop off with Perry and have Perry see if there was anything useful in it while he was meeting with Lang. When he arrived at the Capitol, however, Perry wasn't in his office. He found Jane Rosen in her cubicle and placed Brian's laptop case on her desk. He said, "That's Brian's laptop. When Perry gets back, you and he need to see what's in it. You know, see if there's some sort of report or memo related to what these politicians were doing."

"Will we need a password?" Jane asked.

"No," DeMarco said. "I gotta get going. Have Perry call me after you've looked at the computer." He decided not to tell Jane what Neil had said about a pro having deleted information from the laptop.

"All right," Jane said.

DeMarco could tell she didn't like taking orders from him. Too bad.

DeMarco turned on the car radio, which was set to a twenty-four-hour news station. After a few minutes, he changed the station. The news was just too depressing. Wars, pestilence, and famine. Rising prices.

Homelessness crises. Mass shootings. Political gridlock. He found the station broadcasting the Nationals game against the Rays. That was better. Some announcer quietly calling balls and strikes, and in between pitches, telling amusing stories of kids in their twenties being paid several million bucks every summer because they could hit a hundred-mile-an-hour fastball. The fact that the Nationals were losing didn't mar the experience.

Lang lived in a two-story colonial that had a massive oak tree in the front yard and a big front porch. The oak tree looked as if it was over a hundred years old, and DeMarco bet the people who lived in the house prayed during every windstorm that it didn't come crashing down on the roof. A little girl, maybe nine, her dark hair tied in pigtails with pink ribbons, was sitting on the front steps with a black Labrador. DeMarco walked toward her, keeping his eye on the dog. The girl saw where he was looking and said, "Don't worry. Riley won't bite you." Then she gave DeMarco a small, wicked smile and added, "Unless I tell him to."

Great. "I'm here to see Professor Lang," DeMarco said.

"I'll go get him," the girl said.

As she bounced through the front door, she called out, "Daddy, there's some man here to see you."

Riley was staring at DeMarco. The dog seemed docile enough, and DeMarco thought for a second about patting it on the head, then decided not to. He didn't trust dogs. One minute they're just looking at you—and the next minute they decide your face is lunch.

A slender man in his mid-thirties, wearing a faded red T-shirt, baggy gym shorts that reached past his knees, and sandals that looked as if they'd been made from old tires, came to the front door. He had his dark hair tied up in one of those samurai, sumo wrestler manbuns, a hairstyle DeMarco had always thought looked ridiculous. Except on samurai.

He said, "Mr. DeMarco?"

"Yes," DeMarco said, and showed his congressional ID to Lang.

"Please come with me."

DeMarco followed Lang into the house, which was delightfully cool, as Lang had a functioning air-conditioning system—reminding him again that he had to do something to jack up Rick, who still hadn't responded to any of his phone calls to tell him when his new compressor would be arriving.

Lang led him to a room that appeared to be his den. There was a desk with a computer on it and shelves stacked with books. Lots of books. In one corner was a large globe on a stand; DeMarco had always wanted one of those so that when he heard someone mention Tajikistan on the news, he could go to his globe and spin it around and find out exactly where Tajikistan was located. Lang took a seat behind his desk and DeMarco sat down in a comfortable armchair.

Lang said, "I can't believe Brian's dead. How did he die?"

"A drug overdose. Heroin laced with fentanyl."

"Brian? He's the last person on earth that I would have expected to use drugs."

"Yes, that's what everyone says. And which in a way is the reason I'm here."

"What do you mean?"

DeMarco said, "Did you know that Brian had a summer job as an intern in Congress?"

"Yes."

"Well, he worked for John Mahoney, the former Speaker, and Mahoney asked me to look into the circumstances surrounding his death."

"Why would Mahoney do that?"

DeMarco decided to tell Lang the truth. "Because Brian's mother asked him to. Before he died, Brian apparently learned something at work having to do with politicians taking bribes or receiving illegal campaign contributions. He told this to both his mother and his girlfriend, but he didn't tell either of them exactly what he'd found. And they're both convinced that Brian was killed because of whatever he'd learned, even though there's no evidence that he was murdered and the police aren't treating his death as a homicide. So she asked Mahoney to look into it, and Mahoney assigned me. The reason I wanted to meet with you is that his mother told me that Brian admired you, and I wondered if he might have confided in you about these politicians."

"He tried to," Lang said.

"What do you mean 'tried to'?"

Lang said, "He called me one day and basically said what you just said, that he'd learned that a group of politicians had been bribed and he wanted my advice on what to do about it. When he called, I was on a hiking trip with a colleague, barely had a cell phone signal, and I told him I'd talk to him when I got back. When he didn't call again, I didn't think too much about it. I figured he'd changed his mind. But I didn't know he'd died until you told me."

"So you don't have any idea what he might have uncovered?"

"No. He didn't get into the details."

DeMarco said, "Based on what his girlfriend told me, Brian was documenting what he found, but I haven't been able to find a report or memo or anything like that. Did he email anything to you?"

"No. Nothing."

It looked as if DeMarco had just wasted two hours driving to Charlottesville and would waste two more hours driving back to Washington.

"Do you think Brian was killed, Mr. DeMarco?" Lang asked.

DeMarco decided not to tell Lang what he really thought. He said, "I don't know. Kids OD all the time, and quite often the people closest to them didn't know they were drug users. And the cops said it didn't look like he was murdered, and so far I haven't been able to find a motive for murder. All I have is this vague story about politicians being bribed. But campaign contributions aren't technically bribes, and I doubt that Brian knew enough about campaign finance laws to know what was illegal and what wasn't. So I don't know."

DeMarco stood up. "Thanks for taking the time to talk to me, Professor. And I'd appreciate it if you'd not talk to anyone about the discussion we just had. If the media finds out about Brian's mother's concerns, and if these politicians, whoever they are, actually did do something illegal, that could give them an opportunity to cover up whatever they did."

And it could cause Mahoney an enormous political headache, which he didn't say.

"I understand," Lang said.

DeMarco wished he could think of something to threaten Lang with if he didn't keep his mouth shut, but threatening a law professor when it came to his First Amendment rights would just be asking for trouble. He was going to have to trust him. And other than the manbun, Lang seemed like a good guy.

<hr />

As DeMarco was driving back to D.C., his phone rang. He didn't recognize the number but decided to answer the call.

He said, "Hello, this is Joe."

"It's Honoré. I got a photo of the girl. The camera in the nail place picked her up."

"Great. Is there any way to ID her?"

"Not without making this thing a big fuckin' deal. I mean, if I go to the FBI and say that this woman might have killed a congressional staffer, they'll pull out all the stops and start running her photo through databases using facial-recognition software like she's some kind of terrorist. But for that to happen I'll have to talk to my boss, Mahoney will probably have to push on people, and a whole bunch of folks at the bureau will get involved and someone will leak it to the media. You ready for that to happen?"

"No, not yet. Can you text me a copy of the photo?"

"Yeah."

"Then do that, but don't do anything else until I've had a chance to talk to Perry Wallace."

"Okay," Honoré said.

"And thanks," DeMarco added, thinking that Perry had definitely sent him the right cop.

———◆———

An hour from Washington, DeMarco turned the radio station back to the news to hear if the D.C. traffic was gridlocked and if he'd have to find an alternate route back to the Capitol. The newscaster was talking about some slimeball in New York who'd bilked a few thousand working-class folks out of their savings with a Ponzi scheme. The guy had been caught because one of his employees, who was pissed off that he didn't get a bonus, ratted the schemer out to the SEC—and it was at this point that something occurred to DeMarco, something that should have occurred to him a lot earlier.

It was like a cartoon lightbulb going on over his head.

He drove a few more miles in the bumper-to-bumper traffic, trying to figure out a way to prove that he was right.

Finally, he called Elaine, almost rear-ending the guy in front of him as he looked up her number. He asked her, "How did Brian back up his computer files?"

She said, "He used an external hard drive because one time, when he was in high school, he had some kind of computer glitch that wiped out everything on his laptop."

"Did he also use the cloud?"

"No. He didn't trust the cloud. He said he'd read too many articles about how it could be hacked. Why are you asking?"

"Oh, just something I'm trying to figure out."

He asked Elaine a few more questions before hanging up, drove a bit farther, thinking about the next step he'd take, then called Honoré back. He asked her to meet him in his office at the Capitol at eight p.m. that night.

When she asked why, he said, "Not on the phone."

26

It was after seven by the time DeMarco arrived back at the Capitol, but Perry was still there, as DeMarco had known he would be. He was with Jane in a small conference room near his office looking at Brian's laptop.

DeMarco said, "Did you find anything?"

"No," Perry said. "Jane and I both looked at it—Jane spent all afternoon on it—and there's nothing in it pointing to the kid finding anything underhanded while he was working here. Almost all the files in it are related to stuff he was doing at UVA. Law school papers he wrote, notes he took in class, law school case studies. Stuff like that. There were no emails where he sent a report to someone. Anyway, it looks like he followed the rules and didn't use his personal computer here."

"Well, there's something I didn't tell you," DeMarco said. "Before I gave the laptop to you, I gave it to a guy who was able to get around the password. This guy, who's a pro, told me that it looked as if another pro had wiped a bunch of files off Brian's machine."

"You serious?" Perry said.

"Yes. Whoever stole his laptop made sure there wasn't anything incriminating in it before they turned it over to the cops. Now let me tell you what I learned today."

DeMarco told Jane and Perry how the cops got the laptop from a barista at a coffee shop, the barista claiming that a woman had given the computer to him, saying that Brian had left it at her place after having spent the night with her.

DeMarco said, "The story's bullshit. Brian never spent the night with this woman. He wouldn't have cheated on Elaine, and he never would have forgotten his laptop anywhere. So she's working with the people who stole the laptop, or maybe she stole it. And when the cops found out I was looking for it, they told somebody, I don't know who, and the word eventually got back to the people who killed Brian. And that's when they decided to wipe the laptop and return it, thinking that when I saw there was nothing in it, I'd stop looking into his death."

"So you're convinced he was killed," Jane said.

"Yeah, I'm convinced. I can't prove it, but I'm convinced."

"What about the woman?" Perry said. "Was Celeste able to ID her?"

"Who's Celeste?" Jane asked.

"A Capitol cop," Perry said.

"Not yet," DeMarco said in response to Perry's question. "Celeste got a photo of her from one of the stores near the coffee shop but hasn't made an ID yet. Anyway, today I also talked to a professor at UVA who was Brian's adviser. Brian had told him that he'd uncovered a conspiracy and wanted to talk to him about it and get his advice, but then Brian died before he could meet with the professor, and the professor doesn't know anything."

Perry said, "So we still have no idea what he learned?"

"No, but I think come tomorrow I'll know."

"Why's that?" Perry said.

"On the way back from Charlottesville, I talked to his girlfriend again. I wanted to know how Brian backed up his files. She said he used an external hard drive, and he backed up his files to it continuously as he worked. He didn't back them up to the cloud, because he didn't trust the cloud."

"Where did he keep the hard drive?"

"In his laptop case," DeMarco said. "But there was no external hard drive in the laptop case. Whoever stole his laptop got rid of it."

"Then I don't understand," Perry said. "If the external drive is gone and the laptop has been wiped, how will you be able to find out what he learned?"

"I'm getting there," DeMarco said. "Elaine told me that when Brian was in high school his laptop was stolen. It was sitting in his mother's car, and someone broke into the car and stole it along with a bunch of other stuff. According to Elaine, the reason Brian used the external hard drive was in case his computer got a virus, or the operating system went bad or something like that. But because he used the external drive every time he used the computer, he knew if his laptop case was stolen, he'd lose everything. In fact, Elaine said he was almost paranoid about his laptop being stolen again, and because of that, he backed up important files to a flash drive and he kept the flash drive separate from his laptop."

"And you know where the flash drive is," Perry said.

"I think so. Elaine remembered that one time when she was at Brian's apartment, she had to charge up her phone and she plugged the charger into an outlet and the outlet didn't work. When she told Brian, he said, 'Oh, yeah, that's my little hidey-hole.'"

"Hidey-hole?" Perry said.

"Yeah. Brian got the idea from watching a movie where a drug dealer put his drugs or his cash into an outlet box." He pointed to an outlet in the room. "That outlet and all the wires running to it are in a little box in the wall called an outlet box. What you do is cut off the wires going to the outlet and tape over the stubs with electrical tape. Without all the wires inside the box, you have enough room to store small things. Well, Brian didn't have a bunch of cash lying around or any jewelry, and I'm sure he didn't have drugs. So Elaine thought that's where the flash drive might be if he wanted to hide it. In that dead outlet box."

"And she just remembered this now?" Perry said.

"Hey, the girl just lost her fiancé. She's not thinking straight. But when I asked her about how he backed up his files, she remembered."

"So you're going to take the covers off all the outlets in his apartment?" Perry said.

"Don't have to take the covers off all of them. I'll just take a circuit tester with me and find the outlet that doesn't have power going to it. I'd do it tonight but I'm tired from driving down to Charlottesville and I'd have to go to Silver Spring to get his apartment keys from his mother."

"I thought she already gave you the keys."

"She did, but I gave them back to her. Anyway, tomorrow morning I'll head over there and see if he hid a flash drive in an outlet box."

———— ◆ ————

DeMarco left Perry's office and descended the steps to reach his office in the subbasement of the Capitol. Not the basement, the subbasement. Nearby was a room holding an emergency diesel generator, another room filled with big, noisy copy machines, and a maintenance shop used by the janitors. The location of the office was Mahoney's idea; he wanted DeMarco close at hand, but in the bowels of the building where he'd go mostly unnoticed. On the frosted-glass door of his office, in flaking gold paint, were the words "Counsel Pro Temp for Liaison Affairs"—a completely meaningless title that Mahoney had invented to further obscure DeMarco's true function. As for the office itself, it wasn't much larger than a backyard tool shed. It contained a battered wooden desk, two old wooden chairs, and a metal four-drawer file cabinet that had nothing in it because DeMarco didn't keep records that someone in law enforcement might eventually get a subpoena to look at.

Honoré showed up at eight. She looked around his office and said, "You're not exactly a big shot, are you?"

Before DeMarco could come up with a clever response, she said, "So why'd you want to see me?"

DeMarco said, "I want you to help me do something tonight. And I don't want you to tell anyone, including your boss."

DeMarco had figured that Honoré might balk at doing what he wanted, but she didn't. In fact, the idea seemed to please her. He suspected that when there wasn't an insurrection taking place, being a Capitol cop was fairly boring, and she was eager to do something more exciting than provide directions to tourists and protect a bunch of people she probably didn't like all that much.

27

Grady was sitting on his patio enjoying a good French red—he allowed himself one glass of wine a day—and a Cuban cigar. As it was after eight, the temperature had dropped into the seventies, and it was pleasant outside. He was thankful that his wife was with her book club and that he was able to enjoy the evening in solitude. As he sat there, he thought about everything going on at work. As usual, he was juggling a million different things but most of them were going well. And hopefully, the Lewis problem was behind him and, at least for a while, he wouldn't have to deal with Carson Newman. Fucking Newman. The man was dangerous.

He'd just had this thought when he received a text message. He ignored it while he took another puff on his cigar and tried to blow a smoke ring—and, as always, he failed. He wondered if his lips were too thin or shaped wrong and that's why he couldn't blow a ring. He looked at the text.

Oh, no. It was from his source, the one who had forewarned him about Lewis. All the text said was *911*. Meaning there was an emergency.

He called the source, and when they finished speaking, he hung up and yelled into the otherwise silent evening: "Son of a bitch!"

Wouldn't this fucking thing ever end?

He sat for a moment, stewing, trying to decide if he should call New-man. No, what would be the point? He knew what he needed to do and there was no time to waste, and there wasn't anything Newman could do from Boston.

He called Morgenthal.

He told Morgenthal what he wanted him to do. And that it had to be done tonight.

"No way," Morgenthal said. "I told you I wasn't going to have anything more to do with this."

"I'll pay you twenty thousand dollars."

As Grady said this, it occurred to him that he'd have to find a creative way to get Newman to pay the twenty grand. Newman was notorious for dodging bills and was constantly being sued by subcontractors for fail-ing to pay them. So what he'd do was pad Newman's bill. His firm billed Newman almost a million every year and tacking on another twenty thousand wouldn't be hard.

Morgenthal had gone silent, thinking over Grady's offer.

Grady said, "Well, will you do it or not? And if you don't do it, you can forget about my firm sending any more business your way."

"Yeah, I'll do it," Morgenthal said.

———◆———

Morgenthal parked outside Lewis's apartment building at midnight but remained in his car. There were still too many people walking the streets on a warm summer night. He set the alarm on his phone for two a.m. Until then he'd just put his head back and try to sleep.

He felt like shit—his head ached, he was still nauseous, and he also felt weak because he'd hardly eaten—but he figured he should have the stamina to do the job. It wasn't like there would be any heavy lifting involved.

If Grady hadn't offered to pay him so much, he would have turned him down. But he wanted the money. Not for himself, but for Sydney. He needed to pile up as much money as he could for her before he was gone. And he needed to help Sydney figure out what she was going to do after he was gone. What she should do was enlist in the military, as he'd mentioned to her more than once. The military had been good for him and for her dad. And the military would be good for her. She needed the discipline the military offered. She needed the routine. And more important, she needed a mission of some kind. The fact that she had a record wouldn't be a problem. She didn't have any violent felonies on her record and the military was desperate for bright people and she'd probably get a good-size enlistment bonus. The next time he talked to her, he'd bring the subject up again.

He'd spoken to her earlier that evening and learned she was staying in a cheap motel on the Maryland shore about an hour from D.C. He could tell when he talked to her that she was feeling antsy being cooped up in a small room by herself. He told her to just relax, go for a walk on the beach, get a good book to read.

"How long do I have to stay here?" she'd asked.

"I don't know. I know a guy in D.C. Metro, and I trust him. I'll get ahold of him tomorrow and find out if the cops are looking for you. But plan on staying there a few more days, and try to stay out of sight as much as possible. And when you do go out, disguise yourself in some way. Wear a hat, wear sunglasses, cover up the tats. But for now, just sit tight. If I learn the cops have ID'd you, we'll come up with a plan."

The plan would most likely be to use Grady's twenty grand to send Sydney to Mexico for a couple of months.

Morgenthal's phone chirped at two a.m. and woke him up. He was surprised that he'd actually slept a bit, and he felt refreshed. He looked around and didn't see anyone. Fortunately, there were no nearby bars that dumped a bunch of drunks onto the street when they closed.

He left the car and walked up the steps to the front door of the apartment building. He looked around again, and still didn't see anyone nearby. It took him less than a minute to pick the cheap lock.

Lewis's apartment was on the third floor, and as there was no elevator, he had to take the stairs. When he finally reached the third-floor landing, he had to stop and rest for a couple of minutes. After his breathing returned to normal, he walked down the hallway to Lewis's apartment. Again, it took him less than a minute to pick the lock.

The apartment was dark, as the lights were off, so he found a light switch and turned on the overhead light in the living room. A light inside an apartment looked less suspicious than a flashlight bouncing around. He was surprised at how small the apartment was; he'd been in hotel rooms that were larger. The job shouldn't take long.

He took the circuit tester out of his pocket along with a Phillips-head screwdriver. The circuit tester was a simple device consisting of two wire probes attached to a plastic case about the size of his thumb. You pushed the two probes into an outlet, and if there was power going to the outlet, a light would come on in the plastic case.

He went to the first outlet he saw in the living room, one on the wall near the kitchen, and knelt down and pushed the probes into the outlet.

He heard the door behind him open and spun his head around and saw a black woman with short hair and light blue eyes pointing a gun at him.

She said, "Show me your hands. Now!"

Standing behind the woman was DeMarco, a small smile on his face. He knew it was DeMarco because Sydney had sent him photos of the guy.

Fifteen minutes later, Morgenthal's hands were cuffed behind his back, and he was placed in the back of a MPD cruiser. Before he was placed in the cruiser, he heard the woman tell the Metro cop who'd handcuffed him that she was a member of the U.S. Capitol Police, then DeMarco pulled the cop aside and spoke to him. He had no idea what DeMarco said to the cop.

At the station, he was told to empty his pockets. His wallet, his phone, his keys, and his watch were placed in one plastic bag. His lockpicks, the circuit tester, and the screwdriver were placed in another bag. An evidence bag.

He was dumped into a holding cell with a bunch of drunks, a couple of them passed out on the floor. He found an empty spot in a corner, sat down on the floor, leaned back against the wall, and closed his eyes.

After the D.C. Metro cops departed with Morgenthal, DeMarco called Olivetti. He woke Olivetti up because it was almost three in the morning.

"Why in the hell are you calling me at this time of night, DeMarco?" Olivetti asked. "I should never have given you my cell phone number."

DeMarco said, "I just caught a guy breaking into Brian Lewis's apartment. I used an armed U.S. Capitol policewoman to make a citizen's arrest, and a couple of your cops just hauled him away."

"What in the fuck are you talking about?" Olivetti said, still not fully awake and understandably confused.

DeMarco told Olivetti that Barista Bob had lied to him about how he'd gotten Brian's laptop. He explained that a young woman was the one who gave Bob the laptop and convinced him to turn it over to the cops. He told him how, with the help of the same Capitol cop who arrested the intruder, he'd gotten a photo of the woman but didn't know her name.

DeMarco said, "I'm going to text you her photo. This woman, whoever she is, was involved in some way with stealing Brian's laptop."

"What does this have to do with someone breaking into Lewis's apartment?"

"I'm getting there," DeMarco said. "After I got Brian's laptop from his mother, I took it to a pro to have him get around the password. Well, the laptop didn't have anything incriminating in it. It probably contained a report at one time that backed up Brian's story that some politicians had taken bribes, but the pro I used to crack the password told me that somebody had deleted a bunch of files from it. So that's when I planted a story that there was a flash drive hidden in Brian's apartment."

"Planted a story? How'd you plant a story?" Olivetti said.

"I can't tell you that, not yet anyway. And it doesn't matter. What matters is that after I planted the story, a guy broke into Brian's apartment to get the flash drive."

"Is there a flash drive?"

"No. But you need to ID the guy and see if he's working for anyone. He may be the one who killed Brian, or he might know who did. And you need to see what he knows about the woman who gave the laptop to the barista." DeMarco paused and said, "Olivetti, Brian Lewis's death needs to be investigated as a homicide."

An hour after he was placed into the holding cell, Morgenthal was led to an interrogation room containing a small table and two chairs and handcuffed to a ring in the center of the table. A moment later a man came into the room and introduced himself as Detective Olivetti.

Olivetti read him his rights. When he was finished, he asked Morgenthal if he understood his rights. Morgenthal didn't answer. He asked if Morgenthal wanted a lawyer. Morgenthal didn't answer.

Olivetti said, "Mr. Morgenthal, can you tell me what you were doing in that apartment tonight?"

Morgenthal figured he must have gotten his name from his wallet, because he hadn't told anyone his name. He hadn't said a word since he'd been arrested—and he didn't say anything now.

Olivetti said, "Mr. Morgenthal, you're going to be charged with breaking and entering and trespassing. But you need to know something, if you don't already know it. A young man named Brian Lewis died in that apartment. His death was thought to have been self-inflicted, caused by an overdose. But now we're going to investigate his death as a homicide and you're our prime suspect. So I would strongly suggest that you talk to me. If you had nothing to do with his death, say so. If someone hired you to break into his apartment, it's in your best interest to tell me who it was."

Morgenthal didn't say anything.

"I also need to know what you know about a young woman giving Lewis's laptop to a barista."

Morgenthal didn't respond.

Olivetti showed Morgenthal his cell phone. On it was a photo of Sydney.

Olivetti said, "This is the woman. Do you know her?"

Morgenthal didn't answer.

Olivetti spent ten more minutes asking the same questions and threatening him with all the dire things that could happen to him. When Olivetti realized that talking to him was futile, Morgenthal was led back to the holding cell. He sat down again on the floor and closed his eyes.

Olivetti called DeMarco, this time waking DeMarco up because it was six a.m.

"The guy who broke into Lewis's place is a private detective named David Morgenthal. He's ex-military. After he retired from the army, he and another guy, who was also ex-military and who's now dead, set up a detective agency in D.C., which has been in business the last twelve years. He has no criminal record. Morgenthal refused to talk to me. He wouldn't say a word about why he broke into the apartment. He wouldn't admit he knew the woman in the photo you sent me. He wouldn't tell me shit. He's going to be arraigned sometime this morning, where he'll plead not guilty and be released on bail."

"Do you think he could have killed Brian?"

"I don't know," Olivetti said, "but my gut tells me he didn't. Like I said, he doesn't have a record, and although he's not that old, he's sort of frail, like he might be sick or something. If Brian was killed, and there's still no proof of that, whoever killed him would have had to subdue a healthy young man to inject the shit into him, and I have a hard time seeing Morgenthal doing that."

"So what are you going to do next?"

"I don't know, and that's the truth. I need to talk to my boss. And you need to tell me more about how you planted the flash drive story."

"I can't do that yet."

"Why not?"

"What you need to do, Olivetti, is get a warrant to look at Morgenthal's phone and business records and see who he's been talking to."

"I don't know if I have probable cause for that kind of warrant. All he's guilty of is trespassing."

"Olivetti, Brian was killed. I have no doubt about that now. And if this guy, Morgenthal, didn't do it, he's the best lead you've got. So get a bunch of smart lawyers in a room and figure out a way to get a warrant."

———◆◆◆———

Olivetti waited until eight, until his boss arrived at work, and then told him what had transpired and what DeMarco wanted.

His boss called the chief of detectives, who called former congressman Jimmy Cooper, who called Grady.

Grady's secretary heard something shatter against the wall in Grady's office.

28

DeMarco walked into Perry's office and closed the door. He was exhausted, as he'd gotten only a couple of hours of sleep the night before. Perry was slurping coffee and eating a vending machine donut while speed-reading a document thicker than a King James Bible.

DeMarco said, "Your pal Jane's a rat."

"What are you talking about?"

"Last night I used Honoré to arrest a guy who broke into Brian's apartment."

"You what?"

"He was looking for the flash drive I told you and Jane about. And you and Jane were the only people I told about it. Well, the flash drive doesn't exist. I made up that story to see if I was right about Jane."

"Right about her? What are you—"

"Yesterday, something finally occurred to me. How did anyone know that Brian had information pointing to a bunch of crooked politicians? Somehow, somebody learned that he had found things that could cause people problems, and one or more of those people had him killed to stop him from talking and stole his laptop. Well, Brian, as near as I can tell, only told three people what he'd found. He told his mother, his girlfriend, and this professor at UVA, but he didn't tell them anything specific. Now he may have talked to people I don't know about, but there was most likely a fourth person he talked to, and that person was Jane. She told us that he asked a lot of questions. And she was his immediate supervisor. She had to have had some idea about whatever it was he'd learned.

"So yesterday, I told you and her about the flash drive—and like I said, you and she were the only ones I told—and last night a guy breaks into Brian's place and tries to find it. Which means either you talked or Jane did. Did you tell anyone about the flash drive?"

"No," Perry said.

"I didn't think so. And the guy that broke in was using a circuit tester when we caught him."

Perry shook his head. "I can't believe this. The woman's worked for me for years."

"Yeah, well, get her ass in here and let's find out who else she's working for."

"Wait a minute. What about the guy who was arrested? Who is he?"

"He's a private detective named David Morgenthal. He was most likely hired by someone to retrieve the flash drive. I don't think he would have had any motive for killing Brian. But Morgenthal isn't talking. The cops interrogated him, and he refused to say anything. But let's deal with Jane first, and then we'll talk about Morgenthal and what to do next."

* * *

Perry called Jane and told her to meet him in a conference room near his office. She was already sitting in the room when Perry and DeMarco arrived. Perry slammed the door shut so hard that Jane was startled. Perry and DeMarco didn't sit down. DeMarco went and stood in a corner and leaned against a wall. Perry placed his knuckles on the table and leaned over and glared at Jane.

"What's going on?" Jane said.

Perry said, "Who have you been feeding information to?"

"What?" Jane said. "I don't know what you're talking about."

"Don't you dare fuckin' lie to me," Perry said. "I'm going to fire you, there's no doubt about that, but I can fire you in one of two ways. The first is I kick your ass out the door and spread it all over this town that you're not to be trusted. And if anyone calls and asks for a reference, I'll tell them not to hire your treacherous ass. You'll be lucky to get a job at Walmart. The other way is I can pretend you resigned, and when someone asks about you, I'll say you were a great worker, salt of the earth, and all that shit. But I won't ever let you work on the Hill again. Now who have you been leaking to?"

"Perry, I swear—"

"Yesterday, DeMarco told us there was a flash drive hidden in Brian's apartment. There was no flash drive, but the only ones DeMarco told that story to were you and me. Well, last night, a guy broke into Brian's apartment to get the drive and DeMarco caught him. Who did you tell, Jane?"

Jane put her head in her hands and started crying.

Perry slammed his hand on the table and said, "Stop blubbering. I don't have time for that shit. Who did you talk to?"

The way Perry went at Jane surprised DeMarco. He'd always known that Perry was a tough, shrewd, cynical political operative capable of dealing with the backstabbing and conniving common to Capitol Hill, but he was usually soft-spoken. He'd never seen Perry this angry before and now realized there was a hard side that the man would unleash if the occasion called for it. And betraying Mahoney the way Jane had, called for it.

Jane blew her nose into a Kleenex. She said, "Three years ago, I was in a financial sinkhole. I had all kinds of things go wrong at the same time. I had to buy a new car. My roof leaked and I had to replace it. My furnace broke and—"

"Jane, I don't give a shit about your problems. Tell me—"

"A lobbyist somehow found out about me owing so much. I don't know how he found out, but he did. He came to me and said he'd help me get out of debt. All he wanted in return was to be kept abreast of what was happening in Mahoney's office. He wanted the inside scoop on whatever the Speaker was doing and thinking about when it came to certain things, anything that wasn't being reported in the press. He's been paying me three hundred bucks a month to keep him informed."

"You've been talking to this guy for three years?"

"Yes."

"Jesus," Perry said. "So who is he?"

"Patrick Grady."

To DeMarco, Perry said, "Grady's a partner at Kellogg, Long & Meyer, the biggest lobbying firm in this town. And I've heard stories about them paying people who work in sensitive positions to pass on inside dope. Getting a source inside the Speaker's office is exactly the kind of thing they'd do, and three hundred bucks a month would be pocket lint to them."

Jane said, "Perry, I didn't tell him anything that was really important. It wasn't like I was giving him classified information. I just told him a few things I'd hear you and Mahoney talking about on bills that affected his clients. If I hadn't been so far in debt—"

"What did you tell him when it came to Brian?" DeMarco said.

"I told him that Brian was looking into the dirty dozen and he'd found out that they'd been compromised. I didn't have a lot of details, because Brian didn't share a lot of the details, but I told Grady that I got the impression Brian was thinking about going public with what he found."

"What gave you that impression?" Perry asked.

"Because he started asking questions about how the House Ethics Committee works. But I never thought anything bad would happen to him. I just thought that once Grady knew that he was looking into something that could affect one of his clients, he'd find a way to make the problem go away. I mean, using lawyers or something. Or maybe by trying to buy Brian off."

DeMarco said, "Who was the client?"

"Carson Newman."

"The billionaire in Boston?" DeMarco said.

"Yes," Jane said. "I knew KL&M represented Newman, and that was the reason I told Grady. But I didn't think—"

Perry said, "Get out of here. Go clean out your desk and—"

"No," DeMarco said. "You're going to go back to your office and just sit there until we tell you otherwise. I haven't decided what we're going to do next, but we might need you to feed something else to Grady, something we want him to know. So until we tell you otherwise, you come to work every day like you usually do, then just sit in your office. You can work on your résumé. But if I find out that you told Grady that we're on to you, then getting fired is going to be the least of your problems. Brian's death is about to be turned into a homicide investigation, and if you tell Grady anything other than what we tell you to tell him, you're going to be dragged into that investigation as a suspect. I don't know what your finances look like now, Jane, but just wait until you have to start paying lawyers to keep from going to jail."

After a weeping Jane left, DeMarco said, "I suspect she knew more about what Brian found out than she just told us, but at this point it doesn't matter. Do you know Newman?"

"Yeah. He used to contribute heavily to Mahoney, but they had some kind of falling-out. He's a prick."

"But is he the kind of guy that would have had Brian killed?"

"I don't know," Perry said. "I can see him paying off a bunch of congressmen to stop that tenants' rights bill because the bill would have affected his bottom line. But Newman would be smart about it. He wouldn't do anything overtly criminal that could come back to bite him. But the thing about Newman is that he's one of those people who never seems to pay the price for anything he does. Nothing ever sticks to him. He declares bankruptcy and companies he owes money to don't get paid and go out of business, but Newman never suffers personally. He gets sued, and his lawyers always win, or they delay things long enough that the other guy eventually folds. One time, a few years ago, a guy was about to appear before a grand jury and testify about some shady shit that Newman had pulled, but then the guy died before he could."

"Maybe Newman had him killed."

"No, he committed suicide. But what I'm saying is that Newman's an arrogant bastard who thinks that he can get away with anything because in the past he always has. So maybe a murder isn't out of the question, but I can't imagine that Brian would have found anything that would have pushed him to that extreme."

"Perry, Mahoney's going to have a political nightmare on his hands, and you need to talk to him and see how he wants to play it. The cop who investigated Brian's death is a detective named Olivetti. Last night after we nabbed Morgenthal inside Brian's apartment, I called Olivetti. I told him that I'd planted a story that there was a flash drive and that's what Morgenthal was looking for when he broke in. I had to tell him that so he'd know that Morgenthal breaking in was connected to Brian's death. What I didn't tell Olivetti is that I planted the story with Jane because I suspected her."

DeMarco continued, "Olivetti doesn't think Morgenthal killed Brian, and he's probably right. The guy didn't strike me as a professional killer either. He was probably only hired to retrieve the flash drive. And what I'm hoping will happen is that Morgenthal will eventually tell Olivetti who hired him and that will lead to whoever killed Brian. But at some point, it's going to get out that the reason Brian was killed was because he'd found dirt on a dozen politicians. And that's going to be the break-ing news on CNN—that a dozen Democrats took bribes, and a kid was killed because they did. You're going to have FBI agents asking to look at your files. They're going to question you, me, Mahoney, and Jane. They're going to question the dirty dozen. We can tell them that we don't know exactly what Brian found—and because his laptop was wiped, that'll be the truth—but that's not going to stop the FBI from investigating and it's not going to stop the media from turning this whole thing into a spectacle."

"Maybe you should have checked with me before you told Olivetti anything."

DeMarco decided to ignore that comment. He said, "Because Mor-genthal isn't talking, I told Olivetti that what he needs to do is get a warrant to look at Morgenthal's phone records. If he can find out who Morgenthal's been talking to, maybe that will lead him to Brian's killer, and maybe that will happen without anyone talking about dirty politi-cians. But I doubt it. At some point, the motive for Brian being killed will come out—and we're back to the political-nightmare scenario. Then there's another possibility. If Olivetti can't get a warrant and if Morgen-thal doesn't talk, then as far as I'm concerned, we have an obligation to tell the cops that even if we don't know exactly what Brian uncovered, we know that he pointed the finger at Grady and Newman and twelve politicians. We have to tell them that, because even if we don't have any evidence, these people need to be investigated."

DeMarco sat back. "So talk to Mahoney and tell him a firestorm is headed his way."

"What if Mahoney tells you to keep your mouth shut?"

DeMarco looked at Perry for a beat. "I never met Brian, but I got the impression he was someone I probably wouldn't have wanted to be friends with. Too intense, too serious, too self-righteous. Based on what I heard about him and the way he looked, he made me think of a young

Ralph Nader, and I know I wouldn't have wanted to be friends with a young Ralph Nader. But I really like his girlfriend and I like his mom, and they loved him. And he was a good kid trying to do the right thing. So, Perry, no matter what Mahoney says, I'm going to do whatever it takes to make sure someone pays for killing him."

29

Morgenthal was barely able to stand by the time he returned home. He walked into his house and collapsed into the first chair he came to in his living room. He didn't have the stamina to go any farther. He was supposed to have had another chemo treatment that day, but he'd missed it due to his arraignment and the time it took for him to be processed out of the jail.

The arraignment had gone better than he'd expected, thanks to an aggressive public defender. He didn't tell the public defender anything. The charging documents contained the whole story, the story being that he was arrested for picking a lock to get inside an apartment. When his lawyer asked why he broke in, Morgenthal didn't answer the question. He said, "I didn't steal anything. I didn't damage anything. The only thing they can convict me of is trespassing." When the judge asked him how he wanted to plead, Morgenthal said, "Not guilty." You always said "not guilty." When the judge asked for recommendations regarding bail, the prosecutor said, "Your Honor, we recommend that the defendant not be released on bail. It's complicated, Your Honor, but a young man died in the apartment Mr. Morgenthal broke into. The police initially assumed the young man died because of an accidental drug overdose but now believe that he may have been murdered. The police asked Mr. Morgenthal why he broke into the apartment, to see if his actions were connected to the young man's death, but he refused to answer any questions. And—"

"As is his right," the public defender said.

"And the police want Mr. Morgenthal to remain in custody while they continue to investigate, and hopefully he'll cooperate with the investigation. So this isn't about trespassing, Your Honor. It's about a possible homicide and I believe Mr. Morgenthal constitutes a flight risk."

"This is nonsense, Your Honor," the public defender said. "All my client did was pick a lock to get into an apartment. He didn't steal anything or damage anything. And there's no evidence whatsoever that he's involved with someone's death. What the prosecutor is really saying is that they want to detain my client indefinitely so they can force him to talk."

"We're not going to *force* him to talk," the prosecutor said. "The police simply want his cooperation, and because this is now a murder investigation, they don't want to take the chance of him disappearing."

"Well, remand is out the question," the judge said. "Do you have a bail recommendation?"

"A hundred thousand," the prosecutor said.

The public defender also knew that the judge had a problem in that the jail was already holding twice as many people as it had been designed to hold. She said, "That's absurd. He trespassed, for Christ's sake. He didn't assault anyone. He didn't murder anyone. And my client doesn't have that kind of money." She said this having no idea how much money Morgenthal had.

The judge said, "Bail is set at five thousand." Meaning Morgenthal had to come up with five hundred to pay a bail bondsman.

After the arraignment, Morgenthal contacted one of the bail bondsmen who hung around the courthouse like flies around a carcass, and his bond was posted.

As Morgenthal sat there trying to decide what to do next, his phone rang. The caller ID said it was his oncologist. Morgenthal figured that she was calling to find out why he'd missed his chemo session. Turned out that wasn't the reason she called. After his last chemo session, they'd done a CT scan. The scan showed that there was no reason to continue with the chemo. Morgenthal needed to call in hospice.

Morgenthal sat for a while, contemplating his imminent death. The news the oncologist had given him hadn't really been a surprise; he'd been expecting it ever since he was diagnosed with cancer. Looking back on his life, he had to admit that he hadn't left much of a mark on the world. He'd served his country without distinction, then used the skills he learned in the military to spy for people like Patrick Grady. His only marriage had failed because he'd been unfaithful. He had no children who would mourn for him. It seemed as if the only positive and unselfish thing he'd done during his time on earth was take care of Sydney after her father died.

He called Sydney. He wasn't going to tell her that he'd been arrested. Nor was he going to tell her about the news he'd just gotten from his oncologist. They'd have that discussion face-to-face. All he wanted was to hear her voice.

"How you doing, kid?" he asked.

"You don't sound good, Dave. Are you okay?"

"Yeah, I'm fine. Just a little tired."

"Why did you call? Have the cops ID'd me?"

"Not yet," Morgenthal said. He knew this because that cop, Olivetti, had asked who the young woman was who'd returned Lewis's laptop. "But they got a photo of you," Morgenthal said.

"How do you know that?" Sydney asked.

"I told you, I know a guy I trust in D.C. Metro. I'm guessing they got the photo off one of the security cameras near the coffee shop."

"Shit," Sydney said.

"But they don't have your name, and they might never get it. And even if they do ID you, you still don't really have a problem. You just admit that you gave the laptop to that barista. You may have lied to the barista, but you didn't do anything illegal. And when they ask where you got the laptop from, you tell them the truth. You tell them you got it from me."

"But that'll cause you a problem," Sydney said.

"Not much of one. Because if I have to, I'll point to the client who gave me the laptop, and he's the one who will have a problem."

He didn't want to tell Sydney, not over the phone, that the other reason he wouldn't have a problem was because before long he'd be dead.

"But for now," Morgenthal said, "just stay where you are. Do you have enough cash so you don't have to use a credit card?"

"Yeah. I hit the ATM before I left D.C. But I'm going out of my mind with boredom."

"You're not getting the urge to drink or anything, are you?"

"I've always got the urge, Dave. I'm an addict. But I'm okay."

"Good. And while you're there, think about your future. You know you can't keep working for me forever."

"Why not?"

"Well, for one thing, I'm not going to be here forever. The other thing is, and as you can see with the predicament you're in, this is a business that can land you in trouble. You need to find something else to do. Have you given any more thought to enlisting?"

"Not really. I just can't see myself in one of those uniforms, taking orders from some asshole with a crew cut. Plus, what would I be doing if I was in the army? Standing guard someplace? Driving a truck?"

"The military has all kinds of things you can do that are interesting and they'll give you the education to do them. Like me and your dad.

We were in intelligence, and these days intelligence means tracking bad guys with their cell phones and using satellites and drones to spy on them. But you know what I can see you doing, Sydney? I can see you flying a helicopter."

The idea came to him when he was leaving the jail and saw Marine One, the president's chopper, in the sky above him, maybe taking the president to Camp David or Andrews Air Force Base.

"A helicopter?" Sydney said.

"Yeah. You got the brains for that. And you'd love it."

"You know, that would be kind of cool," Sydney said.

"You tell 'em the only way you'll enlist is if they put you into choppers. Like maybe you can start out in chopper maintenance—you're handy with tools—which will give you a chance to apply for flight school."

"Choppers. Huh," Sydney said.

He could tell the idea appealed to her. "Think about it. And I'll get back to you soon. But for now, just stay where you're at and stay out of sight."

After he spoke to her, Morgenthal thought a bit more about what would happen with Sydney after he was gone. His will was current, and he'd told her what the will said—that he was leaving her everything he had. But he only had around fifty thousand in savings, plus the twenty thousand he still had to collect from Grady. He'd never been a saver—when he'd been younger, he'd had a bit of a gambling problem—and he wished he had more to leave her. Money would give her options, like going to college if she wanted to.

Then it occurred to him that there was a way he could significantly increase Sydney's inheritance. He mulled it over for a few more minutes and, considering what his oncologist had just told him, decided he didn't have anything to lose.

He called Grady.

"I was arrested last night," Morgenthal said.

"I know. I already heard. What did you tell the cops?"

"Nothing. I didn't tell them why I was in the apartment or anything else. I didn't say one word to the cops. Not yet."

"What does that mean, *not yet*?" Grady said.

"There's two ways I can play this. One, I plead guilty or I get convicted for breaking and entering, and I do the time or pay the fine and keep my mouth shut. Or two, I tell them I was working for you and let the cops start talking to you about Lewis. You see, I've decided to retire, Mr. Grady. I've got some health issues. If you pay me half a million, which I know your firm can easily afford, I'll keep my mouth shut. If you don't pay, then I won't. It's up to you, but I figure I'm in this mess because of you and I want enough so I can walk away and not have to work anymore."

"You son of a bitch."

"Let me know by tomorrow what you want to do. I'm sure I'll be seeing the cops again soon because they're looking for answers about what happened to Lewis and why I was in his apartment."

30

Grady sat staring at the ugly, brown coffee stain running down the wall across from his desk. He'd asked his secretary to clean up the mess he'd made by throwing his cup at the wall after he'd heard about Morgenthal's arrest, but she'd told him that she was a secretary, not a bloody janitor.

Everything he'd spent his whole life working for would be destroyed if Morgenthal talked to the cops. KL&M would fire him, and no other lobbying firm would hire him. He'd lose his house. His mortgage was based on his current salary, and if he was fired, no one would match that salary. There'd be no more first-class trips to the Caribbean where he'd be paid to sit in the sun and drink and bullshit with the fools on the Hill. There'd be no more five-hundred-dollar dinners at the Capital Grille where the firm's clients picked up the tab. He also had no idea what kind of job he'd be able to get if he was fired; the only thing he'd ever done was lobbying work, and he didn't know how to do anything else.

He'd told the senior partners what he'd done to get the tenants' rights bill defeated and they'd been pleased, and particularly pleased that he'd managed to satisfy a difficult client like Carson Newman. And what had benefited Newman had also benefited some of the firm's other clients. So the senior partners had been happy. He didn't, however, tell them about Brian Lewis. At first, he didn't tell them because he didn't know what

Lewis had learned. And after Lewis died, there was no way he was going to tell them that he might have helped Newman plan a murder. And then Morgenthal goes and gets arrested. The senior partners wouldn't care about the things he'd done when it came to Lewis—hiring Morgenthal to follow Lewis and DeMarco, and hiring Morgenthal to retrieve the flash drive—but they would care if Morgenthal ran to the cops and told them what Grady had done. The firm didn't reward bad publicity. It rewarded success, not failure, and he'd be out the door.

And there was no way he could pay Morgenthal half a million. He didn't have half a million in cash lying around—and there was no way in hell the firm would pay. The firm spent other people's money to solve problems, not its own. Which meant Newman would have to pay. But even if Newman was willing to pay, which he doubted, Morgenthal would still be out there, like the sword of Damocles, sharp and pointed, forever dangling over his head. No, paying Morgenthal wouldn't ensure his silence forever. Morgenthal had to . . . well, he had to go away.

He called Newman, and when Newman didn't answer, he left a voice mail saying: *Call me ASAP. We have a big problem.*

"What problem?" Newman asked when he called back five minutes later.

He hadn't told Newman about the flash drive and hiring Morgenthal to retrieve it. Now he did—and Newman was of course outraged that Grady had acted without consulting him and became even more outraged when he learned that Morgenthal had been arrested.

Cutting off Newman's rant, Grady said, "The problem now is that Morgenthal is trying to blackmail us."

He used the word *us* deliberately, making sure Newman understood that Grady wasn't the only one liable to be exposed.

Grady said, "He wants half a million dollars, and says if I don't give it to him, he's going to tell the cops everything he knows."

"What about the flash drive?"

"There is no flash drive." Grady knew this because DeMarco had told this to Olivetti, who had relayed the information up his chain of command—and Grady was wired into the top of the chain of command. "DeMarco invented the flash drive. It was a setup. He told my source about it, who told me, and I made the mistake of sending Morgenthal to retrieve it. The fact that the flash drive doesn't exist is good because that means no one knows what Lewis learned. But now the problem is Morgenthal."

Newman said, "Are you suggesting we pay this asshole?"

"No." Grady paused, then said, "I don't know exactly what happened to Lewis but maybe something similar needs to happen to Morgenthal."

He was telling Newman, *I know you had Lewis killed and now you need to kill Morgenthal.*

Newman went silent for a long time. Grady just waited. When he finally spoke, Newman said, "Tell Morgenthal you'll pay him, but it will take a couple of days to come up with the money."

"You want to pay him?"

"I want you to tell him you'll pay him."

Newman disconnected the call.

31

When Grady called, Carson had been about to get a massage. His masseuse came to his office once a week, lugging a folding table that probably weighed fifty pounds, and she was now waiting outside his office. He'd started having back problems a few years ago and a friend had recommended her, saying there was no one in Boston who could match her.

When he saw her the first time, he was repulsed. Her name was Olga Gunnarsson, and because of the name, he'd been expecting a tall, gorgeous, blond Swede. The masseuse may have been Swedish, but she had dark hair cut in a mannish style and a slight mustache, was built like a block of concrete, and was so ugly she made his eyes hurt. He came to think of her as an appliance, not a human. But her hands, strong enough to bend rebar, worked magic on him, and following a session with her, he always felt hornier than a billy goat, and would usually go see his mistress immediately afterward.

But now, thanks to fucking Grady—

He took one of the three burner phones out of his desk and texted: *Need to see you ASAP. Same place as before. How soon can you get there?* There was a five-minute delay before he got a response: *45 minutes.*

Shit. He'd have to leave in half an hour. There wasn't enough time for his massage. He called his secretary and told her to arrange for the masseuse to come back tomorrow. Then he called his mistress and told her he couldn't make it today. He noticed she didn't sound disappointed.

Fucking Grady.

Three years ago, one of Carson's top executives, his chief financial officer, was arrested in an FBI sting operation for attempting to have sex with a thirteen-year-old boy he met online who was actually a thirty-year-old FBI agent. The man, who had worked for Carson for twenty years, decided that his best option to keep from going to jail for pedophilia was to tell the FBI everything he knew about Newman Enterprises' business practices.

When Carson learned that the pervert was scheduled to testify to a grand jury, he knew that he had to do something to stop him. And the only solution that occurred to him was to have him killed.

But like most people, Carson didn't know any professional killers.

He did, however, know Gabriel Dushku.

Gabriel was his next-door neighbor on Cape Cod.

The beach house Gabriel Dushku now lived in had been owned by a movie star, who had to sell it when she could no longer afford the taxes. The movie star's problem was simply that she'd grown older, and no casting director wanted her after she turned forty. When Gabriel bought her place, Carson naturally wanted to know who his new neighbor was. And he didn't like the name *Dushku*. It was definitely, well, *foreign*.

He asked one of his in-house lawyers to find out who he was living next to on the Cape. He'd expected that it would take the lawyer a couple of days to do the research, but the lawyer called him back in less than an hour.

He said, "Gabriel Dushku is from Albania."

"I don't think I know any Albanians," Carson said.

"You might know one. Mother Teresa was an Albanian. And there's an actress named Eliza Dushku. She played in a television series called *Buffy the Vampire Slayer*."

"Never heard of her," Carson said.

"Anyway, back to Dushku. He's a criminal. Allegedly. A simple Google search showed that he was the head of the largest, most violent organized crime group in the Balkans. Allegedly. But he retired from his, uh, activities five years ago and turned everything over to a cousin. Allegedly."

"Quit saying *allegedly*, goddamnit," Carson said.

"There was no way for me to determine his net worth, but it's significant. He has a town house in London, a farm in Tuscany, and a yacht that's over a hundred feet long. He paid cash for his place on the Cape."

Carson's place on Cape Cod was worth five million and he expected that Gabriel's, being a bit larger, was worth even more.

"What did this organized crime group do?" Carson asked.

"All the things you'd expect," the lawyer said. "Drugs. Sex trafficking. Smuggling illegal immigrants and weapons. Bribing politicians and judges. Extortion. Murder. That's according to the Internet. But Dushku has never been convicted of a crime, and like I said, he's no longer in the business. Alleg . . . Supposedly."

"Well, I don't like him living near me," Carson said.

But when Gabriel invited him and his wife to a housewarming party, Carson decided to go. He was curious. He was surprised to find a couple of famous professional hockey players at the party and then learned Gabriel was a part owner of a team. Also attending were several actors—Gabriel had invested in a Broadway play—plus a few investment bankers who looked uncomfortable in beach attire, the owner of a fast-food chain, and the CEO of a tech company who was constantly being pho-tographed with women twenty years his junior.

As for Gabriel, Carson was surprised to see he was white. He'd been expecting someone with a darker complexion. He was a handsome man in his early sixties, just a few years older than Carson. He had short white hair and clear blue eyes and an infectious smile. And his wife was absolutely stunning.

When he asked Gabriel what he did for a living on the first occasion they met, Gabriel said he was retired.

"But what did you do before you retired?" Carson asked.

"Oh, imports and exports," Gabriel said.

Carson soon found that he enjoyed Gabriel's company. The man was charming, with a subtle sense of humor and impeccable taste, and he began to socialize with him on regular basis when they were both on Cape Cod.

When Carson learned that the pedophile was scheduled to appear before a grand jury, he called Gabriel and said he needed to speak to him urgently about a personal matter.

"Sure, come on over," Gabriel said.

They sat by Gabriel's swimming pool, looking out at the ocean, sipping gin and tonics while Gabriel's wife sunned herself in a nearby lounge chair. The fact that she was topless normally would have distracted Carson, but not that day.

Carson said, "I've got a problem. There's a man who's about to testify to a grand jury and I don't want him to testify."

"I see," Gabriel said.

"I'm not going to beat around the bush here. Do you know someone who might be able to help me?"

Gabriel gazed out at the ocean as he thought the question over. "I do," he said. "But I need a favor in return from you."

"What sort of favor?"

"You see, I have a cash problem."

"So how much do you want?" Carson said. He couldn't believe a man as rich as Gabriel, a man he thought of as a friend, was going make him pay a referral fee. But then again, the man was a criminal.

"No, you misunderstand me. I don't need cash. I have cash that needs to be, uh, cleansed."

He meant laundered.

"How much cash are we talking about?"

"Not much. Only fifty million."

"Fifty *million*?"

"Yes, it won't be hard at all. Some of your companies would be ideal for this sort of thing. And I'll loan you an accountant who knows what to do."

Oh, Christ. He didn't want to go into business with an Albanian gangster. But he was desperate, and he couldn't think of anyone else to help him. "Okay," he said. "But I'll only do the fifty."

"Good, that's all I need," Gabriel said.

He knew, in his heart, that Gabriel was lying and would ask him to launder more for him in the future. Considering who Gabriel was, he might even threaten to harm him if he didn't. That's what gangsters do. But what choice did he have?

"Now what about my problem?" Carson said.

Gabriel removed a business card from his wallet; the only thing on it was a hand-written phone number. "Call that number. I'd suggest you use a burner. No one will answer. Leave a voice mail giving your number and ask the man to call you. After that, you and he can make arrangements. I'll contact him as soon as you leave today and tell him I know you and that you're a friend. That way he'll know you're not an undercover cop."

"I don't want this person to know who I am."

"You'll have to sort the details out with him. Oh, and don't be surprised by his appearance if you meet. He's very good at what he does."

At that moment, Gabriel's wife got up from the lounge chair where she'd been sunbathing and walked toward the house wearing only her bikini bottom and sunglasses. Gabriel and Carson followed her with their eyes.

"She's magnificent, isn't she?" Gabriel said.

"Yes," Carson said, his voice thick.

"I just can't understand why I can't remain faithful to her."

———————◆◆◆———————

Carson didn't have a pay-as-you-go phone with him at the Cape and had to drive to a Walmart to purchase one. He called the number Gabriel had given him and left a voice mail: "A mutual friend referred me to you. Please call. The matter is urgent."

Ten minutes later Carson's new phone rang.

"Hello?" Carson said.

"Hello!" the man said, sounding cheerful.

Carson said, "I've never done anything like this before and I'm not sure how to go about it, but I don't want you to know who I am."

His biggest concern was that if the man was arrested for murdering the pedophile or for any other crime, he'd give him up to the cops to get a better deal for himself.

The man said, "I don't need to know your name. But I don't do business over the phone."

The man was worried about the call being intercepted and recorded, which also worried Carson.

The man said, "Where are you located?"

Carson didn't want to tell him where he lived. He said, "I can be in Boston by tomorrow morning. Can you meet me there?"

"Yes. Boston's ideal. Is noon acceptable?"

"Yes."

"Good. I'll text you a location and how much money to bring with you. I don't do wire transfers."

Carson could appreciate this, too. Banking transactions were traceable.

The man said, "How will I recognize you?"

Carson said, "I'll be wearing a Red Sox baseball cap."

"Half the men in Boston wear Red Sox baseball caps."

That was true. Carson thought about his wardrobe for a moment and said, "I'll be wearing a blue baseball cap that says *Yellowstone* on it."

"Good," the man said. "And from now on you'll be Mr. Yellowstone."

The next day, Carson was sitting on a bench in the Boston Common near the statue of George Washington mounted on a horse. In a white Walgreens plastic bag on the seat next to him was fifty thousand dollars in cash. Even though he wouldn't tell the man his name, he was still concerned about being recognized. He'd been on television at least a dozen times and his photo had appeared numerous times in the *Boston Globe*. In addition to the baseball cap, he had on sunglasses and hadn't shaved that morning, hoping those things would make him less recognizable. And it wasn't as if he was a nationally known figure or a movie star. He'd also dressed down for the meeting, wearing faded jeans and a plain blue T-shirt.

He'd been sitting for only a couple of minutes when a man sat down next to him. He figured the man must have gotten there early to make sure he was alone or to see if anyone was following him. The man smiled and said, "Hello, Mr. Yellowstone."

Gabriel had told him not to be surprised by the man's appearance but nonetheless he was. He was a homely man with a broad face, a bulbous nose, and thick lips, and his eyes protruded slightly. He was wearing a floppy tennis hat, a bright yellow sports shirt, cargo shorts, and sandals. He had hairy legs and big feet. He was over six feet tall and fat—he probably weighed more than 250 pounds—but at the same time Carson got the impression that he was quite strong. He reminded him of Russian weightlifters he'd seen in the Olympics. Smiling, as he was now, he seemed friendly and cheerful, and Carson suspected that this was his normal demeanor.

Carson said, "I'll be frank with you. I'm concerned about you getting arrested and giving me up to the cops."

"That's understandable. All I can tell you is I've been doing this a long time and have never been caught. And the man who recommended me wouldn't have done so if I were incompetent. Then there's the fact that I don't know your real name."

"I also don't like the idea of giving you the entire amount up front."

"Mr. Yellowstone, it's the way I do business and you're going to have to trust me. Or you can hire someone else if you wish."

"No, I'll trust you," Carson said. Of course, he didn't trust him, and the man knew it, but he had no other choice.

"Who's the subject?" the man said.

Subject sounded better than *target*.

Carson gave him the pedophile's name and home address and told him he could find a photo of the creep online. He said, "The job has to be done before next week. And it would be best if this looked like a suicide or an accident."

Four days later, the executive was found in his garage, which had been hermetically sealed with duct tape, sitting in the front seat of his car. The car had been running for so long, it ran out of gas. That a man likely to spend years in a federal prison for being a child molester would commit suicide wasn't surprising. Nonetheless, the FBI did take a hard look at Carson to see if he might have been involved. Unsurprisingly, they couldn't prove a thing.

When Brian Lewis became a problem, Carson had sent the man a text: *This is Mr. Yellowstone. I need to see you.*

32

Lev Belushi was having lunch in his modest home in Dorchester with his wife of twenty-five years and his four adoring daughters, his chubby, dark-eyed beauties.

Lev had been born in Tirana, Albania, and had lived and worked there until he was twenty. But when he did something foolish and impulsive, as young men tend to do, the bosses decided he should move to America to assist their associates there. If he'd stayed in Albania, he would have been killed by the man he'd offended, who was also a boss, although thankfully not a major one.

So he'd moved to Boston—only New York and Michigan have larger Albanian populations than Massachusetts—and he felt comfortable there. He was forty-seven now and no longer the rash young man he'd been. When people pointed out that there were two famous Americans— John and Jim—who bore the name Belushi, Lev always said that he knew that, adding that the famous Belushis' father had been born in Qytezë, Albania. He sometimes wondered if the famous American Belushis could be distant cousins, and if he hadn't been terrified of having his DNA in any database, he would have done one of those ancestor searches.

As they were eating the fried chicken he'd prepared—he loved to cook—his phone chirped that he had a text message. He read the message and said, "Excuse me, my darlings," and left the table to respond to the text.

After they finished eating, he said, "Girls, I'm sorry but I'm going to have to miss the game this afternoon." They'd been planning to play croquet on the lawn his wife had just mowed; she did most of the yard work. Actually, she did all the yard work. "Oh, no, Papa," his daughters cried. "I'm sorry," he said, "but if Papa doesn't work, we don't eat." His wife knew what he did for a living; his daughters thought he was a salesman who sold machines to factories and traveled frequently but often worked from home.

Lev met Mr. Yellowstone on the same bench in the Boston Common where they'd met twice before. Lev arrived first, and while he was waiting, a pretty girl walked by with an unusual breed of dog, one that looked more like a lamb than a canine. Lev asked the girl about it and learned it was a Bedlington Terrier. They chatted awhile before the girl went on her way. She told Lev, as she was departing, that he reminded her of her favorite uncle.

A moment later, he saw Mr. Yellowstone coming toward him, holding a plastic shopping bag. He was wearing his disguise, a baseball cap and sunglasses, as he'd done on the other times they'd met—but Lev knew that Mr. Yellowstone was Carson Newman. Before the first time he met him, Gabriel Dushku had called and given him his name, and told him he should do whatever Newman asked.

Newman sat down on the bench next to him and placed the shopping bag between them.

Lev said, "I'm surprised you need my services again so soon."

And he was surprised. It had been less than two weeks since he'd dealt with Lewis. He was beginning to wonder if Newman didn't know any other way to solve his business problems than by having people killed.

Newman said, "Yeah, well, I do." He handed Lev a piece of paper, where he'd written down the details Lev needed. Lev asked a few questions, then picked up the shopping bag. He went home and packed, kissed his wife and daughters goodbye, and took a cab to Logan. He was in Washington, D.C., three hours later.

— ❖ —

When Lev had killed Brian Lewis, Newman had insisted that the death be made to look like an accident. It was Lev's idea to use heroin laced with fentanyl. He obtained the drugs and the drug paraphernalia he needed from an Albanian dealer in D.C. He followed Lewis for a couple of days, saw him with his pretty girlfriend and saw him working on his laptop in the coffee shop near his apartment. On a Friday night, he picked the cheap lock on Lewis's door and waited for him to come home. When he heard the key turn in the lock, he stepped behind the door, and when Lewis stepped into the apartment, his laptop case slung over his shoulder, he put one thick arm around Lewis's neck and clamped a handkerchief saturated with a liquid over his mouth and nose.

The chemical used to incapacitate Lewis was a marvelous substance. Lev didn't know who manufactured it; he got it from an associate of Mr. Dushku's. The rumor was that it was produced by scientists who worked for the Russian FSB and was used by the agency to carry out state-sponsored assassinations and kidnappings. Lev didn't know if that was true or not. What he did know was that the chemical almost instantly rendered a person unconscious and left no trace during a routine autopsy. It acted so quickly that Lewis barely struggled and Lev's thick, soft arm around his throat didn't leave bruises.

After the boy was unconscious, Lev removed Lewis's sport jacket and shirt and tie, sat him on the toilet, injected the heroin into him, and left the rubber tubing around his arm and the needle and cooking spoon on the bathroom sink. He planted an extra bag of heroin, a couple of marijuana joints, and three tabs of ecstasy in a place they'd be found easily. This had also been Lev's idea: to leave evidence showing the boy was a drug user. He picked up Lewis's laptop case and locked the apartment door behind him when he left.

As he was leaving the building, he encountered an elderly lady coming up the steps. He held the door open for her, smiling at her, and she thanked him and smiled back. He made no impression on the woman other than being large and friendly, and the police never questioned her. They didn't question anyone in the building.

The subject this time was a man named David Morgenthal.

Lev spent part of the day parked in a car near Morgenthal's home. Morgenthal never left the house while Lev was watching. And it appeared as if Morgenthal lived alone, as Lev never saw anyone else in the house or enter it or leave it.

Lev walked past the house and around the block a couple of times. Because of the heat, he was wearing a polo shirt, Bermuda shorts, and his floppy tennis hat. He didn't look at all out of place. On his second trip past the house, he saw a man inside, the man moving slowly as he sat down in a chair. He didn't see any security cameras on the exterior of the house or any signage indicating Morgenthal had a monitored security system.

He'd been told that Morgenthal's death didn't need to look like an accident or a suicide. The job just needed to be done quickly. So he texted a man he knew in Virginia that he'd done business with before, and that evening when he returned to his motel, there was a package waiting for him at the front desk. He opened the package in his room. Inside it was a nine-millimeter semiautomatic, a magazine containing eight bullets, and a silencer for the weapon. The weapon was used, and was an older model, but Lev deemed it functional after inspecting it.

He returned to Morgenthal's house at one in the morning. As there were still lights on in nearby homes, he decided to wait awhile. At two thirty, he put on a ski mask. He still had on his shorts and sandals—it was a hot, muggy evening—but he was now wearing a black T-shirt and had black leather gloves on his hands. He'd decided that the ski mask was prudent in case he was wrong about Morgenthal not having cameras.

He walked around to the back of Morgenthal's house. In one hand he was carrying a small duffle bag. It took him five minutes to pick the lock on Morgenthal's back door; he had a better lock than Lewis. He opened the door and listened. As expected, he didn't hear anything. At two thirty in the morning, Morgenthal should be sleeping.

The back door opened into a kitchen. He placed the duffle bag on the floor near the door, then, holding a small flashlight in his left hand and the gun in his right hand, he walked slowly through the kitchen and found himself in a living room. When he stepped into the living room, a voice said, "What the hell." He saw Morgenthal try to rise from the chair where he'd been sitting. Why Morgenthal would be sitting in the chair at that time of night, he had no idea.

He shot Morgenthal twice in the chest before he could rise from the chair.

He returned to the kitchen and picked up the duffle bag and began to search the house for things to steal that were easy to carry—and to take what he'd been told to take. He found Morgenthal's cell phone near the chair where he'd been sitting. He dropped it into the duffle bag. He found Morgenthal's wallet in a bedroom on the second floor with an unmade bed, sitting on top of a dresser. He took the cash from the wallet. He opened all the drawers in the bedroom and left them open to give the impression someone had been searching for things to take. He wanted the police to think that Morgenthal had been killed by a burglar.

In a room on the first floor that had been converted to an office, he saw a laptop computer on a desk. That went into the duffle bag. He opened all the drawers in the desk. He found a second bedroom. In this room, the bed was made. Based on the clothes he saw in the closet, the second bedroom was occupied by a slim woman. He wondered where she was and was glad that she hadn't been home. He'd been paid to kill one person, not two. He opened all the drawers in the bedroom and found some jewelry in one drawer, but nothing that appeared valuable. Nonetheless, he dumped the jewelry into the duffle bag. He didn't see a laptop or an iPad or any other electronics in the room. In a closet on the first floor, he found a safe bolted to the floor. He made no attempt to open the safe but left the closet door open. He left the house a few minutes later, leaving the back door unlocked.

He'd dump the gun and everything he'd stolen on the way to the airport.

He should be back with his wife and daughters before noon.

33

After a late and leisurely breakfast in Georgetown, DeMarco decided it was time to go see Brian's mother again. He not only wanted to tell her what he'd learned, but he also still had the job of making sure she didn't run to the media.

He found Caroline outside her house mowing her small lawn with a push mower. Her sister was trimming bushes with an electric hedge trimmer.

"Let's go inside and talk," she said when DeMarco arrived.

Good idea, DeMarco was thinking. It wasn't even noon, but it was almost ninety degrees outside, and he couldn't believe the two women were out there in such heat doing yard work.

She called to her sister, "Irene, take a break before you have a stroke. I need to talk to Mr. DeMarco."

As they were walking toward the house, she said, "We've got a real estate agent coming over later to take some pictures. We're trying to spruce up the place as best we can."

She led DeMarco to the kitchen, where she added ice to three glasses and poured in lemonade from a pitcher. She handed one to DeMarco, then excused herself while she took a glass to her sister. When she came back, she said, "I still have to clean out Brian's apartment. I've been putting that off. I'll do it this week, unless you think I should leave things as they are. You know, in case the police need to get back in there again."

"You should talk to the cops about that," DeMarco said.

"So, what did you come to tell me?"

"I came to tell you that the cops are going to investigate Brian's death as a homicide."

Caroline closed her eyes briefly. "Finally," she said. "How were you able to make that happen?"

"First, let me start with the fact that I still have no idea what Brian learned that made him a threat to anyone. I've been through his computer at work and there wasn't anything there. His laptop probably contained the information I needed to see, but there was nothing in it either."

"What do you mean?"

"The guy I used to get around the password said that a lot of files had been deleted from the machine. In other words, whoever killed him deleted whatever Brian learned. But I found out that the story of how the police got his laptop was false. Brian didn't leave it at a coffee shop. A woman gave the laptop to a barista who worked at the coffee shop and convinced him to turn it over to the cops and say that Brian left it there."

"Who was the woman?"

"I don't know. Yet. I got a photo of her from a security camera near the coffee shop and right now the cops are looking for her and trying to ID her. But that's not the big news. I planted a fake story that there was a flash drive in Brian's apartment that contained his important files, and the night before last, a guy broke into his apartment to get the drive and he was arrested."

"My God. Is he the one who killed—"

"I don't know. But I doubt it. The guy who broke in is a private detective with no criminal record, and I suspect someone hired him to retrieve the drive. His name is David Morgenthal. He was charged with trespassing because that's the only crime he committed. And right now, he's out on bail."

"Out on bail!" Caroline shrieked.

"Caroline, the cops couldn't detain him. And there's no evidence that he killed Brian. But because of him breaking in, the cops are now treating Brian's death as a homicide and they'll try to get warrants to look at Morgenthal's phone records to see if they can figure out who he's working for."

DeMarco paused. "So, Caroline, you got what you wanted. The cops are now looking for a killer. But I don't know what's going to happen next, and there isn't much for the cops to go on since we don't know what Brian learned and since the killer didn't leave any evidence behind. We're just going to have to wait and see what happens. If they can get Morgenthal to talk, or if they can find something in his phone records, then maybe that will lead them to the killer."

"But what if they don't get any leads?"

"Then that'll be because the killer was smart enough not to leave a trail, but it won't be because the cops aren't trying. And Mahoney will make sure they keep trying. And I'm going to stay in touch with the police, so I'll know what they're doing. But for now, you're going to have to be patient."

Caroline said, "All right, Mr. DeMarco. And I want to thank you for everything you've done. Please keep me informed."

"I will," DeMarco said.

DeMarco left feeling somewhat guilty for not telling Caroline that Brian's research pointed to a dozen politicians, a lobbyist, and a billionaire in Boston. He still wanted to delay the political firestorm that he'd predicted for as long as possible.

34

Sydney woke up at six, earlier than she liked to. She tried to go back to sleep but couldn't. The small motel room felt like a prison cell and the walls were closing in on her. She decided to go for a walk on the beach.

She was staying in the small town of Mayo, Maryland. She'd picked it because it was only an hour from D.C. and she'd been there once before and had enjoyed the views of Chesapeake Bay. She tried to remember why she'd gone there before and who she'd gone with, but couldn't, so it had most likely been back when she was doing drugs and drinking.

She got into her car and drove to a spot where she could access the beach and where the only person she saw was one guy walking a dog. She walked about half a mile, until she came to a log that was scorched black on one side, as if somebody had used it for the back of a campfire. She sat on the log and looked out at the bay and saw a lone sailboat that had to be forty feet long. It was heeling so far over that the deck rails on one side were almost touching the water. The guys sailing the boat were either good or just lucky they didn't capsize it. It occurred to her then that she'd never been on a boat of any kind, not even a canoe or a rowboat. There were a lot of things she hadn't done.

As she sat there, she thought about Dave saying she ought to become a military chopper pilot. She had to admit the idea intrigued her. She'd known for some time that she had to decide what she was going to do with her life. Like Dave had said, he wasn't going to be there forever, and she couldn't rely on him supporting her forever. She wished she could become a formal partner in his business but knew that wasn't realistic. With the sort of sensitive work he did, it was unlikely his clients would accept a twenty-three-year-old woman as his stand-in.

Having nothing better to do, she decided to use her phone to see what it would take to become a helicopter pilot. But the first thing she did was look at photos of military helicopters. She'd seen helicopters before, of course, news choppers and medevac choppers, but they didn't look anything like the Black Hawks and Apaches she saw online, these awesome machines bristling with machine guns and missiles and that had a top speed of over two hundred miles an hour. It would be an absolute kick to fly one.

One article she looked at said that an Apache attack helicopter cost about sixty million dollars, so the military was picky about who flew them. You didn't have to have a college degree to become a chopper pilot—just the demonstrated aptitude and intelligence, followed by months of training designed to wash out the incompetent. Nor did you have to be a military officer; army helicopters were flown mostly by warrant officers, a rank that was sort of in between the officers and the enlisted soldiers as best as she could tell.

She spent an hour looking at articles talking about careers in the army, trying to figure out what it would take to get into chopper school. There was obviously no guarantee that she'd make it, but she concluded it was doable, and the best way to improve her chances was to learn to fly a helicopter before enlisting. From what she could see online, that could take as much as fifty or sixty grand, which she didn't have, and several months of training.

She glanced at her watch. It was now almost eight and she decided to call Dave—not to talk about choppers; she'd talk to him about that once she was home—but just to see how he was feeling. He'd really sounded weak the last time she spoke to him. Those chemo sessions beat the crap out of him. She called his number, but he didn't answer. She left a message saying, "Call me. Want to see how you're doing." She wondered if today was one of the days he was supposed to get another dose of poison to kill the cancer and maybe that's why he wasn't answering. Then she thought no, those sessions didn't start this early.

She drove back to the town, found an espresso place where she could buy a breakfast sandwich, and ate in her car. She called Dave again, and again he didn't answer. Not wanting to go back to the motel, she decided to drive up the coast for a bit, north toward Annapolis, just to kill time and take in the scenery. Half an hour later, she called Dave again. No answer. Now she was starting to get worried. Something wasn't right. She turned around and went back to the motel and called Dave again, and when he didn't answer, she checked out of the motel and started driving toward D.C. She called him half a dozen more times in the hour it took to make it back and continued to get his voice mail, and her anxiety increased with each passing mile.

She arrived home about eleven and saw Dave's car parked on the street in front of the house where it was usually parked. But that didn't necessarily mean he was home, as he hardly drove since he'd started chemo and might have taken a cab somewhere. The front door was locked, as it usually was. She unlocked it and stepped into the house and saw him immediately.

He was sitting in the armchair where he normally sat and where he sometimes slept if he didn't have the energy to walk up the stairs to his bedroom on the second floor. There were two red spots on the white T-shirt he was wearing. She knew they were bullet holes. There wasn't much blood, which meant that his heart had stopped pumping almost instantly.

She dropped to her knees, her hands clamped over her mouth. She didn't know how long she knelt there, unmoving, looking at him. Her head felt as if a train were roaring through it.

He'd been like a father to her. He'd been her best friend. He'd put up with an unbelievable amount of shit from her when she'd been drinking and drugging and never quit on her. And some son of a bitch had killed him.

She finally forced herself to think. She had to do something, but what should she do?

What she should do was call 911 and report that she'd found his body. She couldn't just leave him sitting where he was. They weren't close to any of the neighbors, and Dave didn't have friends likely to wonder where he was if they didn't hear from him. He could sit there until he rotted, and she couldn't bear the thought of that. At the same time, if she called the cops, they might arrest her. She knew, thanks to DeMarco, that the police were looking for the woman who'd given the barista Lewis's laptop and that they had a photo of her. So she might get arrested.

If someone else did find the body, as unlikely as that seemed, the cops would quickly realize that she'd been living with Dave. All her clothes were in her bedroom and there were photos and paperwork in the house that could be used to identify her. Then there was Dave's will, which named her as his sole heir. If she didn't report the murder—and maybe even if she did—she'd become the cops' prime suspect for killing him.

So should she call the cops now or not? No. Not yet. She needed to be free to figure out who'd killed him, and she wouldn't be able to do that if the cops detained her. And after she found out who killed him, she was going to kill the killer. If it was the last thing she did, she was going to deal with the bastard who'd killed her one and only true friend.

She went into Dave's bedroom. The first thing she noticed was that all the drawers in the bedroom were open, as if someone had been searching for something. She saw Dave's wallet lying open on top of the dresser. She picked it up and saw that there was no cash in it, but Dave's credit cards were still there. She put the wallet back where it had been and went to the bedroom closet and pulled a metal box off the top shelf. The box was a gun safe, but Dave didn't keep it locked, as he used to when she was younger and using drugs. In the box was a loaded Beretta with a spare clip and a box of ammunition. Dave had taught her how to shoot the gun a couple of years ago during a period when she'd been sober. She took the gun and the spare clip and went to her room.

Someone had searched her room, too. All the drawers were open. She didn't bother to see if anything had been taken and packed a knapsack with a couple of changes of clothes and put the gun and the spare clip inside the knapsack. From her bedroom she went to a closet on the first floor. She noticed the door to the closet was open but the small safe anchored to the floor didn't appear to have been broken into. She entered the combination into the keypad and opened the safe. Considering her problems with addiction, she couldn't help but think that Dave giving her the combination had been a tremendous act of faith. Inside the safe was an envelope holding a couple grand in cash—their rainy-day stash for the day when the banks collapsed and the ATM machines didn't work. She took the cash.

She went to Dave's office next and saw that all the desk drawers were open and that his laptop was missing. Whoever had killed him had wanted to make it look as if Dave had been killed by a burglar. But she wasn't buying that. Why would a burglar pick their house to rob? It was an average house located in a run-down neighborhood. And why wouldn't the killer have taken other items that could be pawned, like Dave's watch, which was still on his wrist. Or his credit cards, which could have been used until Dave's death was reported? And it was difficult to pawn laptops because those devices were password-protected and of no use to someone who didn't have the password. Also, she'd noticed when she was in Dave's bedroom that all his medications, some of which were powerful painkillers, appeared to still be on the night table next to his bed. A junkie would have taken the medications.

She looked for his phone next but couldn't find it. It wasn't sitting next to his chair in the living room, and he always kept his phone close to him in case she called. And it hadn't been in his bedroom. She called the number again, hoping to hear it ring, but didn't hear it and her call went to voice mail. Whoever had killed him had taken his phone.

She realized then that everything that had been taken was a device that contained information—maybe information that the killer didn't want anyone to see.

Dave's death had to be connected to the last cases they'd worked: following Lewis and then DeMarco. Someone had wanted to silence Dave because he knew something damaging to someone. What other reason could there be? And the only person that could be was the client who'd hired Dave to follow Lewis and DeMarco. But she had no idea who the client was, because Dave hadn't told her.

Considering what he did for his clients, Dave had always been secretive when it came to their identities. He didn't advertise for business, he worked on a referral basis, and work wouldn't be referred his way if he ever disclosed the name of a client or what information he'd provided the client. As a licensed private detective, he could claim, as lawyers do, that communication between him and a client was privileged. That might or might not work if he was subpoenaed to testify, and if a judge decided to toss him into jail for contempt for refusing to cooperate, Dave had been willing to do the time. But he'd never wanted to put Sydney in that position. For one thing, she wasn't licensed and couldn't claim privilege. And although Dave would have denied it, Sydney also suspected that Dave didn't tell her his clients' names in case she fell off the wagon. Maybe if he'd lived longer and she continued to work for him, and continued to stay sober, he would have told her who his clients were, but in the case of Lewis and DeMarco he hadn't.

He kept files on his clients in the desk in his office, but Sydney didn't bother to look at those. The only thing in the files was billing information: hours worked and expenses billed to the clients, and regarding the expenses, Dave's records were deliberately vague. And if the cops obtained a warrant to seize or search his files, they wouldn't find the clients' names. The clients were identified by code names—names like Rain

Man, Sunset Boulevard, Casablanca, Moneyball, short movie titles—but only Dave knew who the titles represented, and he kept that information in his head. Sydney knew that the code name for the latest client, the one who'd hired Dave to follow Lewis and DeMarco, was Kingpin—after a goofy movie starring Woody Harrelson as a bowler with an artificial hand—but that's all she knew.

She had to find out who the client was. She had to know the reason Dave had been killed.

And she could only think of one person who might know more than she did.

35

---◆---

DeMarco pulled his car into his garage unsatisfied after talking to Olivetti.

He'd called Olivetti on the way home after speaking to Caroline and learned that Olivetti had made no headway in getting warrants to obtain Morgenthal's records. Olivetti had spoken to a prosecutor who said that she'd look into the warrants, but she had a trial starting tomorrow and Morgenthal wasn't her first priority.

He'd call Perry later and get him to call the prosecutor. To motivate her, Perry could promise her that Mahoney might be there for her in the future if she had political aspirations. If Perry was unsuccessful, or if the prosecutor couldn't get the warrants, then DeMarco was going to be forced to tell Olivetti that Brian's research pointed to Grady and Newman and twelve congressmen—which would unleash the political and media nightmare that he'd warned Perry about. And who knows how Mahoney would react.

DeMarco's garage sat beneath his house in what was essentially his basement. He trudged up the stairs to the doorway and entered his kitchen. After leaving the comfort of his air-conditioned car, he felt as if he'd stepped into a sauna.

He took off his suit jacket and hung it over the back of a chair near his kitchen table and opened the refrigerator. As he bent over to pluck a beer from a shelf—lingering longer than necessary to enjoy the coolness—a voice said, "Turn around."

Oh, shit.

He turned and saw the woman who'd given Brian's laptop to the barista. She was holding a gun in her right hand and it was pointed at his chest.

The photo pulled from the security camera didn't do justice to her. She was a gorgeous young woman. She was tall and well built, wearing tight blue jeans and a sleeveless white T-shirt. With her short, spiky hair, the vine tattoo winding around her throat, and her jade-green eyes, the first word that occurred to DeMarco was *exotic.* The second word that occurred to him was *dangerous.* She was not only holding a gun, but she looked mad enough to use it.

"Sit down," she said, gesturing to the chair where'd he hung his jacket, "and place your hands on your knees."

DeMarco figured she wanted him sitting instead of standing to make it harder for him to lunge at her and try to take the gun. Not that he had any intention of doing that. She was young, her arms and legs were muscular, and she looked athletic. The last thing he was going to do was try to take the gun.

He said, "What do you want?"

"Sit down, goddamnit, or I'll put a bullet in your knee."

DeMarco sat.

"Now what do you want?" DeMarco asked. "Why are you here?"

"I want to know who killed Dave Morgenthal."

"What are you talking about? Morgenthal's dead?"

"Yes. He was shot, probably last night, in his house. And I want to know who killed him."

"I have no idea who killed him," DeMarco said. "I didn't even know he was dead."

"But you know something, and I know you know more than I do, because you've been running around poking into Brian Lewis's death. I know you talked to some guy named Perry. I know Perry was going to look at whatever was in Lewis's computer at work. I know Lewis wrote some kind of report. I heard you tell Perry about the dirty dozen, and I want to know what that means. I also know that Lewis had been planning to talk to some professor about what he found and that you were planning to talk to the professor, too. And I know you got Lewis's laptop and I want to know what you found in it."

"How do you know all this stuff?"

"Because I was following you and listening in on your cell phone calls."

"You're shittin' me," DeMarco muttered. It had never occurred to him that someone might follow him, but he'd been right to be paranoid about someone tapping into his calls.

"So, I want answers, and if you don't tell me what I want to know, I'm going to put a bullet in one of your kneecaps. And if you still won't tell me, I'll put a bullet in your other knee, and you'll be walking with crutches for the rest of your life. Unless I kill you."

"Hey, you don't have to shoot me full of holes," DeMarco said. "I'll be happy to tell you everything I know. I want to get to the bottom of what happened to Brian as much as you want to find out who killed Morgenthal."

"So who's Perry?"

"Just a minute. What's your name and what's your relationship to Morgenthal? All I know about you is that you're the one who gave Brian's laptop to that twit at the coffee shop."

"I worked with him, and I lived with him. He was like a father to me. And you don't need to know my name."

DeMarco shrugged. "I'm going to get it eventually. Unless you kill me, that is. I gave your photo to the cops, and they'll ID you."

The woman hesitated. "My name's Sydney Roma. My father was Dave's partner, and after my dad died, he took care of me. He became my guardian. Now start answering my questions. Who's Perry?"

"He's Perry Wallace, John Mahoney's chief of staff, and Brian worked for him."

"And what did you find in Lewis's computers?"

"Nothing."

"Hey! Goddamnit, if you're not straight with me I'll—"

"I am being straight with you. Brian was doing research on a dozen congressmen who voted no on this one bill. Perry called them the dirty dozen and Brian was trying to figure out why they voted the way they did. He suspected they were bribed. And I know from talking to his girlfriend, he was documenting what he learned. But there wasn't a report or a memo, or anything like one, in his computer at work, and it wasn't in his laptop. His laptop had been wiped by a pro before it was returned to the cops."

"Wiped? What does that mean?"

"It means a bunch of files had been deleted from his laptop before I got ahold of it. Meaning before you gave it to the barista. All I know is that Brian got dirt on some people, but I don't know who killed him or even exactly why he was killed. Maybe if you'd tell me what you know, we could work this thing out together. Like who hired you to follow me?"

"No one hired me. A client hired Dave, and Dave told me to follow you and tap your calls."

"Why would he ask you to do that?"

Tears welled up in Sydney's eyes. "Because he had cancer and needed help."

"So who was the client?"

Sydney wiped away the tears. "I don't know. I never dealt directly with Dave's clients, and he wouldn't tell me their names. It was a thing with him, maintaining the client's confidentiality. So I don't know who he was working for."

"Who gave you the laptop you handed off to the barista?"

"Dave did. But I don't know who he got it from."

"And I suppose you don't know who paid him to break into Brian's apartment to get the flash drive."

"What are you talking about?"

"You don't know about the flash drive?"

"No. I didn't know there was any flash drive."

"I planted a story that Brian had left a flash drive in his apartment that contained the report he wrote, and Morgenthal broke into the apartment to get it and was arrested."

"Arrested? He didn't tell me that. I've been hiding out since you started trying to track me down, and today when I couldn't get ahold of him, I came home to see if he was okay and found him dead. But he never told me that he broke into Lewis's apartment or that he'd been arrested."

"Well, he was. Somebody, I'm guessing the same client who hired him to follow me, hired him to get the flash drive. But after he was arrested, he wouldn't talk to the cops. He wouldn't tell them anything—about why he broke into the apartment or who hired him or anything else."

"What's on this flash drive?"

"There is no flash drive. I leaked the story that one existed to see what would happen. And what happened is someone told Morgenthal to get the drive and he got caught. What I'm wondering is if him getting arrested posed a threat to whoever he was working for and that's why he was killed."

Sydney shook her head. She appeared not to know what to do or say next. The woman was holding a gun in her hand, but it suddenly occurred to DeMarco how young she was. She wasn't any older than Brian. She was also a young woman who'd just lost someone she cared about.

He said, "Sydney, would you mind if I got a beer? It's hot in here and I'm thirsty."

"Go ahead, but if you try anything—"

"I'm not going to try anything. You want one?"

"Yeah. I mean no. I don't drink."

"How 'bout a Coke?"

"Yeah, okay."

DeMarco got a beer for himself and a Coke for Sydney. He handed the can to her but then saw she couldn't open it because she was holding the gun in her other hand.

He said, "Sydney, why don't you put the gun down before you accidently shoot me. And why don't you sit down. I'm not going to try to force you to do anything, and when you want to leave, I'm not going to try to stop you. And based on what you're telling me, you haven't done anything illegal."

Other than breaking into my house and pointing a gun at me.

DeMarco said, "You followed me, and you gave Brian's laptop to that dork at the coffee shop, but it sounds like that's all you've done, so you're not in any legal trouble. Yet. So sit down and let's see if we can figure this thing out together."

After a moment's hesitation, she put the gun down on the counter—where she could easily reach it—and opened the Coke. But she remained standing.

"There's got to be a way to find out who hired Dave," she said. "But whoever killed him took his cell phone, so I don't have a way to figure out who he was talking to."

"Well, there's a couple things I didn't tell you. This report Brian was working on apparently pointed at two men in addition to the congressmen he was researching. Their names are Patrick Grady and Carson Newman. Do you know who they are? Did Dave ever mention them?"

"No. Never heard of them. Who are they?"

"Grady's a lobbyist here in D.C. Newman's a big-shot businessman in Boston. Brian apparently thought they were involved in bribing these congressmen, and so one of them might have hired Dave to follow me after they found out I was looking into Brian's death."

"Why do keep saying *apparently*?"

"Because I don't know for sure. Brian's supervisor said that Brian had mentioned their names in conjunction with the research he was doing but he didn't provide any specifics."

DeMarco decided not to tell Sydney about Jane. As pissed off as she was, she could show up at Jane's house next with her gun.

DeMarco said, "But there's no direct evidence that Grady or Newman bribed anyone or would have had a strong motive for killing Brian."

"I don't need evidence," Sydney said. "I'll go talk to this guy Grady, since he's here in D.C., and make him tell me what he knows."

"You mean you'll stick a gun in his face. That would be a stupid thing to do, Sydney. You need to let the cops do their job and look for Dave's killer."

Before Sydney could respond, DeMarco's phone rang. He looked at the caller ID. He said to Sydney, "It's Brian's mother. Let me see what she wants. I won't tell her you're here."

"Put your phone on speaker," Sydney said.

"Hi, Caroline. What can I do for you?"

"I'm at Brian's place with my sister. We're clearing it out, packing up all his clothes and things."

"Okay," DeMarco said.

"I found a flash drive."

"You what?"

"There's only one closet in the apartment. Brian hung all his clothes in it, and beneath the clothes on hangers there's a small chest of drawers for his underwear and socks and T-shirts and things like that. The flash drive was in a sock."

DeMarco couldn't believe it. He'd invented the flash drive thinking it would be logical for Brian to have used one to back up the report on his computer. But now it looked as if that's what Brian had actually done. If anyone—including Brian's killer, the cops, or himself—had done a thorough search of the apartment, they would have found it.

DeMarco said, "I'll be over as soon as I can to pick it up. It's probably password-protected and I'll get my guy to unlock it. Can you wait there for a while? I'm in the middle of something and need to deal with it first."

"I'll wait," Caroline said.

36

What DeMarco was in the middle of was trying to figure out how to handle Sydney.

As soon as he hung up from Caroline, she said, "I thought you said there was no flash drive."

"As far as I knew, there wasn't. I made up the story that Brian stored important files on one because it sounded plausible, but I didn't know one actually existed. I should have searched his place better."

"I want to know what's on that drive."

"So do I, and I'll find out what's on it after I get it. But what you need to do is report Dave's death."

Sydney shook her head.

"Sydney, whether you believe it or not, we're on the same side here. I want to get the people responsible for killing Brian and you want to get whoever killed Dave and it's probably the same people. But you need to report his death. You need to give the cops a chance to do their job and see if they can find the killer. That's what they do for a living and they're better at it than you and me."

"If I report his death, they might think I killed him and then they'll arrest me. At a minimum, they'll detain me for questioning, and I don't want to be detained."

DeMarco was thinking she might be right about that, but then said, "No, they won't. And the reason why is I'm going to get you a lawyer to keep that from happening. But you have to tell the cops he's dead. If you don't, then it's like you said. When his body's found, they're going to suspect you killed him and hunt you down and arrest you. But if you'll let me, I'll get you a lawyer to keep you out of jail, and while you're dealing with the cops, I'll go get the flash drive from Brian's mom. And I'm not going to cut you out of the loop, because I need you to help me catch whoever killed Dave and Brian."

"I don't believe you."

"Sydney, I don't have a plan yet, but I'm thinking that there may be a way to use you to expose the people who killed Brian. What I'm saying is, since you were working with Dave, maybe there's a way we can play that to draw these people out. But that's not going to happen if you're on the run from the cops or in jail. So let me get you a lawyer."

Sydney looked away and DeMarco could tell she was wavering. She knew she needed help.

Finally, she said, "I can't afford a lawyer."

"You won't be paying," DeMarco said. "I will." Meaning the U.S. tax-payers, the poor suckers, would foot the bill.

When she didn't respond, DeMarco picked up his phone.

"Who are you calling?"

"Your lawyer."

He punched in a number. Naturally, considering who he was call-ing, his call went to voice mail. He left a message saying, "Janet, it's Joe DeMarco. Call me. It's urgent."

When he hung up, Sydney said, "Who's Janet?"

"Janet Evans is one of the best, and most expensive, attorneys in this town. A few years ago, I was framed for killing a congressman and Janet was one of the people who kept me from going to jail. And not too long ago, I was arrested in Wyoming by some hick sheriff out there, and Janet helped me out of that mess, too. And she's going to help you."

DeMarco's phone rang. It was Janet.

He answered the phone, saying: "I need your help. There's a young lady who's about to report finding a dead man in her house and the cops might consider her a suspect and arrest her, which I don't want to happen. So I'd like you to be there when she calls the cops. Or if you can't do it personally, send one of the hotshots who works for you."

"What's the whole story, DeMarco?"

"The whole story's complicated. But the only thing that matters is that she didn't kill anyone. I'll tell you the rest of the story later." *Maybe*, he said to himself. "I'll text you the woman's phone number and address so you can set up a meeting with her."

"All right, DeMarco, but I can't meet with her myself because I'm in New York. I'll have one of my associates deal with this."

"Thanks, Janet. I'll owe you."

"You already owe me, DeMarco."

DeMarco hung up and said to Sydney, "Give me your number and address, then go to your place, wait for the lawyer to get there, and then call the cops. And you can trust the lawyer. She's *your* lawyer, she'll keep what you tell her to herself. Okay?"

Sydney didn't answer.

"Sydney, you have to trust somebody. And like I already said, we're on the same side here."

"Okay," Sydney said, "but I swear to God if you don't—"

"Yeah, I know. You'll come back and shoot me in the knees."

37

Sydney didn't go inside the house. She couldn't bear to look at Dave again. She sat down on the front steps and her lawyer arrived fifteen minutes later. The lawyer introduced herself as Bridget Shaw. She was a trim woman with short blond hair, dressed in an expensive gray suit, and she just *looked* smart. She also wasn't much older than Sydney, and Sydney couldn't help but think that if she'd lived her life differently, if she'd gone to college instead of doing drugs and getting into trouble, she could have been the one standing there in the expensive suit.

She told Bridget that Dave had been her guardian when she was younger and that she'd lived with him, and that when she came home from the Maryland shore, she found his body. She said that he'd been shot and that the house had been searched. Thinking it was information the lawyer needed to know, she also told Bridget that Dave was a private detective and that his death could be related to his profession. She didn't, however, say anything about Lewis or his laptop or following DeMarco. She'd discuss those things with her lawyer if necessary and depending on what the cops did, but would prefer not to tell Bridget any more than she had to.

When she finished, she asked Bridget if she wanted to see the body.

"No," Bridget said. "The house is a crime scene and neither of us should go in." She paused, then asked, "Do you own a gun, Sydney?"

"No. But Dave did."

"Where's it at right now?" Bridget asked.

Sydney hesitated. "It's in my car." Sydney decided not to tell Bridget that she took Dave's gun to threaten DeMarco and to kill whoever killed Dave. She said, "When I saw Dave, I got scared and went to his room and got it."

"Will there be a problem if the police do a ballistics check?"

What Bridget was really asking was: *Did you use the gun to kill Dave?*

"No, there won't be a problem," Sydney said.

"Okay, after the police get here, we'll tell them you have the gun and I'm sure they'll take it."

Sydney called 911 and reported finding Dave's body, and things moved quickly after that. A patrol car arrived ten minutes later. A uniformed cop had Sydney unlock the front door, went into the house holding his gun, saw the body, checked for a pulse, then backed out of the house. Half an hour later, two detectives arrived. They both went into the house. Fifteen minutes passed before the older of the two detectives, a husky guy in his forties who looked like Forest Whitaker wearing Clark Kent glasses, came back out and walked over to Sydney. He said his name was Jim Cave.

Cave asked Sydney about finding the body and she told him that she'd been away from home for a couple of days, relaxing at a place on the Maryland shore. She gave him the name of the motel so he could confirm she'd been there.

"Why did you go to Maryland?" Cave asked.

Sydney said, "I was just taking a break from the heat. I figured it would be cooler on the shore."

Before Cave could ask another question, she said that while she was away, she called Dave a number of times, and when he didn't answer, she became concerned, so she came home. She added that he was being treated for cancer and she'd been worried that he'd had some sort of complication related to the disease. She said that when she saw the body, and saw that the place had been searched, she became frightened, got Dave's gun, called her lawyer, and then called the police.

"Why did you call your lawyer first?" Cave asked.

"Because I've had some bad experiences with cops, and it seemed like a prudent thing to do." She knew Cave would see she had a record, but all he'd find were arrests for disorderly conduct, possessing drugs, and shoplifting. And a couple of DUIs.

"And who she called first is irrelevant," her smart lawyer said.

"Where's the gun now?" Cave asked.

"In my car," Sydney said. "In the glove compartment. I thought it would be better not to be holding it when you guys got here. Do you want me to go get it?"

"No. We'll get it. And we're going to have to take it with us to do a ballistics test, unless you object for some reason."

"I don't object," Sydney said.

"And we'd like to do a GSR test. That's a—"

"I know what it is," Sydney said. "Go ahead and do one."

Cave said, "After the CSIs arrive and do the GSR test, and after I'm done here, I'd like you to come down to the station with me. I've got a bunch of other questions to ask."

"No," Bridget said. "My client isn't going to sit in an interrogation room like a suspect, not unless you arrest her. Are you planning to arrest her?"

"No, but—"

"So ask your questions now," Bridget said, "and if you have more later, call her and she'll get ahold of me and she'll cooperate."

Cave wasn't delighted with that response, but he got on with the questions. He asked her if Dave had any enemies. No, Sydney said. He asked if she'd seen any strangers lurking about. No, she said. He asked if Dave had anything worth stealing, like a bunch of cash. No, she said.

Cave said, "I know Mr. Morgenthal is—was a private detective. I saw his license hanging on a wall in his office. Would any of his clients have had a reason for killing him?"

Sydney decided not to mention Patrick Grady or Carson Newman. At least not until she talked to DeMarco again, who'd said he might have some way to use her to get to them.

She said, "I don't know who his clients were. There's a bunch of client files in the desk in his office, and you have my permission to look at them, but Dave used code names to identify his clients because he was worried about his records getting subpoenaed."

Cave asked a few more questions, but he never asked a thing about Lewis's laptop, and it occurred to Sydney that Cave and Olivetti hadn't talked to each other. And since Dave's house was quite a ways from Lewis's apartment, Cave and Olivetti probably weren't in the same precinct. Eventually, one part of the police bureaucracy would connect with the other part, and when it did, Sydney and her smart lawyer would deal with the situation. But until then, she wouldn't say anything about Lewis or his laptop.

Cave asked Sydney if she had someplace to stay for the night, as she wouldn't be allowed into her house until probably tomorrow. Sydney said no, that she'd find a motel, then asked what was going to happen with Dave's body. Cave said it would be removed from the scene in a couple of hours after the CSIs did their examination and then taken to the morgue for an autopsy. It might be quite a while after that before they'd be able to release the body so she could bury Dave.

Sydney hadn't given any thought to Dave's funeral, and they'd never discussed it. She didn't even know if he wanted to be buried or cremated. She supposed what she should do was bury him at Arlington National Cemetery because he'd been a veteran. He probably would have wanted that. But she had no idea how much that would cost or how to go about it.

As Bridget was leaving, she told Sydney to call her if the cops questioned her again. "And if they read you your rights, the only thing you say is *I want my lawyer.*"

38

Caroline and her sister had finished cleaning out Brian's apartment by the time DeMarco arrived. Brian had only lived for twenty-two years, and all of his earthly possessions had fit into four cardboard boxes.

Caroline gave DeMarco the flash drive after making him promise to tell her what it contained. He promised he would—a promise he might or might not keep.

His next stop was Neil's place. He told Neil to see if the drive was password-protected and, if it was, to crack it. Neil stuck the drive in one of his computers and said, "There's no password." DeMarco told him, "Move out of the way so I can see what's on it."

The only thing on the drive was a single file with the name "Tenants' Rights Conspiracy."

DeMarco printed out the file, all ten pages of it.

DeMarco waited impatiently as Perry read Brian's report for a second time.

After he finished, Perry waved the pages at DeMarco and said, "There's nothing in this thing worth killing someone for."

Before DeMarco could say otherwise, Perry said, "I can see what Brian did. He started looking at the twelve guys that voted no, and right off the bat, he found that a couple of them got campaign contributions from people or companies he could easily link to Newman. Then he kept going and found that *all* of them got something from Newman, although none of them got anything from Newman directly. Like the thing with the bighorn sheep tag."

One of the congressmen, an avid hunter, had gotten a hunting permit —called a tag—to kill a bighorn sheep. The tags were extremely hard to get and were also expensive, and the manager of one of Newman's construction firms had transferred a tag he'd obtained to the congressman so the congressman could shoot a sheep. But Newman hadn't personally given the congressman the tag.

Perry said, "I have no idea how he got some of this stuff, but he must have researched the hell out of these people. Like this one about the congressman's kid getting into a pricey preschool. Maybe he found out about that by looking at the congressman's or his wife's social media and then pulled the string to tie it to Newman. And he had to have called people and asked questions, and I suspect he misrepresented himself when he did. I mean, the kid was a fucking bloodhound."

DeMarco said, "But if his report got out, it would show that Newman, through proxies, made a concerted effort to influence all twelve congressmen. It was a conspiracy."

"So what?" Perry said. "Lobbyists and rich guys conspire every day of the week to get politicians to vote the way they want. And there's no proof of a quid pro quo. There's no evidence that these congressmen voted the way they did because of what Newman did. Or supposedly did. And they probably got campaign contributions from other people who also would have wanted them to vote no, too. I mean, this thing might have been embarrassing for Newman, but he certainly wouldn't have gone to jail, and I can't imagine him or Grady killing Brian to keep what he learned from being made public."

"You're forgetting something, Perry. Brian was killed *before* anyone saw what he'd learned. All Newman or Grady knew, thanks to fucking Jane, was that Brian thought he'd found something that implicated Newman. But they didn't know what he *actually* found until they got their hands on his laptop. Once they got his laptop and looked at that document, they probably said the same thing you did, that it hadn't been worth killing him for, but by then it was too late and Brian was dead. So they didn't kill him because of what he found. They killed him because of what they *thought* he might have found. And even after they knew what his report said, they still didn't want it getting out, so they sent Morgenthal to get the flash drive."

"But why would they kill Morgenthal?"

"I don't know. Maybe Morgenthal had evidence tying them to Brian's murder. Maybe he threatened them in some way. Maybe he tried blackmailing them. Whatever the case, I'm sure his death is connected to Brian's."

"So what do you want to do, DeMarco?"

"I don't know," DeMarco said again. "I was thinking there might be some way to use Jane, to get her to leak something to Grady that might make him do something that'll prove he was involved in Brian's death. But now with Sydney involved, she might be even better than Jane because Morgenthal worked with her. Like maybe Sydney could say that Morgenthal passed something on to her before he was killed and she's going to the cops with it unless they pay her not to."

"But what would he have passed on to her?"

"I don't know," DeMarco said for a third time. He was getting tired of saying that. "I need to sit down with Sydney and see if I can figure something out."

Holding up the pages in his hand, Perry said, "And what do we do with this?"

"For now, we keep it to ourselves until I can come up with a plan."

"What about Brian's mom?"

"I don't want to tell her about it yet, because she might talk to the media or the cops, and I don't want that to happen until I've got a plan for dealing with Grady and Newman. When she asks me what was on the flash drive, I'll tell her it was encrypted, and my computer guy is still trying to get around the encryption. The problem we have isn't Brian's mom. It's Sydney. She's a loose cannon. She's pissed off and was running around with a gun and she wants to avenge Morgenthal's death, and I'm not sure she can be controlled."

DeMarco's phone rang. He looked at the caller ID and said, "Speak of the devil."

39

DeMarco told Sydney that he was at the Capitol and to meet him at his place so they could talk.

He found her sitting on his front porch. He said, "Why didn't you just let yourself in like you did the last time? How did you do that, by the way?"

"You got shitty locks," Sydney said.

Inside the house, Sydney said, "Jesus, it's hot in here."

"Yeah, my air conditioner crapped out. Have you eaten?"

"No," Sydney said.

"I've got some leftover spaghetti. We can eat while we talk."

They went into the kitchen and DeMarco took a bowl of spaghetti from his refrigerator. He'd made the spaghetti a day ago and made enough to last a couple of days so he wouldn't have to cook again. When his mother, who was a fantastic cook, made spaghetti, she'd buy handmade pasta from an Italian market and make the sauce and the meatballs from scratch. DeMarco did it the easy way. He bought pasta that came in a box, a bottle of Paul Newman's marinara sauce, and frozen meatballs. The end result wasn't as good as his mother's but good enough. He warmed up two plates of spaghetti in the microwave while Sydney mixed a Caesar salad that came in a bag with all the ingredients. As she was mixing the salad, she told DeMarco about how things had gone with the police at her house and how her smart lawyer had helped.

They sat down to eat, and Sydney said, "So. Did you get the flash drive?"

"Yeah. And a document Brian wrote was on it, and it points to Carson Newman doing some things that might have made these twelve congressmen vote the way Newman wanted on a bill he didn't want passed. The problem is that Brian was an intern and didn't understand the law and how much bullshit sitting politicians can get away with, and he really didn't find anything incriminating when it comes to Newman personally."

"But he was killed because of this document?"

"Yeah. But he was killed before anyone knew what it said. Someone overreacted or had some bad information."

Bad information that Jane probably gave them.

"And you think it was this guy Newman?"

"Not Newman personally. If he wanted Brian dead, he'd hire someone. Or maybe Grady was the one who wanted Brian dead, and he's the one who hired a killer. This whole thing started when Grady learned that Brian had found something that implicated Newman."

"How did Grady find out what Brian learned?"

DeMarco again decided not to mention Jane. He said, "He had a source—a spy—in Congress who told him. And it was right after Grady learned about Brian that Brian has a drug overdose, and then Dave gets hired to follow me when I started looking into Brian's death."

"That wasn't the order in which it happened," Sydney said. "Before Dave was hired to follow you, he was hired to follow Brian. Although I was the one who did the actual following."

"I didn't know that. Why didn't you tell me?"

Sydney shrugged. "I thought you knew."

"Well, I didn't," DeMarco said.

"Anyway, I followed Brian for a few days, listened in on his calls, recorded his calls, and reported back to Dave. Nothing happened while

I was following him. He'd go to work, see his girlfriend, and work on his laptop in the coffee shop sometimes. The last thing that happened when I was following him was that I recorded him talking to this prof at UVA. On the call, Brian said he'd found out that some congressmen were committing crimes and he wanted to talk to the professor about it, but the professor couldn't see him right away. Right after that, Dave was told to stop following Brian, so I stopped following him. And a few days later Brian was dead."

"So whoever Dave was working for knew about the call to the professor?" DeMarco said.

"Yeah."

"And that was probably when they decided to kill him. They didn't want him passing on what he knew to anyone."

"I guess. And then you started looking into Brian's death and Dave was hired to follow you. And when I told Dave you were looking for Brian's laptop, the next thing that happens is someone gives Dave the laptop. Then you know what happened after that. I got the laptop to the barista, he gave it to the cops, but you didn't buy the story and went hunting for me. Then Dave was killed."

DeMarco didn't say anything for a while. "You still have the recording of Brian talking to the professor?"

"Yeah. It's on my phone."

DeMarco went silent again. "Here's what we're going to do," he said after a couple of minutes. "We're going to assume that Dave's client was Grady. We don't know that for sure, but it makes sense."

It made sense because Jane had passed on what she knew to Grady.

DeMarco said, "I suppose Dave could have been working for someone else, like he could have been working directly for Newman, but Newman's in Boston and he probably wouldn't know who Dave was. So what you're going to do is call Grady and tell him that you were the one who was really following Brian and that you recorded his calls. You're going to play him the call Brian made to the professor. You're going to say that you know

Dave got Brian's laptop from Grady. You're going to say that you know Grady hired Dave to break into Brian's place to get the flash drive. And you're going to say that you know that Grady had Brian and Dave killed and that you're going to tell the cops everything you know unless Grady pays you a shitload of money. Then one of three things will happen."

DeMarco said, "One, Grady denies everything and doesn't do anything. And if that happens, well, then we're screwed."

"I'm not going to stand for that," Sydney said.

DeMarco decided to ignore that comment. "Two is Grady pays you. If he does, we got him, because that proves he's guilty and the cops start squeezing him about the murders."

Sydney nodded.

DeMarco said, "Or three, Grady tries to have you whacked and we catch the guy who tries to kill you and he gives up Grady or Newman."

"We're going to catch the killer? You and me?"

"Oh, hell no," DeMarco said. "The cops are going to catch him. You're just going to be the bait."

They batted DeMarco's idea around for a while, DeMarco telling Sydney what he was going to do next. He said that they'd meet up again tomorrow after he saw some folks at the Capitol.

Sydney said, "Okay. I need to go find a motel room. The cops said I couldn't go back into my house until the forensics guys were finished, which probably won't be until tomorrow."

DeMarco said, "Why don't you spend the night here? I got an extra bedroom."

Sydney hesitated.

"Hey, if you're worried about me trying to, uh, take advantage of you—"

Sydney laughed, which DeMarco found somewhat insulting. "It's not that," she said. "I was thinking that a motel would have air-conditioning. What's wrong with your air conditioner, by the way?"

DeMarco told her how the compressor failed after less than two years and how it would be a couple of months before a new one was available. "This goddamn company said I should have gotten the extended warranty."

Sydney said, "Compressors don't usually go bad after only a couple of years. You probably have an electrical problem and there's nothing wrong with the compressor."

"You know anything about compressors?" he asked.

"Yeah, a little. Dave was a really handy guy. Our house doesn't look like much from the outside, because Dave didn't like to paint, but he could fix just about anything that broke, and he liked fixing things, and he taught me a lot." Sydney paused, probably thinking about the times she and Morgenthal had done things together. She looked out the window and said, "It's still light out. Why don't we go look at your air conditioner? You got a multimeter?"

"A multimeter?"

"A gizmo that measures current, voltage, resistance, those sorts of things."

"No, but my neighbor across the street probably does. He's a retired engineer that used to work for NASA."

"Go ask him if you can borrow it," Sydney said.

Ten minutes later, Sydney and DeMarco's neighbor—who DeMarco thought looked the way Jimmy Stewart would have looked if Stewart had been seventy years old and bald—were huddled around the air conditioner, ignoring DeMarco. They'd taken off a sheet metal cover that exposed the unit's wiring and were using the multimeter to measure whatever it measured.

"Yep," his neighbor said to Sydney. "That's the problem."

Sydney turned to DeMarco and said, "Come over here."

She pointed and said, "You see that little metal cylinder there with the three wires running to it?"

"Yeah," DeMarco said.

"That's a capacitor. That's what failed, not your compressor. A new one will cost you about forty bucks. Tomorrow while you're meeting with people, I'll go get you a new capacitor and install it. It'll take five minutes."

"I'm going to kill Rick," DeMarco said.

"Who's Rick?"

The next morning DeMarco woke up before Sydney and was dressed and ready to go to the Capitol to talk to Perry about his plan for Grady and to see if they could get the Capitol cops to cooperate. After Sydney had figured out the problem with his air conditioner, she changed her mind about spending the night, probably to save the money she'd have spent on a motel room. And after DeMarco moved the fan from his room into the spare bedroom and forced open a window that was stuck shut with old paint.

As he was having a cup of coffee, she sat in his kitchen, eating a bowl of Cheerios. He thought she looked so incredibly young without her makeup on and with her hair clean of gel from a shower and in disarray from sleeping. She looked like a little kid.

With her mouth full of cereal, she said, "By the way, who's Leah? When I was listening in on your calls, she called and said she wouldn't be able to see you because she had to go to Ohio and see her mother. She your girlfriend?"

"She'd like to be, but I'm not sure I'm ready to make the commitment."

"Are you, like, one of those confirmed bachelors?"

"No. I was married once. My wife had an affair with my cousin."

"Ouch. That had to hurt."

"Yeah."

"So why aren't you sure about Leah?"

DeMarco said, "Because I'm a coward. She's beautiful and she's bright and she's fun to be with but she has twin daughters from her first marriage. They're thirteen years old and I think they were spawned by Satan and they scare the hell out of me."

"Aw, I was probably like them at thirteen. They'll grow up."

"Yeah, and look how you turned out."

"Hey!"

"Anyway, I need to get going. And you'll fix the air conditioner while I'm gone?"

"Yeah. Me and the old guy across the street, who's dying to help out."

"Okay. I'll call you right after I talk to Perry and let you know if we're good to go or not."

40

Mahoney was back.

DeMarco learned this when he went to see Perry and was informed that he was in Mahoney's office, most likely briefing Mahoney on everything that had happened in D.C. while he'd been off cavorting with America's defenders.

Mahoney's last stop on his tour of military bases had been a remote outpost in Uganda. Mahoney had learned that Special Forces operators were going to assist the Ugandans in capturing a Somali warlord who was running around killing people and kidnapping young girls. He'd insisted on being in the command center during the operation so he could watch it via the body cameras the soldiers were wearing. A photo of Mahoney high-fiving a colonel after the warlord was reported dead had been published in the *Post*.

DeMarco figured that Mahoney being back could be good or bad when it came to catching Brian's killer. Mahoney could either use his influence to make folks do what DeMarco wanted or he could order DeMarco to do nothing because he didn't want to face the political backlash that would occur if Brian's report was made public. And if he ordered DeMarco to do nothing, DeMarco would have a hard decision to make. Should he or should he not disobey the order—which could cost him his job? On second thought, that wasn't a hard decision. He was going to keep going after Brian's killer whether Mahoney approved or not. The hard part would be finding a way to do it without Mahoney knowing what he'd done. Well, he'd cross that bridge when he came to it.

DeMarco told Mavis that he had to see Mahoney and Perry at the same time and that it was urgent. She told him to plant his ass in a chair and wait. While he was waiting, he asked her, "How's he doing?" Mavis, the guardian of all Mahoney's secrets, ignored the question—but DeMarco saw a small smile flit across her face.

Mavis's phone rang, and she picked it up, listened for a moment, and said something DeMarco couldn't hear. She hung up and said, "You can go in now. You got fifteen minutes."

"Yes, ma'am," DeMarco said.

Mahoney looked good. His eyes were clear, his complexion less florid. He seemed relaxed and not seething with the perpetual anger that had been boiling inside since he'd lost his job as Speaker. In fact, he looked as if he could have spent his time away from D.C. at a spa instead of sleeping in tents and eating mess hall chow. Spending time with people who literally put their lives on the line every day seemed to have put things in perspective.

He said, "Perry's told me about all the shit you've uncovered when it comes to Brian. He's told me about the kid's report and how Jane's been spilling her guts to Patrick Grady for years and how it looks like Carson Newman could have maybe hired someone to kill him. And he told me the flash drive story and how this guy Morgenthal was arrested. So you don't need to go over all that. Just tell me what you're planning to do next."

Before DeMarco could respond, Mahoney shook his big head and said, "That fucking Newman. I knew something was off when those guys all voted no, but it never occurred to me that Newman was involved, although it should have. I got a text message from him a few days after the bill failed saying, *How do you like them apples?* But I didn't know what the text meant at the time, and I didn't care, because there was so much other shit going on right before the midterms."

And probably because your brain was pickled with bourbon, DeMarco thought.

DeMarco said to Perry, "Did you tell him about Sydney?"

"No, I hadn't gotten to that part of the story yet," Perry said.

DeMarco told Mahoney about Sydney finding Morgenthal's body and his meeting with her, and how Sydney was the one who'd actually followed Brian and DeMarco. And how she was the one who'd passed off Brian's laptop to the barista.

"She stuck a gun in your face?" Mahoney said.

"Yeah, but I think she's all right. I actually kind of like her."

"So what do you wanna do?" Mahoney said.

"I want to use her to set up Grady."

DeMarco told Mahoney what he had in mind. When he finished, he said, "I know you probably don't want this to happen, but at some point, it's going to get out that this whole thing started with Brian looking at twelve congressmen who sold their votes. And the congressmen are all Democrats."

Mahoney didn't say anything. He pulled open the file drawer in his desk and stuck his big hand into it—and DeMarco knew he was reaching for the bottle of Maker's Mark he kept there. Then he surprised DeMarco by pulling his empty hand out of the drawer and turning around and picking up a carafe off the credenza behind his desk and pouring coffee, instead of bourbon, into his coffee cup. DeMarco knew that there was no way that Mahoney would remain alcohol-free, but at least for the moment, he was showing some restraint.

Then Mahoney surprised him a second time. He said, "You know something? I don't give a shit if the kid's report gets out and these twelve assholes are embarrassed. Or worse. If they'd shown some goddamn loyalty, then maybe I would, but they didn't." Looking at Perry, he said, "In fact, the way I want to spin this is that I had Brian doing what he did because I was trying to root out corruption in my own house."

Perry, who'd been sipping from his own coffee cup when Mahoney made this announcement, almost spit his coffee out. The idea of Mahoney as a crusader against political corruption was beyond his grasp. But all he said was, "I can make that happen."

DeMarco said, "I may need your help when it comes to the Capitol cops."

"Not a problem," the new and reformed John Mahoney said.

DeMarco had decided to use the Capitol Police to help him trap Grady, figuring that D.C. Metro might not be willing to play along but that the Capitol cops might, particularly if Mahoney was twisting their arms.

41

Mahoney said, "Bill, I'm hoping you can help me out here. This is important to me since it involves a kid who died while he was working for me."

William Foster, chief of the U.S. Capitol Police, reacted to this statement without commenting. Foster was a mountain of a man with a shaved head who reminded DeMarco of Anthony "Booger" McFarland, an NFL defensive tackle who won two Super Bowl rings. But Foster had never played football; in college, he'd carried the tuba in the marching band. Prior to becoming the head of the Capitol Police, he'd commanded the police department in Richmond, Virginia, and he had a law degree.

Mahoney said, "So I'd just like you listen to what DeMarco has to say and if you can assist him, I'd really appreciate it."

Mahoney knew he couldn't order Foster to do what he wanted, and he'd never be dumb enough to give him an order. If anything went wrong, DeMarco and Foster would get the blame and Mahoney could honestly say, under oath if necessary, that he hadn't been involved. He also knew that Foster owed him, as he'd been instrumental in getting him his current job.

"Now I gotta run to a meeting," Mahoney said.

———◆◆◆———

"So what does Mahoney want, DeMarco?" Foster said.

Foster knew who DeMarco was. He knew the official line that he was an independent lawyer who worked for Congress—and he knew the truth.

DeMarco said, "Mahoney doesn't want anything. What I want is your help in keeping a girl from getting killed."

DeMarco told Foster about Brian's report and what Sydney Roma and Dave Morgenthal had done and how Morgenthal had been arrested and killed. He concluded with, "I know Patrick Grady and Carson Newman are involved in Brian's death, but I can't prove it. What I want to do is use Sydney to threaten Grady and see what he does. And I'm guessing what he'll do is try to have her killed, and I want your cops to keep that from happening." He then told Foster what he planned to have Sydney say to Grady.

Foster rubbed his bald head for a moment. "D.C. Metro is going to be mighty pissed if I send a bunch of my cops into the city. That's their jurisdiction, not mine."

"I don't want to use D.C. Metro, because I want to keep this in house as much as possible."

Foster was bright enough to know that what DeMarco meant was that Mahoney thought he might be better able to control any political fallout if the Capitol cops were involved and not the city's police force.

DeMarco said, "And all your people will be doing is protecting someone who can help solve Brian's murder. And finding out what happened to him, a guy who used to work for Congress, definitely falls under your jurisdiction."

That was mostly bullshit, and Foster knew it, but he also knew it provided some rationale for his cops becoming involved.

Foster said, "Yeah, okay. But if Grady decides to give Sydney the money, we'll do the money exchange on the Capitol's grounds so there's no question when it comes to jurisdiction."

"That's fine," DeMarco said. Although he doubted there'd ever be a money exchange.

DeMarco looked at his watch. It was eleven a.m.

He said, "I'm going to have Sydney call Grady at four this afternoon. That gives you five hours to put a net around her. And my guess is that if Grady tries to have her killed, it will happen tomorrow night."

Tomorrow was a Friday.

42

A woman with a British accent told Sydney that Mr. Grady wasn't available.

Sydney said, "You tell him that I was Dave Morgenthal's partner and he better call me back before I call the cops."

"I beg your pardon?" the woman said.

"Here's my number," Sydney said.

Sydney was sitting with DeMarco and Celeste Honoré in DeMarco's kitchen—and Celeste was somewhat pissed at DeMarco.

Her boss, William Foster, hadn't known about her role in helping DeMarco get a photo of Sydney and helping him arrest Morgenthal when Morgenthal broke into Brian's apartment. For one thing, DeMarco and Perry had asked her not to tell anyone. The other thing was that she'd been on her own time the night Morgenthal was arrested, and she'd figured that her part in nabbing a guy for breaking into an apartment in one of the poorer parts of D.C. wouldn't get any media attention—which it hadn't—and therefore her boss would never know what she'd done. But when DeMarco asked that she be assigned as part of the team to protect

Sydney, Foster had asked him how he knew Celeste, and DeMarco made the mistake of telling Foster what she'd done—which resulted in Celeste getting her ass royally chewed by Foster for working outside the chain of command. Fortunately, Foster liked Celeste and she was one of his best officers, and in the end he'd agreed to DeMarco's request, and Celeste was glad he agreed because she wanted to help catch a killer. DeMarco also didn't tell Sydney that Celeste was the one who arrested Dave; he didn't want Sydney holding that against her.

Sydney's phone rang. She said, "It's him."

She hit the speaker icon so DeMarco and Celeste could listen in on the call and they heard Grady say, "Who are you?"

"Like I told your secretary, I was Dave Morgenthal's partner."

"What's your name?"

"You don't need to know my name. All you need to know is—"

"You're lying. Morgenthal didn't have a partner. His partner died years ago."

"That was his old partner. You see, Dave had cancer and was getting chemo, and because of that, he needed help. And I'm the one who helped him. I'm the one who followed Brian Lewis and Joe DeMarco."

"I don't believe you."

"I'm going to play you a recording of Lewis talking to a law professor at UVA named Adam Lang."

Sydney hit another icon on her phone, and they all heard Brian say, "Professor Lang, it's Brian Lewis."

Grady didn't interrupt as Brian went on to tell Lang that some politicians had been bribed and that he needed Lang's advice.

When the recording finished, Sydney said, "I know you're the one who hired Dave because, like I said, I worked with him and he told me. I know Dave sent you that recording. I know you're the one who arranged for Dave to get Lewis's laptop and I know you're the one who hired him to break into Lewis's apartment to get the flash drive that DeMarco said was there. Right now, the cops are trying to figure out who killed Dave and Lewis, but they don't know about you. But they will find out about you if you don't give me what I want. And, by the way, I'm the one who found Dave's body, so I'm already talking to the cops."

"And what do you want?" Grady asked.

"I don't know who you were working for when it came to Lewis, but I know that all your clients are people and corporations worth billions, maybe trillions. So what I'm saying is, I know you can easily spare a million bucks, which is what I want. I want a million bucks. In cash."

DeMarco had told Sydney to ask for an outrageous amount of money, thinking that would make it even more likely that Grady would try to have her killed.

Grady didn't say anything.

"Now I know it takes a while to round up that much in cash, so I'll give you forty-eight hours. But at four p.m. the day after tomorrow, I'll be sitting on a bench near the entrance to the Botanic Garden by the Capitol. You'll bring the money yourself. It should fit in one of them rolling carry-on bags. You don't know what I look like, but I know what you look like. And I'm picking the garden because there will be a lot of people there and if you decide to send the guy who shot Dave instead of bringing me my money, he'll have a hard time pulling that off without getting caught."

Grady still didn't say anything.

"All right. I'm guessing you're not talking because you don't want to admit to anything, and you think I might be recording this call. But that's okay. I don't need you to say anything. I just need you to be there with the money, and if you don't come, I'm going to the cops. That's a promise."

DeMarco had told Sydney not to tell Grady her name, because he didn't want to make it too easy for Grady. He said all she had to say was that she'd found Dave's body and Grady, with his connections, would be able to identify her. And once he'd identified her, he'd be able to find out where she lived because the address on her driver's license was also Morgenthal's address.

And that's where DeMarco figured they'd try to kill her.

43

At six p.m., Celeste, armed with a pistol and a shotgun, was sitting with Sydney inside Morgenthal's house. The Capitol Police's protective cordon was in place outside the house.

DeMarco figured that nothing would happen that night. It would take Grady some time to figure out who Sydney was and where she lived, and then Grady or Newman would have to dispatch someone to kill her. So he figured nothing would happen Thursday night, and most likely nothing would happen during the day on Friday. He believed that if they tried to kill her, it would happen after dark on Friday. But if they did try to kill Sydney Thursday night or during the day on Friday, Foster's cops were ready.

Morgenthal's house sat in the middle of the block. The house had a detached one-car garage, but Morgenthal had never put his car in it because he stored things there and used the garage as a workshop. The entrance to the garage was down a narrow alley that ran behind the house. The backyard was surrounded by a five-foot-high chain-link fence. An unlocked gate in the fence led to the alley.

The Capitol cops thought that what the killer would most likely do was wait until the wee hours of the morning. He'd walk down the alley and through the backyard gate and enter through the back door, which was what they suspected he'd done when he'd killed Morgenthal. But to reach the back door, he'd have to walk past the garage. So two cops were stationed inside the garage and they had a view of the back door through holes they'd drilled through the walls. In a beat-up van parked on the street near the house, two cops watched a monitor that showed the feed from a night-vision camera pointing at the alley. There were four more cops in unmarked cars, lurking in the neighborhood, looking for anyone casing the house, and these cops would descend on the house if anything happened. All these officers were SWAT trained and armed to the teeth.

Thursday evening, Sydney stayed in the house. She made herself visible by walking several times past the front windows. When it got dark, she turned on all the lights in the house. At eleven she turned off the lights to give the appearance that she'd gone to bed. The following day, she again made herself visible through the windows, so in case anyone was watching, they'd know she was home. She went out onto the porch a couple of times, while wearing a bulletproof vest under an extra-large T-shirt, and pretended to talk on her phone.

Sydney's guardians saw only one person who might have been casing the house. It was a fat man walking a dog. The guy let the dog take a dump on the sidewalk in front of Sydney's place, and while the dog was doing its business, he appeared to be studying the house. And it seemed as if he took an inordinate amount of time before he continued on his way. So one of the cops followed him. It turned out that he lived two blocks away. Using his address to ID him, the cop did a criminal record check and learned that the dog walker had a conviction for burglary, but the conviction was ten years old. How he currently supported himself was unknown. And although it was unlikely that he was a professional killer, two cops were dispatched from the Capitol to watch him.

While waiting for something to happen, Sydney chatted with Celeste. She learned that Celeste had been raised in a parish outside of New Orleans and that her mother had been a maid and that her father took care of rich people's yards. She'd decided the best way out of poverty was to join the military and had spent four years in the army as an MP. She'd ended up in D.C. because she wanted to work for the feds—FBI, ATF, U.S. Marshals, agencies that arrested major criminals and occasionally got into gunfights—but had to settle for a position with the Capitol Police when the other agencies didn't immediately hire her. When Sydney asked her how she liked the army, Celeste told her that mostly what she did was guard prisoners and arrest drunks but there had been a couple of times in Afghanistan when she'd ended up in unplanned firefights with the Taliban. She said, "Now I can tell you that that got my heart pumping, but most of the time it was pretty boring."

When Sydney mentioned that she was giving some thought to seeing if the military would let her fly choppers, Celeste said, "Now that would be cool."

While the cops were watching over Sydney, DeMarco sat in his now wonderfully cool house waiting impatiently for something to happen. He wanted to be with the cops protecting Sydney, but William Foster, head of the Capitol cops, wouldn't allow that. Foster had said that if there was a gunfight, all DeMarco would do was get in the way and maybe get himself shot. So he piddled around the house. He mopped his kitchen floor, something he did maybe every three months. He changed the filter in his furnace. He cleaned his golf clubs.

One other thing he did was speak to Rick.

Rick hadn't returned his previous calls, but this time, when DeMarco left a voice mail saying he was canceling his order for a new compressor, Rick called him back.

DeMarco told Rick that a twenty-three-year-old girl had figured out that there wasn't anything wrong with the compressor and that all that was needed to fix the air conditioner was a new capacitor, which the girl installed. Rick's response after being accused of incompetence—and possibly fraud—was, "Well, okay, I'll cancel the order, but you're going to have to pay a restocking fee for the compressor."

"How the fuck can that be?" DeMarco screamed. "You said it wouldn't get here for a couple of months. You said they had to build a new one."

"They must have built one and moved it to someplace for shipping. So you gotta pay a hundred-and-fifty-buck restocking fee. It'll be deducted from the money you paid for the compressor."

"I know where you live, Rick," DeMarco said, even though he didn't.

"Well, I know where you live, too," Rick said.

Seeing Rick clearly wasn't intimidated by him, DeMarco was thinking that after this thing with Sydney was over with, he'd see if he could get Celeste to pay Rick a visit.

Friday night came. Because of the heat, Sydney's neighbors were out in their yards or sitting on their porches. Kids were running around all over the place. The neighborhood got quiet at one in the morning, and Sydney's guardians became particularly vigilant.

At two a.m., one of the Capitol cops sitting in a car at one end of the block said into his radio, "This is Carter. I got two guys in a black Jeep Cherokee moving down the block at about ten miles an hour."

A couple of minutes later, Carter said, "They didn't stop at Sydney's place. They're still creeping down the block. They're looking for something, but I don't know what."

A moment later: "They just turned the corner. I'm taking off after them."

"Don't turn on your headlights," Celeste said.

"I won't," Carter said.

"If they turn down the alley, I want everyone ready to move," Celeste said.

Carter said, "They didn't turn down the alley. They're moving on to the next block."

The radio was silent for a couple of minutes.

Carter said, "They stopped in front of a house on the next block. One of them is out of the car. He just rolled under another car."

"What's he doing?" Celeste asked.

"I don't know," Carter said. Five minutes passed.

"He just stole the catalytic converter off the car," Carter said.

"Well, shit," Celeste said. "Get his license plate and the license of the car they hit. But let 'em go on their way. We'll let D.C. Metro know about them tomorrow."

———◆———

DeMarco lay in bed, unable to sleep, expecting the phone to ring any minute telling him that the Capitol cops had nabbed a guy trying to kill Sydney.

At two a.m., he heard a noise outside. It came from his backyard.

He wondered if he'd gotten everything wrong.

He wondered if he'd made himself a target.

He slipped out of bed and, without turning on the lights, picked up an old sand wedge he kept under the bed.

DeMarco didn't own a gun. He didn't like guns. He'd always thought that guns were like throwing a forward pass in football, where three things could happen, only one of which was good. The pass could be caught—the good thing—or it could be dropped, or it could be intercepted. It was the same with guns. You could shoot a bad guy, you could shoot a good guy, or you could shoot yourself. But this was one of those times he wished he had a gun.

He crept to a window where he could see his backyard, parted the blinds with his fingers, and looked out.

Raccoons. Three of them.

They'd knocked over his garbage can.

At eight a.m., Sydney called DeMarco.

"Nothing happened," she said. "Now what?"

DeMarco could hear the frustration in her voice, the same frustration he was feeling.

"Stick to the plan," DeMarco said. "You show up at the Botanic Garden just before four o'clock and we see if Grady brings you the money."

Sydney would be escorted to the garden by half a dozen cops in unmarked cars looking for anyone following her and would be prepared if anyone tried anything while she was on her way there. When she reached the garden, these same cops, in civilian clothes, would stay close to her while uniformed Capitol cops patrolled the area as they normally did.

"Do you really think he's going to bring the money?" Sydney asked.

"I don't know," DeMarco said. The truth was, he didn't.

Grady and/or Newman had apparently decided to do nothing—in which case they'd probably get away with everything they'd done.

DeMarco's phone rang again. It was Perry Wallace.

Perry said, "Did you hear?"

"Hear what?"

"Patrick Grady's dead."

44

Lev Belushi sat at the departure gate in Reagan National chatting with a young mother and her little girl. He'd told the woman that he had four daughters of his own, adding that a man can't have too many daughters. He'd learned that the woman was flying to Boston to see her mother, who was having a knee replaced and needed someone to care for her—which proved Lev's point that a daughter would always be there for her parents. Sons, maybe not so much.

It had been a good year, thanks to the three jobs he'd performed for Mr. Yellowstone—the last one had paid particularly well—and Lev was thinking he might take his family on a cruise, maybe one of those Alaska cruises that departed from Seattle or Vancouver. He'd never been to Alaska but was certain that the scenery would be magnificent and the temperature cooler than in Boston. And he'd book first-class accommodations for his wife and daughters, at least two suites with balconies so they could better enjoy the views.

Yes, he'd executed his assignments flawlessly and he and his family deserved to be rewarded. Morgenthal had been simple, but the Lewis kid and Patrick Grady had posed some challenges and taken some imagination.

When Newman had called and asked for another meeting, Lev had been astounded. It had only been a couple of days since he'd dealt with Morgenthal. But when Newman told him that Grady had to be dealt with in less than forty-eight hours, he told Newman he wouldn't agree to such a deadline. He said, "One of the reasons I don't get caught, Mr. Yellowstone, is that I take my time and don't act until I'm certain I can be successful."

Newman said, "I'll double what I paid you for the last two jobs."

So he took the assignment even though he didn't like rushing things. And in the end, it worked out okay, although that one small thing that happened still bothered him.

Lev had arrived in D.C. on Friday about eleven a.m., rented a car, and drove to Grady's house. He knew from Newman that Grady had an office in D.C. and where it was located and that he might be able to kill Grady in the lot where he parked his car or going to or from work. He thought his best option, however, was to do as he'd done with Morgenthal and break into Grady's house late at night and take care of him there. The only problem with killing Grady in his home was that the man was married, and if he killed him there, he'd most likely have to kill his wife as well. If Newman had given him more time, he might have been able to come up with a more creative solution than a home invasion, but as he didn't have the time, that would have to do.

Grady's house sat on a large lot in an affluent neighborhood in Arlington, Virginia. His neighbors' houses were barely visible from Grady's place, thanks to plants and hedges and fences. Behind the houses on Grady's block was a large green space, a small forest that, for whatever reason, had been preserved and not cut down to build more homes. Lev decided to take a look at the back side of Grady's place and drove around and found a parking lot and a walking trail that led into the green space.

Lev strolled into the forest, moving at a leisurely pace, dressed casually in shorts and a T-shirt and his floppy tennis hat. Just a fat man going for a walk. He wished he had a dog. From the forest, he could see that Grady's backyard was surrounded by a seven-foot stone wall. In fact, all his neighbors had identical backyard stone walls; there was probably a homeowners' association that required that. In Grady's wall was a black, wrought iron gate; it was only about four feet tall, and it could be scaled easily if it was locked. But he could only see a small portion of the back-yard through the gate from where he was standing, and the high stone wall prevented him from seeing the entire yard and the back of the house.

He searched for a tree he might be able to scale so he could look over the wall and saw an oak a few yards off the path he was on. It had a couple of low-hanging branches that would support his weight. He walked through low brush and over to the tree—and heard something snap.

He spun his head in the direction of the sound but didn't see anyone. He wondered if a squirrel or a raccoon or whatever critters inhabited Virginia's forests had broken a branch or stepped on a twig or a dry leaf, but he didn't see anything moving in the nearby bushes. He stayed still for several seconds to see if the sound would repeat itself, but it didn't.

He reached the oak. It wasn't easy for a man of his bulk to do it, but he pulled himself up the tree and then stood on one of the low branches. From the branch, he could see all of Grady's backyard. There was a swimming pool, a patio with lounge chairs, a table shaded by an umbrella, and a large barbecue. A sliding glass door permitted entry to the house from the patio.

He was thinking he might be able to enter the house by using a glass cutter to cut a hole in the sliding glass door and unlatch it, but then saw a much better option. Grady's two-car garage was attached to the house. If he could get inside the garage, he'd be able to get into the house, and the garage had a back door that led to the backyard. What he could do was pick the lock on the garage door, as he'd picked the locks at Lewis's and Morgenthal's places, but if he couldn't pick it, the garage door was far enough from the living areas in the house that he could force it open with a crowbar and without anyone sleeping in the house hearing him.

He climbed down from the tree and went back to his car and thought about a murder weapon. He didn't have a gun, because he couldn't travel with one on a plane, and he'd thrown away the gun he'd used to kill Morgenthal. He could contact the man who'd provided him with a weapon last time but wasn't sure the man could get him one before nightfall. God, he hated this job being so rushed. He decided that when he went to a hardware store to buy a small crowbar, he'd also buy a knife. A knife would do. Or for that matter, so would the crowbar.

He visualized how he would do the job. He'd wait until the early morning hours. He'd creep silently through the forest—he might need a small flashlight to guide him—and climb over the back gate if the gate was locked. He'd pick open the garage back door or force it open with the crowbar. If the door that led from the garage to the house was locked, he'd do the same thing. Then he'd creep silently through the house to find the master bedroom—and stab Grady and his wife while they were sleeping, stabbing Grady first, then the woman. It would be brutal, and it would be bloody, but he was fast, and he was strong, and he had no doubt he could pull it off.

After he killed them, he'd ransack the house and steal a few things small enough to fit into a shopping bag. He'd bring a change of clothes with him in the shopping bag and change his clothes afterward because there was bound to be blood on them. He'd also wash his arms and face and use paper towels to dry off and take the towels with him. In the unlikely event that someone saw him after the killings, it wouldn't do for him to be covered in blood. Then he'd throw away everything he stole, except for any cash he found, and get rid of the knife, the crowbar, and his bloody clothes. Yes, it was doable.

He found a hardware store a few miles from Grady's house, bought what he needed, and checked into a motel. As he hadn't eaten since he'd arrived in Washington, he walked over to a diner near the motel and had a nice meatloaf dinner followed by a slice of apple pie. At seven p.m., he drove back to Grady's house and parked half a block away. He wouldn't stay parked in that spot for very long.

It would be several hours before he killed Grady, but because the job was so rushed, and because he was a cautious man, he wanted to check out the house for a second time and the forest behind it to see if he needed to change his plan in any way. He hadn't seen any security cameras on the exterior of the house the first time he'd examined it, but he wanted to check again to be sure. Cameras these days were small. After he'd done that, he'd return to the motel to take a nap and then come back around midnight. As he was sitting there, a Mercedes pulled into Grady's garage. The person driving the Mercedes was Grady. Good. Newman had told him that Grady would be home tonight, but now he was sure.

He examined the eaves of the house and the area near the front porch and still didn't see any cameras. He did see an ADT sign, indicating that Grady's home had a security system, but he wasn't concerned about that. Most people don't alarm their security systems when they're home. He was just about to drive to the parking lot near the forest and look at the back of the house one more time when the garage door opened and a Lexus backed out. A woman was driving. Lev had found a picture of Grady online but hadn't seen a picture of his wife. He assumed that the woman in the Lexus was her.

He didn't know where Mrs. Grady was going, or how long she'd be gone, but if he acted quickly, he might be able to take care of Grady without having to kill his wife. Even though it was still daylight, the house was secluded, and as Grady's neighbors had backyard stone walls just as Grady did, they wouldn't be able to see him approaching Grady's house from the woods unless they happened to be looking out a second-story window. And once he was in Grady's backyard, they definitely wouldn't be able to see him.

He drove to the parking lot near the forest, parked his car, and headed into the forest. He had the folding knife he'd purchased in one pocket of his cargo shorts and his lockpicks in another pocket. The twelve-inch crowbar was in a back pocket, under his T-shirt, pressing uncomfortably against his back. In his right hand was the shopping bag holding his change of clothes. He didn't know if he was going to do anything, but he wanted to be prepared.

He took the same trail into the forest he'd taken last time and walked directly toward the gate in the stone wall—and through the gate, to his surprise, he saw Grady sitting by the pool. He was dressed in swimming trunks—he must have changed into them as soon as he got home—and sitting in a lounge chair holding a glass of wine and smoking a cigar. On the table next to his lounge chair was a bottle of wine.

Lev looked around—he didn't see anyone other than Grady—and he decided: *Why not?*

He dropped the shopping bag on the ground—he'd retrieve it when he finished—and walked up to Grady's backyard gate. He could see the gate was latched but not locked, and all he had to do was reach over the gate to unlatch it. Had it been locked he would have had to convince Grady to come to the gate to talk to him—and stab him when he did—but now that wouldn't be necessary.

From this point on, he needed to move decisively. He unlatched the gate and stepped into the yard. Grady saw him immediately and put down his wineglass and rose from the lounge chair. Lev was hoping that Grady would think he was harmless: a smiling fat man wearing a floppy tennis hat, a baggy green T-shirt, and cargo shorts. And Grady didn't look alarmed. He just looked annoyed.

Grady said, "Who are you?"

Lev said, "I'm so sorry to disturb you."

As he spoke, Lev continued forward, going around the pool toward Grady, who was standing by the lounge chair. Still smiling, and hopefully looking a bit stupid as well as harmless, he said, "I'm looking for my dog. He ran into the woods." He pointed at the woods behind him. He kept moving toward Grady. "He's a little gray schnauzer. Have you seen him?" He wanted to get close enough to Grady so that if Grady bolted, he could catch him before he ran into the house and locked a door. But Grady, who struck Lev as an arrogant prick, didn't run. He said, "No, I haven't seen your damn dog. You can't see the woods from here."

By now Lev was only about six feet from Grady. "That's okay," Lev said—and pulled the knife from his pocket and flicked it open.

"What the fuck?" Grady shrieked. He turned to run but Lev was on him quickly. Lev was like most NFL linemen; he could cover short distances at an astonishing speed. He threw a big arm around Grady's throat and held him and pressed the blade to his neck. He was about to plunge the blade into Grady's carotid artery, but then he didn't. Sitting next to Grady's lounge chair was a large metal ashtray; Grady's cigar was in it. The ashtray was made of cast iron and looked heavy.

Lev said, "Mr. Grady, I don't want to hurt you. I just want to talk to you. But if you scream, I will kill you. Now what I want you to do is sit back down. I don't want to have to worry about you trying to run. So sit back down and I'll tell you what I need to know."

He loosened his grip on Grady's throat and pushed Grady toward the lounge chair, and Grady slowly sat down. And as soon as he did, Lev dropped the knife and picked up the ashtray—Grady's cigar went flying—and hit Grady hard on the forehead with the ashtray.

Grady wasn't knocked unconscious, but he was stunned. And when Lev pulled him from the lounge chair and dragged him over to the edge of the pool, he didn't resist. Lev laid him facedown on the ground and grabbed him by the hair and smashed his forehead against the edge of the pool. He hit Grady's head in the same spot where he'd hit it with the ashtray. Then he rolled Grady into the pool and held his head under the water for a couple of minutes.

Lev picked up the knife, put it back in his pocket, then used his T-shirt to wipe his fingerprints and Grady's blood off the ashtray. He found Grady's cigar on the pool tiles, where it had landed, and put it back in the ashtray. The cigar was still burning. He grabbed the wine bottle—which was two-thirds full—using the hem of his T-shirt to avoid leaving prints, poured the wine into a nearby bush, put the bottle back on the table near Grady's chair, then broke Grady's wineglass near the spot where he'd tossed Grady into the pool. Grady, by now, was on the bottom of the pool; a small amount of blood was leaking from his forehead into the water. His eyes were wide open.

Lev was hoping the police would think that Grady had drunk a full bottle of wine, slipped as he was walking, hit his head on the edge of the pool, then fell into the water and drowned. If they didn't conclude that his death was an accident, that was okay, but it would be better if they did, as then they wouldn't start hunting for a killer.

Lev used his T-shirt to unlatch the back gate and wipe his prints off the latch, and stepped through the gate. He looked around. He didn't see anyone. Moving quickly now, he walked back into the woods and toward his car, picking up his shopping bag on the way. When he returned to the motel, he might go to the same diner where he'd had dinner and have another piece of pie. The pie he'd had earlier had been excellent. Then he'd get a good night's sleep and catch a plane back to Boston in the morning.

All in all, a good day's work.

And his reward would be a wonderful cruise with his family.

The only thing that bothered him was that snap he'd heard before he climbed the tree. It hadn't sounded like a noise an animal would make. It had sounded . . . mechanical?

45

Carson Newman was sitting by *his* swimming pool.

He was at his beach cottage on the Cape, enjoying the cooling breeze coming off the water as he watched the sunset. The clouds were shades of red and pink, and he remembered the old saying "Red sky at morning, sailors take warning. Red sky at night, sailors' delight."

And it was delight he was feeling because a few minutes ago he'd received a text message on his burner phone saying: *Transaction complete.*

Patrick Grady was dead.

The whole Lewis fiasco—and it had been a fiasco; he never should have had the damn kid killed—was finally over with.

When Grady had told him that Morgenthal had been arrested and was trying to blackmail them, it was obvious that Morgenthal had to go. And Carson had thought that with Morgenthal gone, that would be the end of it. But then it wasn't. From out of nowhere comes a second blackmailer, Morgenthal's partner, a person that idiot Grady hadn't known existed.

Grady had called him in a panic, telling him about Morgenthal's partner and how she knew that Grady had given Morgenthal Lewis's laptop. When Grady said the woman was demanding a million dollars or she'd go to the cops, he'd told Carson that the woman had to be dealt with, and in the next forty-eight hours. Meaning, he expected Carson to deal with her the same way he'd dealt with Morgenthal.

He initially agreed with Grady. There was no way they were going to give her a million, and even if they gave her a million, there was no guarantee that she wouldn't try to blackmail them again. And even if they paid her, she still might talk. But then Carson realized that if the woman was gone, there were still two people who knew his role in killing Lewis and Morgenthal. One of those people was the killer. The other was Patrick Grady. And it wasn't the killer who worried him.

No, the woman wasn't the problem. Grady was the problem. Grady was the linchpin. Everything that had happened with Lewis had gone through Grady. Grady was the one who'd hired the detective to follow Lewis; Grady was the one who'd wiped the laptop; it was Grady who had given Morgenthal the laptop. And if the woman talked to the cops, she would incriminate Grady and there might even be evidence that Grady had paid Morgenthal.

But there was nothing tying him, Carson Newman, to anything that had happened to Lewis or Morgenthal. He hadn't had any contact with either of them. People might suspect that Grady was working for him when it came to Lewis, but they'd never be able to prove it—unless Grady talked. And in the future, even if Morgenthal's partner was dead, Grady still might talk. And he would definitely talk to get a better deal for himself if the cops could prove that Grady was in any way responsible for the deaths of Lewis or Morgenthal or Morgenthal's partner.

Yes, it was Grady who had to go, not the blackmailer.

And now Grady was gone.

Red sky at night, sailors' delight.

46

"So what are you going to do about Newman?"

Three people had asked DeMarco this question: John Mahoney, Perry Wallace, and Sydney Roma.

They all knew, even though it couldn't be proved, that Carson Newman was behind what had happened to Brian, Morgenthal, and Grady—and somehow, bringing Newman to justice had become DeMarco's problem.

And DeMarco knew he needed to do something, because if he didn't, Sydney would. Her exact words had been: "I'll kill that son of a bitch before I let him get away with killing Dave." DeMarco didn't care if someone killed Newman, but he didn't want it to be Sydney. He'd come to care about her, and he didn't want to see her ruin her life.

Finally, he concluded there was only one thing he could do when it came to Newman.

He had to tell the cops everything he knew.

Right now, the cops didn't have the full story. In fact, the cops might not even know that the deaths of Brian, Morgenthal, and Grady were connected. According to the media, Grady's death had been an accident: he'd gotten drunk, fallen, hit his head, and fell into his swimming pool. But the cops investigating his death had no idea that DeMarco had used Sydney as bait to force Grady's and Newman's hands. And according to

Sydney, the cop investigating Morgenthal's death didn't appear to know that Morgenthal and Brian were connected, although Olivetti knew this. And none of the cops knew about Brian's report, because DeMarco hadn't shared the report with them.

Yes, the only way to get the Carson Newman monkey off his back was to transfer the monkey to the cops.

DeMarco called Olivetti and said they needed to talk. He didn't want to try to deal with three different detectives. He'd let Olivetti take the lead when it came to deciding how D.C. Metro's bureaucracy would handle things internally. But Olivetti said he couldn't meet during the day, that it would have to wait until after he got off work, and DeMarco couldn't convince him to change his schedule. Actually, he didn't try that hard to convince him, because he wanted Olivetti's help.

They met at five in a bar called Tony's, a couple of blocks from Olivetti's office. DeMarco arrived first. The bar was on a corner with a view of nothing, as all the windows were covered with neon beer signs and city grime so you couldn't see out. There were only three customers in the place: two old men sitting at a table playing cribbage and a woman at the bar wearing a sweater and a stocking cap on a hundred-degree day, drinking and muttering to herself. Behind a long bar were pull handles for dispensing twenty different kinds of beer, shelves stacked with booze, and a bald-headed bartender wearing a sleeveless T-shirt that exposed the hairiest shoulders DeMarco had ever seen.

DeMarco ordered a plain old Budweiser in a bottle; he'd never been into all the exotic brews. He'd just taken a sip from it when Olivetti walked in. He saw DeMarco and walked over to him. "You want a drink?" DeMarco asked, and then, knowing that Olivetti wasn't going to be happy with him after they talked, added, "It's on me."

Olivetti ordered some beer that DeMarco had never heard of and that cost twice as much as DeMarco's Bud. They took seats at a rickety table that was some distance from the bar and the cribbage players.

Olivetti said, "So, what is it you've got to tell me? And by the way, I only have half an hour. I need to get to my daughter's softball game."

DeMarco was thinking that after he briefed Olivetti, Olivetti might not make the game.

DeMarco told him everything. He told him about Brian's report that pointed at Grady and Newman conspiring to influence the votes of twelve congressman. He told him about Jane being Grady's source. He told him about Sydney, who, while working for Morgenthal, followed him and Brian. When he told him about using Sydney and the Capitol cops to try to set a trap for Grady, Olivetti's response was, "Are you fucking shitting me?"

DeMarco concluded with, "I can't prove that Newman or Grady hired someone to kill Brian and Morgenthal. Nor can I prove that Newman hired someone to kill Grady, but I think that's what happened."

"Can I get a copy of Lewis's report?"

"Probably, but you'll have to ask Mahoney. The thing about the report is, it doesn't prove that Newman committed a crime. All it shows is that people who work for him, or who he knows, made contributions to these congressmen and did a bunch of shady things to influence their vote, but Newman won't go to jail for bribing anyone."

"Then why would he kill the kid?"

"Because he didn't know what the report said at the time he had him killed."

"And why would Newman have Grady killed?"

"I don't know, but I'm guessing it was because he was worried that Grady might implicate him in the murders of Brian and Morgenthal."

"Well, shit, DeMarco. What do you expect me to do with this mess?"

"You need to assume that Grady was murdered and investigate his death as a homicide, and you need to accept that Brian, Morgenthal, and Grady dying are all connected. And what you really need to do is find out if Newman hired someone to kill these people."

"And how in the fuck am I supposed to do that?"

"I don't know," DeMarco said. And he didn't. "But you got a whole police force that can help you, and you can get warrants to look at phone calls and bank accounts and whatever else cops do to catch killers."

Olivetti shook his head, then glanced at his watch. "Thanks to you springing all this bullshit on me, I'm going to have to call about a dozen people and miss my kid's game. And if I can find some way to hang an obstruction of justice charge on you for withholding all this information from me, I'm going to do it."

As Olivetti was leaving, DeMarco thought, *I should have let him pay for his own beer.*

DeMarco called Mahoney and told him that D.C. Metro might be coming to him to ask for a copy of Brian's report. Mahoney said, "That's fine. But what the hell are you doing about Budnick? Did you hear what that prick did yesterday?"

DeMarco had forgotten all about Budnick. "No, what did he do now?"

"He went to Chan's home last night, even though she's got a restraining order against him—"

Emily Chan was the congresswoman who'd fired Budnick.

"—and stood on her front porch screaming that she'd fired him because he'd been planning to expose her as a Chinese spy. He scared the hell out of her kids."

Mahoney concluded with: "This guy needs to be taken off the board. Do your goddamn job."

———————◆◆◆———————

DeMarco called Sydney and told her about his meeting with Olivetti. "What we need to do now is give the cops some time to see what they can come up with."

"How much time?"

"I don't know, Sydney, but at least a few weeks. They're investigating three homicides and one of the suspects is one of the richest guys in Boston. And he doesn't live in their jurisdiction, and if the cops try to get a warrant to look at his phone records or anything else, his lawyers will put up a fight. So it'll take some time."

"Do you think they'll be able to prove Newman did anything?"

"I don't know," DeMarco said. "But they've got trained investigators and CSI guys and a battalion of lawyers who will certainly be able to do a lot more than you and I can."

"Okay," Sydney said. "I gotta deal with Dave, figure out where to bury him and all that. And I need to deal with his will. He left me some money and I'm going to need it. And I have to sell his house, which is now my house. He was paying a mortgage I can't afford, but if I can sell the house, I'll make a profit and be able to pay off the mortgage and have a bit left over. So I got a bunch of shit to deal with, but at some point, if the cops don't do anything, I will."

"Sydney, I'm telling you, you need to walk away from this thing. If you don't, you're just going to end up destroying yourself."

"Well, I'm not walking away."

DeMarco shook his head, a gesture Sydney couldn't see over the phone. "If you need some help when it comes Dave's arrangements or the will, let me know and I'll see what I can do. But the main thing you need to do is focus on the future, not the past. You need to figure out what you're going to do with your life now that Dave is gone."

47

DeMarco was surprised when Olivetti called him only three days later.

DeMarco had told Mahoney that he was in hot pursuit of Karl Budnick, but he still had no intention of doing anything. If Budnick had been arrested for violating a restraining order and was making insane accusations that his former boss, Congressman Emily Chan—who was a veteran and came from a third-generation San Francisco family—was a Chinese spy, it was apparent that Budnick was close to destroying himself, as DeMarco had predicted. So he wasn't doing anything when it came to Budnick, and as he had nothing better to do, he was playing golf.

He was playing with a guy named Marty Hobbs, who was built like a beer barrel with feet but had a six handicap. There were four or five guys he played with frequently, but he played most often with Hobbs because all the other men had regular jobs and they could normally play only on weekends. Hobbs, too, had a regular job. He was a number cruncher for the Commerce Department, but during the pandemic he'd been allowed to work from home, and after most folks had gone back to the office, he'd managed to convince his boss to let him continue working from home. DeMarco had no idea when Hobbs did his job; all he knew was that since he'd started telecommuting, he was almost always available to play.

They were playing for five bucks a hole, and to Hobbs's delight, DeMarco had just sliced his drive into the trees on the right side of the fairway. He was now trying to decide if he should chip out into the fairway or try to hit his ball in between two trees that were only about one foot apart. The smart play was, of course, to just accept that he was going to lose a stroke and chip it into the fairway, but if he could hit it between the trees, he could reach the green in regulation and have a chance at par. The problem was, if he hit one of the two trees, the ball was going to bounce back, maybe hit him in the face, and he'd lose another stroke trying to get out of the trees. So should he make the smart play or pretend that he was Jordan Spieth? He'd just decided to pretend that he was Jordan when his phone rang.

Olivetti said, "You need to get your ass down to the Hoover Building."

"The Hoover Building?"

"Yeah. The FBI is taking over the case."

"The FBI?"

"Quit repeating every fuckin' thing I say. Be at the Hoover Building at three. I'll meet you there. We'll be meeting with an agent named Ransom."

"Ransom?" DeMarco said.

Olivetti was waiting in the lobby of the Hoover Building when DeMarco arrived. When Olivetti saw him, he said, "Is that the way you dress for work?"

DeMarco had come straight from the golf course and was still wearing a sweat-soaked golf shirt and shorts. He said, "I was telecommuting today."

They were given visitors' badges and escorted to a conference room on the third floor. A moment later in walked a woman in her forties wearing a black pantsuit and an open-collar white blouse. She was holding a manila file folder in one hand. She was about DeMarco's height, almost six feet, but probably weighed only 130 pounds. If she had an ounce of fat on her, it wasn't visible. She had dark hair streaked with gray tied back in a tight bun, a high forehead, a pointy nose, and a pointy chin. DeMarco thought that by the time she was sixty, she'd look like the witch who wanted to eat Hansel and Gretel.

She said, "I'm Special Agent Myra Ransom. The only reason I'm talking to you is that John Mahoney told my boss that we had to brief you on what we're doing, and my boss didn't have the balls to tell Mahoney to jam it up his ass. The other reason is Detective Olivetti tells me you're a loose cannon and liable to go off and do something stupid if you don't know what's going on. Like that bullshit you pulled using the Capitol cops and Sydney Roma for bait. So I'm going to brief you, and then you're going to email me a copy of Brian Lewis's conspiracy report, and after that you're going to butt out of this investigation. You got it?"

DeMarco shrugged. "I'll get you a copy of Brian's report if Mahoney says that's okay, but whether I butt out or not will depend on what you tell me."

"No, it won't," Ransom said. "You fuck with my investigation, I'll have you arrested for obstruction of justice."

Why was everyone so intent on slapping an obstruction charge on him? First Olivetti and now this unpleasant woman.

"Why don't you just get on with the briefing," DeMarco said.

Seeing DeMarco wasn't sufficiently intimidated, Ransom started to say something else but then stopped and took a breath.

Ransom said, "We know who killed Brian Lewis and Patrick Grady."

"You do?" DeMarco said.

"Yes. And we suspect the same guy killed David Morgenthal, but we don't have any evidence when it comes to Morgenthal."

"So who did it?"

"A professional hitman named Lev Belushi who's been around for years and who works mostly for the Albanian mob. He's a suspect in more than a dozen homicides."

"The Albanian mob? What does the Albanian mob—"

"Shut up and quit interrupting me. After Grady was killed and D.C. Metro started investigating his death as a homicide, they interviewed all of Grady's neighbors to ask if they'd seen anything unusual the day Grady was killed. No one saw anything, but there's a forest behind the block where Grady lives and one of Grady's neighbors is an amateur wildlife photographer. She'd set up a couple of old motion-detector cameras on game trails in the forest to photograph some kind of fox that lives there. One of the cameras got a picture of Lev Belushi the day Grady was killed."

Ransom took a photo out of the manila file folder and slid it across the table to DeMarco. It showed a homely fat man wearing a tennis hat. Ransom tapped the photo and said, "That's Lev Belushi. And like I said, that photo was taken on the day that Grady was killed. The problem is that it was taken several hours before he was killed. I suspect that what Belushi was doing was reconnoitering the area around Grady's house, trying to figure out the best way to kill him, and later that day, while Grady's wife wasn't home, he got into Grady's backyard, banged him on the head, and tossed him into the swimming pool, where he drowned.

"After D.C. Metro ID'd Belushi from the photo, they canvassed Lewis's apartment building and Morgenthal's neighborhood. No one saw him near Morgenthal's house, but an old lady who lives in Lewis's building is about 50 percent sure that Belushi held the door open for her the day Lewis was killed. And 50 percent is good enough for me. I'm positive Belushi whacked Lewis and Grady."

"How did you—I mean, the FBI—get involved in all this?" DeMarco asked Ransom.

Olivetti answered the question. He said, "Once we ID'd Belushi, we talked to the FBI's organized-crime guys. And that's when the bureau decided to bigfoot us and take the case away from us."

"But why?" DeMarco asked.

Ransom said, "Because we want the guy Belushi works for."

"You mean Newman?"

"Not Newman. Gabriel Dushku."

"Who's—"

"Gabriel Dushku is an Albanian gangster who now lives, among other places, on Cape Cod. He is—or has been—involved in arms trafficking, sex trafficking, drug trafficking, money laundering, and God only knows how many murders. We and Interpol have been after him for years."

"But what does this have to do with Brian and Newman?"

Ransom smiled, reminding DeMarco of the sun coming out briefly on a cold winter day.

"Once we knew Belushi was involved in Grady's murder, we asked ourselves the question: How would Carson Newman know Lev Belushi? Well, it turns out that Newman has a beach house on Cape Cod and his next-door neighbor is Gabriel Dushku and Dushku is at his Cape place every summer, usually until September. So we took a harder look at Newman Enterprises to see if we could find any other connections to Dushku and learned that an accountant who used to work for Dushku now works for Newman. And because of this accountant, we suspect— we *strongly* suspect—that Dushku is laundering money through some of Newman's companies. Now we just have to prove it."

"And so your plan is to get Newman for money laundering and some- how prove he hired Belushi?"

"The short answer to that question is yes," Ransom said. "But I don't really care about Newman. I want Gabriel Dushku. He's the big fish."

"Well, not to me he isn't," DeMarco said. "I want the guys who killed Brian. I want Belushi and Newman."

"I don't give a shit what you want, DeMarco," Ransom said. Before DeMarco could object, she said, "But we both might get what we want."

Ransom said, "What we're going to do is arrest Belushi. With his record and the photo—and he also used a false ID to board a plane—we've got enough probable cause for that. Then we're going to put his family in a safe house and guard them with U.S. marshals. We're going to do that because Belushi knows that Dushku will kill his family if Belushi rats him out. We're also going to pick up Dushku's accountant who is working for Newman and put him in protective custody and then send in a bunch of forensic accounting weenies who are going to go through Newman's books with a fine-toothed comb and get enough to arrest him for money laundering. Then we're going to start playing these guys off against each other. We'll lie to Belushi and tell him we've got enough evidence to convict him of murder. We'll lie to Newman and say we've got enough—or will soon get enough—evidence to show he paid Belushi and communicated with him. And maybe, although I doubt it from what I've heard, we can use Lewis's report to further squeeze Newman. Then we'll start offering deals. If Belushi gives us Newman and Dushku, he gets a get-out-of-jail-free card. If Newman will admit to conspiring with Dushku to hire a killer and laundering money for Dushku, then we might give him a get-out-of-jail card."

DeMarco knew this was the kind of thing the FBI excelled at—and he also knew they'd be willing to let Belushi and Newman get away with murder to get Dushku. The bureau had a long history of making deals with killers to get mob bosses. One of the most famous cases involved Salvatore "Sammy the Bull" Gravano, who confessed to killing *nineteen* people, but he only served five years in prison because he made a deal with the FBI and gave up the mobsters he worked for. And it looked as if Ransom was willing to make a similar deal with Belushi and Newman if she could nail Dushku.

DeMarco also knew that what Ransom was planning would take forever. It would take months, if not years, to do the investigation and get the warrants and the evidence they needed. The bureau was not known for speedy investigations. And in the end, Ransom might not be successful. It didn't sound to DeMarco that she had enough evidence to really get Belushi for murder. All they had was a photo of him in the woods on the day Grady was killed. And there was also the possibility that Belushi would be too afraid to give up Dushku no matter what kind of deal he was offered. As for Newman, his lawyers would shield him from money laundering charges, blaming everything on people who worked for him, and the case would drag on forever. And Newman's lawyers would also be smart enough to figure out that when it came to murder, the FBI's case against him was a weak one and the likelihood of him being convicted was low. Yeah, the bureau might be able to get Belushi, and maybe even Dushku, but the odds were that Newman would—as he'd always done in the past—get off scot-free.

But DeMarco didn't say any of this to Ransom.

And when she told him that he'd better keep his mouth shut about everything she'd told him, he said, "Okay."

48

On his way home, DeMarco drove past a ballfield where there was a baseball game in progress. The players were all around ten or eleven years old, wearing wash-faded uniforms that had probably been passed down to them from last year's teams. He parked his car and walked over and took a seat on the bleachers, where a dozen dedicated parents, mostly women, were sweltering in the late-afternoon sun watching the kids play.

The teams were the Tigers and the Cubs. The Cubs were at bat. The Tigers' pitcher, a small left-handed kid, nodded, a serious expression on his face, after the catcher showed him two fingers—then wound up like CC Sabathia and flung the ball. Strike. The batter, another small kid, stepped back from the plate, adjusted his batting gloves like he'd seen the pros do on TV, and stepped up to the plate again. The pitcher again went through his elaborate windup and hurled the ball. *Whack*.

The ball streaked toward a gap between the shortstop and the second baseman, but the shortstop made a diving play, rolled once in the dirt, and fired the ball to first while on his knees. The game's only umpire, who was standing behind the plate, shouted, "Out!"

DeMarco said to the stout woman sitting next to him, "Now that was a hell of a play."

"That's my grandson," the woman said. "He's gonna be the next Derek Jeter."

And DeMarco thought she might be right.

As the game continued, DeMarco sat there trying to decide what to do about Carson Newman. By the fourth inning, he had an idea, one that might or might not work, and whether it did or not, it might give Ransom the opportunity to send him to jail for obstruction of justice. Or maybe some crime that carried an even bigger sentence.

It took him until the seventh inning to decide that he was going to do it anyway.

———◆———

He called Sydney. He'd decided to kill two birds with one stone.

He said, "I got a job for you."

"What kind of job?"

"The kind you used to do for Dave. You see, there's this nut named Karl Budnick."

DeMarco told her about Budnick being fired from Congress and how he was now running around harassing politicians and following them and broadcasting lies on his podcast. DeMarco said, "Mahoney wants this guy stopped. What I want you to do is follow him and get me something I can use to stop him."

"Like what?" Sydney said.

"I don't know. That's what I want you to figure out. Just find something that can be used to control him or stop him."

"Are you talking about blackmailing him?"

"Not necessarily," DeMarco said. "See if he's up to anything illegal. If he's in jail, he won't be bothering people. Or find something that can be used as part of a lawsuit that might result in him having to shut down his podcast to settle the suit. Or maybe something that can be used to commit him to a loony bin, because I know he's mentally ill. I don't care, just find me something and then we'll talk about it when I get back."

DeMarco doubted that Sydney would be able to do what he wanted. Budnick was a pain in the ass but wasn't committing any serious crimes, and he doubted that it would be possible to have him committed. But stopping Budnick wasn't the point. The point was to keep Sydney occupied. But maybe, bright as she was, she'd actually be able to do something about Budnick.

"Where are you going?" Sydney asked.

"Providence. I need to see a guy. It has nothing to do with Newman. Anyway, get on Budnick. You don't have to do it full-time. I know you got other things you're dealing with. And I'll pay you and pay your expenses, like for gas. You can charge whatever rate Dave used to charge."

Sydney went silent. "You're just trying to give me something to do so I won't go after Newman."

That was exactly what he was doing. But he didn't say that. "No, this is just something that needs to be done and I don't have time to do it myself. And like I said, you'll be getting paid."

"Okay. Text me this guy's details."

"I'll do that."

"Anything new on Newman?"

"No, but it's only been a few days."

There was no way in hell that he was going to tell Sydney about Lev Belushi.

49

DeMarco had decided to fly into Providence, Rhode Island, because he wanted to blur the trail a bit in case the FBI decided to see where he'd been. He doubted it would work, but all he'd be doing was wasting an hour, the hour it took to drive from Providence to Boston.

The FBI's plan was to arrest Belushi for murder and Newman for money laundering. But knowing the way the FBI usually worked—slowly and methodically—he figured it would take the bureau several days to get Ransom's operation up and running. They'd hold a dozen meetings to discuss strategy and how to deploy resources. They had to come up with a plan for putting Belushi's family and the money laundering accountant working for Newman in protective custody. The lawyers would have to write applications for warrants, and those applications would be reviewed and re-reviewed to make sure every *i* was dotted. Then they'd have to line up sympathetic judges to get the warrants approved. But eventually they'd put all the subjects—Belushi, Newman, and Dushku—under surveillance so they could watch their every move and listen in on their phone calls. And what DeMarco was hoping was that two of those three people weren't already being watched around the clock by FBI agents. If they were, and if he wasn't careful, he'd end up in jail for obstruction of justice—and it was indeed his intent to obstruct justice.

The only person DeMarco really needed to meet with was Gabriel Dushku, but before he met with him, he wanted to see Carson Newman. He had to look the man in the eye. He had to.

He was positive that Newman was the person who was responsible for killing Brian because Brian's report pointed to him and him alone. Nonetheless, there was no proof that Newman had hired Belushi to kill Brian. Maybe the FBI would eventually get proof if Belushi flipped on Newman, as Ransom thought he would—but DeMarco wasn't confident that was going to happen. So before he set his plan in motion, he wanted to look Newman in the eye and tell him that he knew what he'd done and he wanted to see how Newman reacted. He also wanted Newman to know that he was responsible for what was going to happen to him.

Before driving to Boston, DeMarco called Newman's office to confirm he was there but didn't ask for an appointment. He wanted to surprise Newman. He made the call from what was possibly the last pay phone in Providence, one in a bus depot, instead of his cell phone, so the FBI wouldn't see that he'd made the call. Then he removed the battery from his phone to make it more difficult for Ransom's minions to track his movements. He had to watch a YouTube video to learn how to remove the battery.

He wasn't too concerned about an FBI surveillance team seeing him go into the Prudential Tower. For one thing, he doubted a surveillance team would know what he looked like; he wasn't a target in Ransom's investigation. The other thing was that he would be just one of scores of people going in and out of the building and wouldn't stand out in any way. Nonetheless, he put on a baseball cap, which looked goofy with the suit he was wearing, and pulled the brim down low to shade his face.

When he entered the Prudential Tower, he had to pass through a metal detector, but the security guards at the entrance didn't stop him or ask where he was going. He was wearing a suit and tie and looked respectable. Before he got on the elevator, he took off the baseball cap and placed it on a chair in the lobby; he'd pick it up on his way out. He doubted anyone would steal it.

He got off the elevator on the thirty-fifth floor, where he was stopped by another security guard. Behind the guard, taking up most of the wall, was a chrome-plated sign, the letters three feet tall, saying NEWMAN ENTERPRISES.

The guard asked DeMarco who he was and who he'd come to see.

He said, "Call Mr. Newman and tell him that Joe DeMarco is here."

Although he'd never met Newman, DeMarco figured that Newman would know his name because he probably knew that Morgenthal had been hired to follow him. And if Newman knew his name, that was further proof that Newman was involved in Brian's death because there was no other reason for Newman to know who he was. It was possible that Newman might refuse to see him, but DeMarco doubted that he would. He would want to know why DeMarco was there. He would want to know if DeMarco posed a threat.

DeMarco waited patiently as the security guard spoke to Newman's secretary. It was five minutes before the security guard hung up the phone, pointed to a chair in the area behind him, and told DeMarco: "Sit down over there. Someone will escort you to Mr. Newman's office when he's available. But before you sit, I need to search you for weapons."

"I passed through a metal detector when I came in the building," DeMarco said.

"I don't care. I'm going to pat you down."

And he did.

Then the guard said, "The other thing is, I gotta take your cell phone. You'll get it back when you leave."

DeMarco didn't protest. He handed his dead phone to the guard and took a seat. Newman must have been worried about him using the phone to record their conversation, not knowing that the last thing DeMarco wanted was a record of his visit.

Fifteen minutes later, a striking blonde in her twenties, wearing black-framed glasses, a tight skirt, and four-inch heels, entered the reception area. She walked up to DeMarco and said, "Are you Mr. DeMarco?"

"Yep," DeMarco said.

"Please come with me."

He followed the blonde down a long hallway, passing a number of closed doors. Almost every door was labeled with the title "Vice President"—Vice President of Finance, Vice President of Acquisitions, Vice President of Media Relations, and so on. They eventually reached an area with a glass-topped desk where the blonde probably sat while she was working and several chairs for Newman's visitors to sit in while they waited to see him. Behind the desk, like the entry to a castle, was a door that had to be six feet wide and twelve feet high. The blonde rapped on the door, opened it, and said, "Mr. DeMarco is here."

DeMarco heard Newman say, "Send him in."

Newman was wearing a blue pin-striped suit with a pink shirt and a shimmering blue tie tied in a perfect Windsor knot, something he'd probably learned to make at whatever prep school he'd attended. In the breast pocket of the suit was a pink pocket hanky that matched his shirt. He was standing behind his desk, looking out a window, and DeMarco was treated to his profile: the hooked nose, the double chin, the large gut. He wondered how much Newman paid his barber to maintain the silver Julius Caesar haircut.

Without looking at DeMarco, Newman pointed and said, "You see that crane over there?"

DeMarco walked over and stood next to him, looked where he was pointing, and saw a yellow construction crane that was probably half a mile away as the crow flies. The boom of the crane was bent down at an odd angle.

Newman said, "That crane has been like that for two months because of some bullshit lawsuit against me, and every time I look out the window, I can see it, and it just drives me fucking crazy."

When DeMarco didn't say anything—he wondered if Newman was looking for sympathy—Newman said, "Why did Mahoney send you?"

"Mahoney didn't send me," DeMarco said. "He has no idea I'm here."

"Then if Mahoney didn't send you, why are you here?"

"I just wanted to ask if you regret having Brian Lewis killed. I mean, after you saw his report and learned that he wouldn't have caused you a serious problem, did you realize you'd made a mistake?"

Newman looked at him now and said, "I have no idea what you're talking about."

But as he said this, there was a glint in his eyes, and he was smiling slightly. No, not a smile. A smirk.

That smirk wasn't good enough for a court of law, but it was enough to satisfy DeMarco. It was all he'd needed to see to know he was right about Newman.

DeMarco said, "The reason I came here is to let you know that very shortly something bad is going to happen to you. And when it does, I want you to know that I'm the one who made it happen."

"Are you threatening me?" Newman said.

As he said this, Newman stepped closer to DeMarco, invading DeMarco's space, his stomach almost touching DeMarco's. He was four inches taller than DeMarco and was looking down at him.

"Not threating. Promising," DeMarco said.

Newman jabbed DeMarco hard in the chest. "You listen to me, you little—"

Before he could complete the sentence, DeMarco stepped back—and hit him in the nose. A short, hard right-handed jab.

Blood spurted from Newman's nose. He staggered backward and collapsed in the chair behind his desk, his hands over his nose. He said, "You hit me!"

"Yeah," DeMarco said. "Couldn't help myself."

Newman pulled the pink pocket hanky and placed it over his nose. Blood had dripped onto his crisp pink shirt. Because he was squeezing his nose, his words were muffled when he said, "I'm going to have you arrested for assault."

He reached for the phone on his desk, probably to call the security guard in the reception area.

DeMarco said, "You do that, I'm going to give the media Lewis's report. It won't cause you a significant legal problem, but it'll be embarrassing and raise a lot of questions."

Newman's hand was still on the phone, but he didn't pick it up.

And the fact that Newman hadn't said *What report?* after DeMarco had mentioned it twice was further proof that he'd been involved in Brian's death. Again, not enough for a court of law, but enough for DeMarco.

DeMarco said, "I'm leaving now, but like I said, I just wanted to let you know that when it happens—"

"When what happens?" Newman screamed.

"—I hope you have time to regret having that kid killed for no good reason."

DeMarco left.

The security guard didn't stop him.

50

It normally took an hour and a half to drive from Boston to Cape Cod, but it took DeMarco twice that long because it seemed as if every person in Boston had decided to go to the beach.

Now what he needed to do was find a way to see Dushku without being recognized. He hadn't been too concerned about the FBI seeing him go into the Prudential Tower but on Cape Cod it would be different because if the FBI already had Dushku under surveillance, agents would probably photograph and attempt to identify every person who visited him.

To keep this from happening to him, what DeMarco wanted was a certain type of vehicle. He didn't know if he'd be able to get his hands on one, and if he couldn't, he'd go see Dushku anyway and just hope that the FBI wasn't already watching him. But before he did that, he'd try to get what he wanted.

The closest town to Dushku's beach house was Barnstable, a town with a population of almost fifty thousand. In other words, a city large enough to have a lot of bars. And, as it was almost five p.m., DeMarco figured there was a pretty good chance a guy driving the kind of vehicle he was looking for would be drinking beer in one of those bars.

He started cruising the main streets, and in the parking lot of the third bar he saw was a van that said "Gunderson Electric" on the side. He went inside and almost immediately spotted the driver—he knew it was him because he was wearing a white, short-sleeved shirt that said "Gunderson Electric" on the back—but he was sitting with three other guys and DeMarco decided to move on.

In the parking lot of the fifth place he came to was a van identified as belonging to Albright and Sons Heating and Ventilation—reminding him of that little prick, Rick. But the bar was packed with a bunch of young guys playing pool and watching a Red Sox game and he couldn't figure out who the driver was.

The next bar he drove by was a small cinder-block box—it couldn't have been more than a thousand square feet—sandwiched in between a tire store and a laundromat. Over the door was a wooden sign saying Paddy's Lounge. There were only two vehicles in the five parking spots in front of Paddy's. One of those was a van belonging to Hendrick's Plumbing.

Inside the bar were three people: the bartender, who was playing a game on an iPad; a woman in her seventies staring bleary-eyed at the muted television over the bar; and a heavyset guy in his fifties wearing blue coveralls and drinking a Sam Adams as he looked through reading glasses at a newspaper. When DeMarco sat down next to him, he saw the man was looking at the section of the sports page showing the upcoming races at Suffolk Downs.

He looked over at DeMarco, annoyed, wondering why he'd sat right next to him and hadn't picked a stool where there'd be some space between them. The bartender started toward DeMarco to see what he wanted, but he shook his head and waved the bartender away.

DeMarco said, "You driving the plumbing van outside?"

"Yeah." When he said this, DeMarco was enveloped in a beer-breath fog. The plumber wasn't on his first beer of the day.

"How'd you like to make two hundred bucks?"

"Doing what? If it's some kind of emergency plumbing job, I'm not interested. I'm done for the day."

"You don't have to do anything but sit here for an hour. I want to borrow your van. And if you have another pair of coveralls like the ones you're wearing, I'd like to borrow those, too."

"What the fuck?"

"I'm a process server and I'm trying to serve a subpoena on an asshole who's dodging me. He lives in a gated community a little ways from here. If I drive up to the gate in my car, the guard at the gate won't let me in until he checks with the asshole, who will refuse to see me. But if I drive up in your van and give the guard the address of a couple I know isn't home, and tell him I'm there to do an emergency repair on the sprinkler system outside their house, I figure I'll be able to get in and serve the papers. And let me tell you one other thing before you tell me to go to hell. The guy's being subpoenaed in connection with a child porn case. He's human scum."

"How do I know you're telling me the truth? How do I know you're not going to use my van to rob a bank?"

"Are there any banks open at this time of day? Anyway, I'm not going to rob anything. Like I said, all I need your van for is to get through a gate. And I'll give you the keys to my car—it's the Nissan sitting right next to your van—and I'll give you the two hundred right now."

"I don't know," the plumber said.

"What if I make it three hundred? And you sit here for an hour picking out whichever nags you'd like to bet on that are racing tomorrow at Suffolk Downs?"

DeMarco, wearing blue coveralls and the same baseball cap he'd worn to the Prudential Tower, stopped briefly on the road in front of Newman's beach cottage—in this case, "cottage" meaning two stories and a three-car garage. He'd found Newman's Cape Cod address online, but he hadn't been able to find Gabriel Dushku's. But he didn't need to find it, as Ransom had told him that Dushku was one of Newman's next-door neighbors.

On the left side of Newman's place, facing the water, was a small one-story house with brown-shingle siding bleached gray by the sun; there were two plastic bubble skylights in the roof. In the Cape Cod real estate market, the house was probably worth a million bucks. On the right side, a quarter mile away, was a home that was even bigger than Newman's. DeMarco figured that this one had to be Dushku's.

He pulled the plumber's van into Dushku's driveway—Dushku also had a three-car garage—and took a toolbox from the back of the van and walked with his head down to the door and rang the bell. He didn't bother to look around to see if he could spot any FBI agents watching the house, because he knew that if they were watching, he'd never be able to spot them. And if they were watching, he was hoping they wouldn't bother to photograph him, as they could ID him from the markings on the van.

He didn't know if Dushku would be home or not. Ransom had said that he stayed on the Cape until September, but he could be out and about. If he wasn't home . . . Well, then he'd have to figure something else out.

The door was answered by a man wearing a tight black T-shirt to show off his body-builder muscles. DeMarco figured he wasn't the butler, as he had a Glock in a shoulder holster. That a gangster would have an armed bodyguard wasn't surprising; gangsters tended to make dangerous enemies.

"What do you want?" the man said. Then he noticed the way DeMarco was dressed and saw the van parked in the driveway. "Nobody here called for a plumber. If you're here to drum up business, you can fuck off."

DeMarco had expected the bodyguard to have a foreign accent, but he didn't. He sounded like your average rude Boston thug.

"I'm not a plumber. My name is Joe DeMarco. I work for Congressman John Mahoney and would like to speak to Mr. Dushku."

"If you're not a plumber, why you driving that truck?"

"Because the FBI might be watching this house."

"What the fuck are you talking about?"

"Go tell your boss what I said. Tell him my name is DeMarco, tell him I work for Mahoney and that the FBI might be watching him."

The bodyguard slammed the door in his face. DeMarco didn't know if that meant he wasn't going to be permitted to see Dushku or if it meant the guy was going to tell Dushku that he had a visitor. He'd wait a few minutes, then ring the bell again if the bodyguard didn't come back.

It was more like five minutes. And the whole time he stood there head down, facing the door, sweating like crazy in the plumber's coveralls. The door finally opened, and the bodyguard gestured him into the house, and when the door was closed, he said, "I gotta pat you down. Put the toolbox down by the door."

DeMarco put the toolbox down and spread his arms and was patted down for the second time that day.

"Give me your phone."

DeMarco figured Dushku, like Newman, must have been concerned about DeMarco recording their conversation. And like Newman, Dushku didn't know that the last thing DeMarco wanted was a recording that could one day end up being played in a courtroom.

He handed his dead cell phone to the bodyguard, who put it on a table near the front door. As he followed the bodyguard through the house, DeMarco didn't pay any attention to the furnishings, as the view through the windows captivated his attention. The back wall of the house was all glass, and he could see the beach and the water and a couple of power-boats. But that wasn't what caught his eye. It was a blonde in a red bikini pulling herself out of a swimming pool. She wouldn't have been out of place on the cover of the *Sports Illustrated* swimsuit issue.

The bodyguard led him down a hallway to what appeared to be a family room. Dushku was sitting on a green leather couch playing a video game on a seventy-five-inch TV screen. In the game was an avatar that looked like Buzz Lightyear running through an apocalyptic landscape shooting a noisy laser gun at things that looked like mutant crabs, which DeMarco guessed were space aliens.

Dushku turned to DeMarco, smiled, and said, "These games can be addictive."

He paused the game and gestured for DeMarco to sit in a chair facing him.

DeMarco hadn't bothered to do any research on Dushku. If the FBI said he was a gangster who ran an organized crime family and killed people, that was good enough for him. Dushku was wearing baggy white swimming trunks and an unbuttoned Hawaiian shirt. He was a good-looking man in his early sixties, short white hair, very tan, and appeared to be in good shape; his stomach was flat and his arms and legs were well muscled. His teeth were so white and perfect, they were either capped or false.

He said, "Do you have identification, something that proves you are who you say you are and that you work for Mahoney?"

DeMarco pulled out his wallet and showed him his congressional ID.

"But this doesn't say who you work for."

DeMarco said, "You can call Mahoney if you want to confirm I am who I say I am. I have his cell phone number."

Dushku studied him for a moment, then shook his head. "No, that's okay. I believe you. But why are you dressed like that and driving a plumber's van?"

"Like I told your guy, the FBI might be watching you and I didn't want them to know I was visiting."

"Why would the FBI be watching me? I'm a retired businessman. And how would you know what the FBI is doing?"

"I know because an FBI agent told me."

"Why would the FBI tell you anything?"

"They told me because of the guy I work for. And you can probably verify everything I'm about to tell you. I imagine a guy like you has contacts in law enforcement."

"I don't know what you mean by *a guy like me*. I told you, I'm a retired businessman."

"Stick to that story if you want. But let me tell you what the FBI's planning to do. They're going to arrest a buddy of yours named Lev Belushi for murdering three people."

"Belushi? I've never heard of the man."

"That's okay," DeMarco said. "You don't need to admit to knowing anyone. So, as I was saying, Belushi is going to be arrested shortly by the FBI for these murders he committed. And your next-door neighbor, Carson Newman, he's going to be arrested for conspiring with Belushi to kill these people. He's also going to be arrested for laundering your money."

Dushku's eyes went from being amused to chips of ice.

DeMarco said, "What the FBI is planning to do is prove that Newman hired Belushi to kill those three people I mentioned. They have all the evidence they need, particularly when it comes to Belushi—he's toast—and then what they're going to do is squeeze Belushi and Newman to get to you. You're the FBI's target, and the bureau is going to offer Belushi and Newman deals in exchange for you. Newman will eventually admit that you hooked him up with Belushi—making you an accessory to murder—and that you pressured him to launder money for you. As for Belushi, I'm assuming he can tell the bureau all sorts of things about you."

"Why are you telling me this, Mr. DeMarco?"

"Because I don't care about you. I care about a twenty-two-year-old kid named Brian Lewis, who's now dead. Brian worked for John Mahoney, and Newman hired Belushi to kill him, and I want them to pay for what they did."

51

DeMarco's plane back to D.C. was supposed to leave Providence in an hour, although these days it seemed as if flight schedules were purely arbitrary, and the plane might or might not leave on time, if it left at all.

Yesterday, after talking to Dushku, he'd returned the plumber's van to its rightful owner, not knowing if the FBI had been watching Dushku or not. He'd done his best not to be identified, but if he'd failed, he was ready to live with the consequences and wondered how many years he could spend in jail for obstruction of justice. When he got back to D.C., he might have a talk with super lawyer Janet Evans and ask, hypothetically, that if he were arrested, could she get him off the hook.

He'd spent the night at a Marriott in Providence, got up late, had a good breakfast, then headed to the airport, and turned in the rental car. One of the things he had to do before he got back to D.C. was come up with a plausible lie as to why he'd spent a day and a night in Providence in case the FBI asked.

To steel himself for the flight to D.C.—or to get into a line to find another flight—he treated himself to a beer while watching the Red Sox play the Yankees on the television over the bar. The truth was that he'd enjoyed watching the Little Leaguers play the other day more than he did watching the professionals who'd spent half a year on strike because they thought they were undervalued. In a baseball strike, it was hard to know who to root for: the millionaires playing the game or the billionaires who owned the teams.

His phone rang and he saw it was Sydney calling. He'd put the battery back in his phone when he'd arrived back in Providence.

"Hi, what's up?" he said.

"This guy, Budnick. He's dangerous."

"Dangerous? He's a nut with a podcast."

"DeMarco, he's got a gun. Last night, he followed that congresswoman into a restaurant. He started screaming that she was a Chinese spy, and her security guys hauled him away and tossed him in jail. This was the second time he violated a restraining order, and he must have made some kind of threat, because when they arraigned him this morning, he was charged not only with violating the restraining order but also for threating a government official. Which is a felony."

"That's great!" DeMarco said. As he'd predicted, Budnick had self-destructed.

"No, it's not great," Sydney said. "He was released without having to post bail, and after that I followed him home. Well, he came out of his house five minutes later and he was carrying a gun in his hand. He wasn't even trying to hide it. And he just looked insane."

"Jesus Christ. Where's he at now?"

"On a bench outside the Rayburn Building, talking to himself. The gun's under his shirt. I think he's sitting there trying to screw up the courage to go into the building and kill that congresswoman. What do you want me to do?"

"I want you to go find a Capitol cop and tell him that Budnick has a gun. Call me back when they've got him. But don't go near him, Sydney. Let the cops handle it."

"Oh, shit," Sydney said. "He's walking toward the building."

The plane boarded half an hour later. He hadn't heard back from Sydney. He spent the flight scanning the news on his phone to see if anyone had been killed at the Capitol. Nothing had been reported. When the plane landed, he called Sydney. She didn't answer. So he called Celeste.

"Who do you need me to arrest now, DeMarco?"

He almost said, *A guy named Rick*. But didn't.

"Has anything happened there at the Capitol, like someone trying to shoot a congresswoman?"

"I thought you knew. Sydney stopped him. She was following Budnick because you'd asked her to, and . . . What the hell is your job, DeMarco? Anyway, she saw him walking toward the Rayburn Building, where two of our guys were standing by the entrance. She was afraid he was going to shoot them, so she tackled his ass and started screaming that he had a gun."

"Do you know where she is now?"

"Might still be in the ER."

"The ER! What—"

"She's okay. She just dislocated her shoulder."

"And where's Budnick?"

"In a cage. And he'll be in one for quite a while. We got him on a gun charge in addition to threatening Chan. He's not going to be podcasting anytime soon."

Other than Sydney's dislocated shoulder, it had all played out perfectly when it came to Budnick. Now what he had to do was take credit for what Sydney had done to stay in Mahoney's good graces.

His phone rang. It was Sydney.

DeMarco answered, saying, "Didn't I tell you to stay away from him?"

"I had to do something. I was afraid he was going to start shooting."

"How's your shoulder?"

"It's fine. They just had to pop it back into place."

"Okay, well, text me how much I owe you."

"I'll do that, but that's not why I called. Do you know anyone that can tell me how to get somebody buried at Arlington? I'm getting the runaround from everyone I've talked to."

"After what you did today, I can go you one better than that. I'll have Mahoney call the Pentagon, and someone over there will take care of Dave for you."

"Thanks, DeMarco. I'd really appreciate that. Anything new on Newman?"

"No, but I got a feeling something's going to happen soon."

52

Lev Belushi walked out of the travel agency, a smile on his broad face. The Alaska cruise, including airline tickets for six people, would cost about thirty thousand—which was just a little more than half of what he'd been paid to dispatch Brian Lewis. His daughters were excited about the trip—they could hardly contain themselves—and were driving his wife crazy. They'd be leaving in a few days, and after that his wife wouldn't have to do a thing for two weeks. Lord knows, she deserved a break.

He opened the door to his car and the heat inside it almost knocked him over. It would be a relief to be away from Boston, and hopefully by the time they returned, the heat wave—heat dome, heat bomb, whatever they called it—would be over. The politicians really should do something about climate change.

He didn't notice the car that pulled up next to him as he was standing with his back to the street.

He heard the four shots, felt the bullets strike his back, but was dead before he hit the ground.

Carson Newman took a helicopter from Boston to Cape Cod. He wasn't about to put up with the traffic. He'd spend tonight alone, but tomorrow the chopper would bring his mistress to the Cape. His wife, fortunately, was attending a fashion show in Paris. He wondered how much that would cost him, not that he cared.

As the helicopter left the city, he glanced over at the leaning construction crane that had caused him so much grief. The criminal charges had been dropped and it looked as if the whole mess would be settled shortly. He would have pay a few million to compensate the families of the two men who'd died, but that money would eventually be written off as a tax-deductible business expense or the cost would be passed on to the people who would lease office space in the building when it was completed. As for the insane attorney general who was determined to get him for tax evasion, her investigation was bogged down and going nowhere. His lawyers had tied the bitch into knots.

So, all in all, things were going well, or as well as they ever did when a man runs an empire. The only thing bothering him was that thug DeMarco's prediction that something bad was going to happen to him. He really should have had the bastard arrested for assault but finally decided it wasn't worth it. The Lewis nonsense was finally over with, and he didn't want to reopen that can of worms. And he didn't see that there was any way that a nobody like DeMarco could cause him a problem, nor, for that matter, could his boss, that loser Mahoney. And one thing he was going to do for sure was help Mahoney's opponent the next time he ran for office. Which reminded him, he needed to talk to KL&M and find out who would be taking over for Patrick Grady.

The chopper landed on the beach in front of his cottage. That was illegal, but he didn't give a shit. It was his beach. The lady who cooked for him wouldn't be there tonight, but he'd asked her to prepare something for him that he could heat up in the microwave. He wanted to spend the night alone. When she'd asked what he wanted for dinner, he'd told her to surprise him. He had no doubt that whatever she made would be marvelous. Yes, he was looking forward to sitting on the deck with a good bottle of wine and enjoying the sunset in solitude. Sometimes, a man just needs a little time to himself to decompress.

He unlocked the beach-side door—and to his surprise, didn't hear the little beeps from the security system letting him know that he had to disarm the system before the alarm sounded. The cook must have forgotten to set the alarm when she left. He wouldn't fire her for such a blunder—she was too good at her job to dismiss—but he would let her know that it better not happen again.

He walked into the kitchen to see what she'd made for his dinner. He was suddenly starving. He opened the refrigerator and saw a dish wrapped in foil. He was just reaching for it when the wire went over his head.

As the garrote sliced into his throat, his last thought, before he lost consciousness, was: *DeMarco*.

53

DeMarco was watching a show on Netflix about a conniving British politician who manipulates and blackmails other politicians and who had just pushed some reporter off a roof because she was also conniving and manipulative. The politician reminded him of Mahoney in a lot of ways, but because of the Limey accent, he sounded more erudite and sophisticated.

His doorbell rang. Then, before he could get out of his chair to answer it, whoever rang the bell started knocking on his door. No, not knocking. *Pounding.*

He opened to door to see Special Agent Myra Ransom. She shoved him hard in the chest, propelling him backward, and screamed, "What did you do?"

"Jesus, calm down," DeMarco said. "I don't know what you're talking about."

"Lev Belushi and Carson Newman were both killed yesterday. And—"

It had only been four days since he'd talked to Dushku. He'd expected Dushku to act quickly, but not that quickly.

"Really?" DeMarco said. "I didn't know that."

Actually, he'd seen on his phone that Newman had been found dead in his beach house by a woman who the press implied—but didn't say for sure—was Newman's girlfriend. He hadn't seen anything about Belushi, however. Apparently, his death hadn't been important enough to get on the news app on his phone.

"And Gabriel Dushku is now on his yacht, which is docked in Moldova, a country that doesn't have an extradition treaty with the United States. He left before the murders, and we couldn't stop him from leaving."

"What does this have to do with me?" DeMarco said, his eyes wide with innocence and ignorance.

"Don't give me that bullshit. You're the only person not in law enforcement who knew I was going after Belushi and Newman to get Dushku. And I know you told him."

"Ransom, there were probably a hundred people who knew what you were doing when it came to Dushku, counting all the cops in D.C. Metro and the FBI and the lawyers in DOJ and whoever else you were working with. Any of them could have told Dushku. Or said something to someone who passed it on to Dushku. The bureau leaks like a fuckin' sieve, and you know it."

Ransom said, "Horseshit! It was you. And if I can prove it was you, I'm going to nail your hide to the wall."

A sense of relief washed over DeMarco. He was now fairly sure that the FBI hadn't been watching Dushku when he did his plumber act. If the bureau had been, Ransom probably would have said so to impress on DeMarco how easily she'd be able to nail him.

"Why would I tell Dushku anything?" DeMarco said.

"To avenge Brian Lewis."

"Hey, I'm not in the vengeance business, Ransom. I'm just a lawyer who works for Congress."

"You're not a lawyer. You're a fucking fixer. And you fixed it so Dushku would kill those people for you. And when I prove that you did, I'm going to have you arrested for obstruction of justice. And for lying to the FBI. And maybe for conspiring with Dushku to kill them. And for any other fuckin' thing I can think of."

She was waving her long arms as she was speaking, making him think of a vulture flapping its wings.

She added: "Because of you, you asshole, one of the biggest gangsters in the world is running free."

"Oh, I'm sure you'll get another crack at him, Ransom. You strike me as a woman who doesn't give up."

"I am. And you better remember that."

Yeah, he definitely needed to talk to Janet Evans.

He said, "Hey, if there's nothing else, I want to get back to a show I was watching. I'm dying to see how it turns out."

54

DeMarco pulled up in front of Caroline's house and parked on the street. Sitting in her driveway was one of those storage pods you pack yourself and that a moving company picks up and hauls to wherever you're moving to. On the front lawn was a real estate agent's sign that had *SOLD* on it. He wondered how soon she would be moving. The good news was that when she did, hopefully she'd have some closure when it came to her son. No, that probably wasn't true. She'd never have a sense of closure, but at least she'd know what her son had done and why he'd died.

DeMarco had spoken to Caroline twice since he'd obtained the flash drive from her at Brian's apartment. She'd called and asked what was on the drive and he'd lied to her, saying that the drive was encrypted. But be patient, he'd said. Now that the cops were investigating Brian's death as a homicide, he'd told her he was still hopeful that they might be able to find his killer.

He lied to her a second time, just before he flew to Providence, and told her that the cops had a lead on who'd killed Brian. He said Detective Olivetti refused to give him the details, as it was an ongoing investigation, but that he, DeMarco, was positive that something was going to break soon. Be patient, he'd said again.

Now it was time to tell Caroline the truth.

He left his car and rang her doorbell. He was holding a manila envelope.

Caroline answered the door dressed as she'd been the first time he'd seen her, in jeans and a faded gray army T-shirt. It looked as if she'd aged ten years since he'd met her. The living room behind her was vacant of furniture. Dust motes were dancing in the air.

She said, "Let's go to the kitchen. It's the only place to sit."

They sat at the kitchen table, where he'd sat with her before. The small cactus plants that had been on the windowsill were gone. The room smelled of Lysol. He placed the manila envelope in the center of the table.

"When are you leaving?" DeMarco asked.

"I have to be out of here by the end of the week. But I'm not sure when I'm driving to Colorado. I wanted to hear what you had to say and see how things were progressing with Brian's case before I made a decision. I'll be staying with a friend, another army widow, until I decide to go."

DeMarco nodded. He said, "Caroline, Brian's case is over with."

Her eyes flashed. "Are you telling me the cops have stopped investigating? If they have, I'm—"

"No, I'm here to tell you that the men responsible for Brian's death are dead. You won't read that in the paper and the cops won't officially say so, but that's the truth."

"What are you talking about?"

DeMarco opened the manila envelope and pulled out the pages inside.

He said, "That's a copy of a report that Brian wrote that started everything. It was on the flash drive."

"So you were able to break the encryption."

"Uh, yeah, but I couldn't share the report with you until now because of the status of the police investigation. But now the investigation is over, and I knew you'd want to see it. And I knew you'd want to keep it because it shows what an incredible young man Brian was."

DeMarco remembered Caroline's sister telling him how Caroline had kept every award and ribbon that Brian had ever won. There was no doubt she'd keep, and cherish, his last significant achievement.

She reached for the report, but DeMarco placed his hand on it. "You can read it after I leave, and if you have any questions, you can call me. But what it reveals is that Brian did an investigation all on his own that revealed that twelve congressmen were bribed by a guy named Carson Newman, who was a big-shot billionaire businessman in Boston. Newman found out about Brian's investigation from a lobbyist who had a source in Congress, and when he did, he hired someone to kill Brian."

Tears welled up in Caroline's eyes. "Oh, my God. I knew it," she said.

"Yes, you were right all along. Anyway, the cops were able to identify the killer. He was a professional hit man named Lev Belushi, and they could link him to Newman. The D.C. Metro cops were working with the FBI to arrest Belushi and Newman, but before they could, they were both killed."

"Why?"

"It's complicated, but Belushi and Newman were both connected to an Albanian mob boss named Gabriel Dushku, and Dushku had them killed because he was afraid they would implicate him in other crimes. But Dushku had nothing to do with Brian's death, and at this point, the FBI can't prove he had Belushi and Newman killed but they know he did. An FBI agent told me. So, Caroline, it's over with. The men who killed Brian were identified and now they're dead, and we know why Newman had Brian killed."

"What's going to happen to the congressmen?"

"Probably nothing."

"Nothing!"

"Caroline, Brian was an incredibly bright young man and a hell of an investigator, and he was right about these congressmen being bribed by Newman, but there isn't sufficient evidence to convict them of a crime. Brian should have discussed what he found with Mahoney's chief of staff, but I guess that Brian didn't trust anyone he worked with, and I can't blame him. In the little time Brian spent in Congress, he learned how corrupt the whole system is."

"What's going to happen to Brian's report?"

"It'll get leaked, and the congressmen will be torched by the media, but that'll probably be the worst of it."

"That's not right."

"No, but that's the way the world works these days. But the main thing is, you can be proud of what Brian did, and although it won't make you feel better, you'll have the satisfaction of knowing that if he'd lived, he would have made a difference."

55

At the Manassas Regional Airport, a blue helicopter with a gold stripe on the side hovered over a helipad near a tan building made of corrugated metal. On the building was a sign saying American Helicopters Inc.

It was a cold day in February and the wind was blowing with gusts of up to twenty miles an hour. The helicopter was maybe thirty feet off the ground and, because of the wind, rocking back and forth a bit, and DeMarco was wondering how hard it was for Sydney to control it. That would be a hell of a thing, if she crash-landed on the day of her graduation from helicopter school. But she didn't.

She landed the helicopter, and a few minutes later she descended from it and was met by a man wearing a parka and a red stocking cap. The man walked toward her and shook her hand—and then he hugged her. Sydney was wearing jeans and a heavy blue sweater; her hair was being ruffled by the wind. She no longer had the spiky, gelled hairstyle. Her hair was short but cut in a more conventional manner and she made DeMarco think of Amelia Earhart. She looked great.

She walked toward him, grinning. He was standing near the building in a ski jacket and a black stocking cap and had gloves on.

"I did it," she said. And then she hugged him and added, "Thank you for being here."

"I wouldn't have missed it," DeMarco said. "Now let's go find some-place warm to celebrate. I'm freezing my ass off here."

———◆———

DeMarco hadn't seen Sydney in six months, not since Dave Morgen-thal's funeral. Dave had been cremated and his ashes were placed in the Columbarium at Arlington National Cemetery. When Sydney had called to thank DeMarco for his help with Dave's arrangements—it had actually been Mahoney who'd helped—DeMarco had asked if she wanted some company on the day of Dave's interment, knowing she had no one. And when she was about to graduate from helicopter school, she'd called him and asked if he'd be willing to come to her graduation, which consisted of her final training solo flight and being given a certifi-cate that said she was certified by the FAA to fly choppers.

The top-of-the-line course offered by American Helicopters Inc. provided more than two hundred flying hours, along with all the written exams, and cost almost seventy-five thousand dollars. After she graduated, Sydney could most likely get a job with several pri-vate companies, like those that transported rich people like the late Carson Newman. But she didn't want to be a flying taxi driver. She wanted to fly a Black Hawk armed with .50-caliber machine guns and air-to-surface missiles. Paying for the course took all the money she'd inherited from Dave plus the small profit she'd made when she sold his house, and for the last six months she'd been renting a room from an old couple who lived in Manassas. Now she was practically broke—but that wouldn't matter.

As they were eating dinner, DeMarco asked, "When do you head for Alabama?"

"Not for a couple of months. Gotta go to basic training first, which is ten weeks. They'll be sending me to Fort Benning for basic. And after that, I got Warrant Officer School, which is six weeks. But that's at Rucker, the same place where they do the chopper training."

"How long is the training?"

"About seven months if they put me in a Black Hawk."

That was the deal she'd made with the army—one that followed a call from Mahoney to a four-star general. Upon completing civilian helicopter training, the army would train her to be a chopper combat pilot. The army would also give her a fifty-thousand-dollar enlistment bonus if she committed to six years of service, which was pretty standard.

"You looking forward to it?" DeMarco asked.

"Not the basic training bullshit, but I'll do what I gotta do."

"I know you will," DeMarco said. "And you'll do great. And when you graduate from the army's helicopter's school, and they give you your wings or whatever they give you, I'd like to be there."

"Really? You'd come?"

"You bet. There're a couple of golf courses in Alabama I'd like to play."